HEARTS
and
thorns

ELLA FIELDS

Editor: Jenny Sims, Editing4Indies
Proofreading: Allison Riley
Formatting: Stacey Blake, Champagne Book Design
Cover design: Sarah Hansen, Okay Creations

For Allie
who actually followed me to the end of the earth

PART ONE

Of all the truths I've ever been told,
the loudest lie was yours.

one

Willa
Six years old

The house shook, and I bolted awake at the sound of a familiar scream, reaching for the cool base of the touch lamp shaped like a castle on my nightstand.

It wouldn't turn on.

A loud crack pierced the silence, followed by a boom so deafening, I jumped as I grappled with my nightstand drawer for the flashlight inside.

He was the worst person in the world.

A bully, a thief, and a liar yet my feet carried me to my bedroom door. I pulled it open before throwing myself down the hall.

Orange flashes of light bobbed off family pictures lining the chestnut-colored walls, and I stumbled as my foot found one of Jackson's stupid toy cars.

Hopping and hissing, I squeaked as another crack sounded right above the house. My ears rang, and the house came alive beneath the eerie glow of lightning, showing me that Jackson's door was open. Three rumbling booms followed me as I ran, my breaths loud in the otherwise silent night, and hurled myself onto his bed.

He sat up, a yell snatched from his throat before I slapped a hand over his mouth. "Quiet, unless you want Mom and Dad to make me leave."

He wasn't my real dad, but ever since my mommy had married him after I'd turned one and I'd learned to talk, I'd called him that. One time, after he'd yelled at me for spilling chocolate milk in the kitchen, I'd uttered his real name, Heath. I was promptly berated by my mother for ten minutes about all the ways I'd hurt his feelings.

Heath liked rules and having a clean house, a whole lot, but that didn't mean I wanted to make him sad. And since then, I'd never ever dared to call him anything other than Dad even though it made my real daddy make a frowny face.

Mommy said she'd taken me to the doctor for a checkup when I was four months old. She'd been so tired, and when I'd continued to chuck all over her, she was barely holding on by a breaking thread. Whatever that meant.

Anyway, that was when Heath stepped into the small office with baby Jackson, who was there for his six-month checkup.

He'd offered to help Mommy clean up, and when she'd burst into tears—hormones, she'd said—he gently took her hand and led her outside for some privacy. Mommy said it was mortifying, the way she'd sobbed in front of this handsome stranger, babbling about how my daddy couldn't change jobs, and how he'd told her he didn't want to be with her.

That made me sad. That my daddy would hurt her feelings like that. That he could make her so upset she'd cry in public and need help from a stranger. My mommy never cried. Ever. So she must have felt awful.

Heath had then gone back inside to cancel their appointments before taking her back to his house for coffee. His fiancée had split when Jackson was only one month old, and she didn't want custody. Whatever that meant. So it was just him and Jackson who lived in what would become Mommy's and my first home. Apparently, we used to live with her friend, but I could never remember what Mommy said her name was.

After feeding me, she'd passed out on Heath's couch with me snuggled into her side, and the rest, as they say, was history.

Jackson's green eyes were narrowed, and he shook his head. Then, rather roughly, he yanked my hand from his mouth. "I don't need you." I made a face that had him sighing. "Fine, just don't get your ugly toes near my face."

I stole one of his three pillows and tossed it to the end of his twin bed. Snuggling beneath his galactic comforter, I tugged it to my chin, shivering as the thumping of my heart slowed.

Jackson tugged it back. "Quit."

I pulled. "I'm cold, you toad."

He grumbled, and his foot nudged my butt as he shifted down the bed so we could both have enough warmth.

I kicked him back. He grumbled again.

Silence wandered into the room, the house, and into the dark sky I could see through the gap in the navy blue curtains behind me. So dark that when lightning crisscrossed through it, my mouth fell open while I waited for the crack of thunder.

Jackson stilled, his fear another blanket to smother us.

"Miss Squires says storms are the skies way of grieving."

The boom sounded over his exasperated, "What?"

"She said that every now and then, just like we do, the sky needs to have a bad day and be upset." I turned my cheek into the pillow, my eyelids heavy. "It's upset, but it needs to be so it can feel better soon, and then its smile will reappear."

Jackson said nothing as the rain began to hammer against the exterior of the house. "You think the sun is the sky's way of smiling?" He'd tried for derision but failed thanks to his curiosity.

"I do," I said. "And when the moon comes out, that means the sky is sleeping."

Some minutes later, the storm but a mere rumble fading beneath the patter of rain, I was almost asleep when he asked, "And the stars? What are they?"

I smiled. "They're nightlights."

"The sky gets scared?" he asked, sounding bewildered.

"Of course, it does. It needs a lot of nightlights because it's ginormous."

Jackson made a humming noise. "Makes sense."

The sun was smiling when I heard voices at Jackson's bedroom door, but I didn't open my eyes.

Heath was talking. "How much longer do you think he's going to be scared of storms?"

Mommy tutted. "For as long as it takes for him not to be. Lots of kids are."

Heath grunted. "We should move them."

Mommy said nothing for the longest time, and I drifted away to the sound of her murmured, "No, let them be."

"You're right. They'll probably be grumpy if we wake them after a rough night."

Mommy's tinkling laughter made me smile, and I hid it by turning my face into the pillow. "Jackson's perpetually grumpy anyway."

Heath laughed at that. "Wonder where he gets that from." He yawned. "Come, I'll make coffee."

I heard them kissing a minute later, and my nose crinkled. I hated watching grown-ups kiss. Unless it was during a movie or inside a picture book. Kissing always looked better in movies and story books.

When the door creaked shut, Jackson's foot nudged mine, and we both ducked under the comforter to hide our giggles.

two

Jackson
Eight years old

A twig snapped, and I crashed to a stop between Mr. and Mrs. Pondersen.

Peering through the frost-sprinkled greenery, I squinted against the light glinting off the headstones.

Close. She was close.

The cemetery stretched and crawled in a wave of hills that gradually rolled toward the creek at the very bottom. Knowing a sea of dead bodies was buried mere meters from our back fence used to freak me out until Willa dragged me back here a year ago under the guise of her favorite hat fluttering away on the breeze.

There was no hat. We'd searched for thirty minutes before she'd told me, and then she'd stood there while I'd berated her, calling her every word I could think of that meant stupid.

She'd glanced up at me beneath the dark lashes that framed her giant hazel eyes, a tiny curl to her pillow-soft lips. I knew they were soft on account of the times she'd pressed them to my cheek after I'd done something nice for her.

She always raced off before I could shove her or pull her hair.

I didn't like her.

She was annoying, too quiet, too content, and too damn nice all the time.

But damn if I didn't love her. She was my sister, so I supposed that was how it was meant to be. You didn't like them, but you had to love them.

In any case, it made our mom smile, which, in turn, made my dad smile. I liked it when they smiled at me. It was a rarity, that was for sure.

A flash of bright blue caught my line of vision, and I spun to the left, almost tripping over Rodger Stempson in my haste to catch Willa.

"If I saw you, that means you're out," I hollered between cupped hands.

No answer. And no sign of her.

I stopped in a clearing with tiny plaques, turning with the rose gardens that lined this section of the cemetery. "Willa?"

I should've known that wouldn't work.

Smirking, I tugged up my shorts and pulled down the brim of my baseball cap, then trudged over to the area I'd last seen her.

"A diversion," I hissed, spying her blue ribbon swaying from a branch. When I plucked it off, some of the satin tore, and I rubbed it between my finger and thumb. "You wicked little witch."

Then I moved, hurdling over the plaques and headstones, gardens and bouquets, the wind singing in my ears as the sun began to melt behind the hills I was scaling.

The sweet sound hit my ears a moment later, like that of wind chimes meeting a flute.

Willa couldn't keep from giggling to save her life. It was one of the things that annoyed me most about her. It was also one of the things that endeared me most to her.

"You tricked me." With my hands on my hips, I spat at the ground beside her head, looming over where she was lying in the tall grass at the very top of the hill.

Willa bit her lip, sinking farther into the sea of green. "You can have two turns at hiding tomorrow."

Groaning, I fell to the grass and laid down beside her, my words labored thanks to running uphill like a madman. "I need to go to my mom's tomorrow."

Willa sighed. "I bet you miss her. I miss my dad."

I didn't miss her, thanks to hardly ever seeing her. Once a week, unless she was busy, I spent half a day at her place. Usually on Sundays after church.

When I visited, she'd park me in front of the TV with a wicked cool PlayStation that belonged to one of her ex-boyfriends, and then she'd go back to speaking to her friends or her current boyfriend on the phone.

Willa, though, she rarely saw her dad. Not because he didn't want to, but because he was a Marine and was away a lot for work. He said that one day, as soon as he could, he was going to set up shop wherever she was and stay put so she could see him whenever she wanted.

I wanted to believe him for her, but grown-ups were good at lying. They lied as if it were a sin to ever tell the truth.

"I like the video games," I finally said.

"Our dad says video games are the work of the devil." Our dad. That was how we differentiated when we spoke of them all at the same time.

I snorted. "Then why does he play one when he's on the toilet?"

Willa gasped. "What?"

"Shh, don't act like you know nothing, Bug eyes. It's a card for my sleeve."

"Do you mean a card up your sleeve?"

I scowled, tearing grass and throwing it at her face. She only laughed, which I was pretty sure was what gave our location away.

The weeds swished, and our parents' faces came into view.

I looked at Willa, who paused in brushing the long strands of grass from her face, looked at me, then gulped.

"The cemetery? Really?" Mom said, brows tugging toward her pert nose.

Dad looked as if he was going to fall over from the long-suffering sigh that shook his shoulders. "Back to the house." When we were too slow to get up, he barked, "Now."

With our heads bent low, we trudged after them through the rows of dead people and the gardens that hummed with life; all the while, our parents grumbled and muttered their displeasure.

"You should know better, Willa."

Stepping onto our property, I tried not to frown at what that implied, but in the end, I scowled.

Dad barely blinked as he slammed the gate behind Willa, then glowered at me. "Well? Nothing to say for yourself?"

I dragged the toe of my sneaker through the perfectly trimmed grass in our backyard. "We wanted to play hide and seek, and the backyard gets boring."

Willa's clasped hands were strangling one another.

"So it was your idea, then," Dad said more than asked.

I nodded, and Willa squeaked, but I kicked her foot and shot her a look of murder that made her shut her mouth.

I lost my dessert privileges for a week, and the next afternoon, I arrived home after dinner to find Willa in her room, watching as Dad bolted up the gate at the back of our yard.

She nudged her half-eaten bowl of ice cream toward me, then let her head flop into her hands, her wavy brown hair getting stuck to the ice cream on her lips before she blew a raspberry to push it back.

"Why the long look?" I spooned some strawberry ice cream into my mouth.

Her bottom lip protruded, wobbling a little. "I just… I liked playing there."

I shrugged. "We were bound to be found out eventually." Our parents could only kiss and whatever it was they did when they sent us outside to play for so long. "Besides, a closed gate means nothing."

Willa dropped her elbows from the windowsill, allowing her gauzy curtains to fall back into place. "What?"

"You really are stupid." I licked the remaining ice cream from the bowl, smiling. "We have a side gate, too, dummy."

Willa giggled, and my chest inflated at the sound.

three

Willa
Ten years old

I tried to keep from wincing as my hair threatened to separate from my scalp under Mom's vicious fingers.

"Stop it," she hissed. "We're running late."

Which always made having my hair done worse than usual, her impatience showing with every tug.

Jackson, who was eating his second bowl of cereal at the counter, made a face at Mom's back.

I bit my lips, but the snort crept free.

"Willa," she said with another hard pull at my hair. I flinched, my eyes squeezing shut. "Unless you want to unload the dishwasher instead of watching cartoons when we get home, I suggest you remember your manners."

I couldn't miss my chance to watch *My Little Pony* while Jackson was visiting his mom, Kylie. "Sorry."

"You're getting a little old for the stupid ponies anyway," Jackson said, jumping down and taking his bowl to the sink to rinse it.

I frowned down at the dark cherry wood floor, my pink Mary Janes shifting.

"Jackson," Mom warned. "Hurry up and get ready, please. And if you've got nothing nice to say—"

"Say nothing." Jackson sighed, rolling his eyes as he

muttered, "I know." He disappeared down the hall and upstairs to get changed.

Dad entered the kitchen, his dark hair combed back over his head and his green eyes scrutinizing his mug when he lowered it to discover he'd finished his coffee already.

He placed it in the sink, then adjusted the long sleeves of his pressed white dress shirt. "Ready?"

Mom hummed, her fingers letting up as she braided the ends of my hair. "Just about."

Heath smiled, and the warmth of it, the approval shining in his eyes, clearing the lines around his mouth, made me smile too. "Beautiful, Willa."

I hated wearing braids, let alone piggy tail braids, but I didn't dare say that. Mom wouldn't listen to me anyway. Instead, I said, "Thanks, Dad."

His smile deepened, his hand brushing over my cheek before he made himself another cup of coffee to go.

A coffee he dropped to the ground at the sight of my father, my real one, standing beside our car in the drive, talking animatedly with Jackson. "Shit. Fucking shit." Heath stormed back inside. "Victoria!"

Shock slowed my feet. Heath rarely cussed. My dad hardly visited.

"Bug eyes," Jackson said, his big teeth on display as he grinned. "Your dad blew a bunch of stuff up."

I stopped a few feet from them, my hands tucked in front of me, clenched.

Dad, scratching the back of his head, laughed a funny sounding laugh. "Ah, yeah. Let's maybe not phrase it quite like that." He clapped Jackson on the back, then took a step closer to me, his hazel eyes swimming with what appeared to be tears. "Willa Grace."

My first and middle name were a rich, croaked song that sounded as if it hurt to sing.

"Daniel." Mom came hurrying outside, her hair a bundle of black curls in a bun atop her head. "What the hell are you doing here?"

Dad winked at me, his smile changing into something more mischievous as he turned to my mother.

Her hand nudged my back. "In the car, young lady. Move it."

I offered Dad a small smile before doing as I was told and sliding in next to Jackson, who was grinning at my dad with clear awe.

I clipped my seat belt on, their conversation entering the window Jackson had cracked open just enough to avoid detection. "You can't just show up unannounced and expect to spend time with her. We have plans. We're a family."

"And god forbid you show up at church with only one of your perfectly coifed children, right?" my daddy said with laughter in his voice.

Mom's face colored. "Daniel Grayson, you get back in that car right now before I—"

"Before you what, Victoria? Pack your things and leave under the cover of darkness again?"

"Shut up," Mom said through clenched teeth, tossing a glance at the house behind her.

My eyes were about to pop out of my head, Jackson's grin slipping away at hearing those words. "What?" he whispered to me.

I didn't answer.

Dad said a slew of bad words so foul that even I flinched. "Of course." He laughed, jerking his head toward our two-story white and gray wooden house. "Jesus Christ, Victoria. You mean to tell me that husband of yours might not know what really happened all those years ago?"

"Daniel," Mom warned.

"Don't cry," Jackson said. His voice sounded stretched, strained, as he fidgeted beside me. He sounded like he used to whenever a storm arrived. "Bug eyes?"

Dad began marching to the house, and I withheld the urge to scratch the wetness itching at my cheeks. "I think it's time we tell him then, don't you?"

Jackson muttered, "Oh, crap," as Heath stepped outside in a fresh shirt. Face hard and clean-shaven jaw clenched, he opened the door to find my daddy standing there.

"Daniel, long time, no see," Heath said, clapping him on the shoulder. Hard. "Where have you been for the past, oh, I dunno, two years?"

I couldn't see my dad's face, but I could still hear his voice. "Yeah, funny story about that."

"Yeah?" Heath asked, stepping closer until he was almost nose to nose with my dad. They were both giant, almost the same height, my mom a flower wilting in the breeze as she stood frozen on the driveway.

"Yeah. You see, I was working, and when I arrived home some months ago, eager to see my kid, I discovered you guys had moved. It took some time, asking around and all that fun shit, but I eventually found out you were here."

Heath took a step back, his eyes flicking to Mom for a beat.

"You didn't know about that either, huh?" He laughed. "Seems she'll do anything to hide her filthy little secrets, won't she? It's too bad they're a little too close to home, which is how—"

Mom marched over then and pushed my dad. "Leave. Now."

"What am I missing here, Vicki?" Heath said.

Dad ignored her efforts to move him as though she was nothing but a fly. "A hell of a lot, I'd say," he said.

Jackson had climbed into the front seat and turned over the
ignition far enough to click through the songs on the CD playing
until he found the right one.

"Enough." Heath glowered. "We need to go. We'll call you."

Crowded House's "Weather With You" crooned through the
car, and my limbs loosened, my cheeks sticky as my eyes dried.

"You'll call me?" Dad hollered as Heath took Mom by the
elbow and led her to the car.

Turning to Jackson, I smiled as best I could in thanks.

He stared at me a long moment, then nodded and faced the
grown-ups again.

"You'll have to excuse me if I don't believe you, but that's
fine." Dad grinned a funny way, and my heart pitter-pattered at
the sight. "I know where you are now, and guess what? I'll be back
if I don't hear from you."

Heath and Mom argued outside the car, their hands gesturing and their lips moving fast as my dad's truck grumbled down
the street.

The drive to church was silent, thanks to Mom turning off
the music, and the tension slowly leeched back in.

I wasn't sure why we bothered since it was already a quarter
past nine. I supposed being late was better than not showing up
at all in the eyes of God.

Heads turned as we snuck inside, Mom's cheeks crimson as
she ushered us into a pew in the back, then took a seat with Heath
in the one in front next to Mr. and Mrs. Turns.

As if we'd not interrupted at all, Father Alfred droned on at
the front, his ruddy cheeks wobbling with every exaggerated word
he read from the opened Bible in his hands, pacing back and forth
upon the red velvet that lined the steps.

I was worried I'd need to confess for paying no attention at all, but the worry over my dad's visit was far stronger than anything else.

I'd missed him. For so long, I'd missed him and wondered why he hadn't called in over six months. Even while on tour, he'd call at least every couple of months.

I suppose I now had my answer, but only one. Questions toppled over one another, vying for prime position at the forefront of my mind as that smile, the parting one Dad had given Heath and Mom, refused to leave my retinas.

Tears pushed at the back of my eyes, and I grew dizzy, staring dazedly ahead.

Then, soft and warm, a hand enclosed around mine, and a body shifted closer.

After peering down at them, I lifted my eyes to Jackson, who was staring straight ahead as if he hadn't willingly taken my hand for the very first time.

four

Jackson
Twelve years old

As the years rolled forward, Willa's questions were left to fade into compliance.

Daniel, though, at least stayed true to his word. He settled into a neighboring town nestled along the outskirts of the cove, but he was deployed again six months later.

But for those six months, Willa smiled brighter than the summer sun each time she returned home from spending time with him. So it was to be expected that glow would dim once he'd gone, and that it would be left up to me to spark it back into existence.

Only, I wasn't exactly equipped for the task.

Cursing under my breath at forgetting my lunch bag, I jerked to a stop when I saw Dash by the stairs, scrunching Alan Myer's shirt in his fist.

"I don't think so. How's about this? You swap me your Bulbasaur for my Charmander, and I'll let you keep your chicken sandwich?"

Alan sniffed, his lips quivering. "But B-B-B-Bulbasaur—"

"B-B-B-But I don't give a crap. I want it. Hand it over or I'll keep the Charmander too."

I grabbed the back of Dash's shirt, tearing him away from Alan.

"What the hell?" Dash sputtered, shoving my hand off him.
Alan scampered off into the playground.

"Bulbasaur sucks, and you looked desperate."

Dash considered that for a moment, then shrugged. "People underestimate him is all."

I smirked. "Sure. So did you find out whether you made the soccer team?"

His eyes clouded, his chin jerking up. "Nah, but I'm probably too good."

He was good, but not good enough that they'd ignore the numerous reports about his behavior and his temper.

We took a seat atop the table beneath the maple tree, and within minutes, Peggy and Willa were walking over, lunches in hand. Willa's smile widened when our eyes met, and I forced mine to the red wood of the table.

"Freckles, have you got a Bulbasaur yet?"

"I don't collect Pokémon cards," Peggy said. "I've told you that a hundred times."

Dash ripped into his cheesy bread, grumbling as Peggy opened her lunch beside him.

"You forgot your lunch, Jack." Willa handed my black lunch box over.

I frowned, snatching it and depositing it on the table next to me.

Laughing, she took a seat on the bench where my feet were shifting and began plucking food out.

She'd taken a liking to preparing food, especially our lunches, since school started back. I loved her packed lunches. They were even better than the ones Mom made, but watching her set all the food out on the table next to my thigh was making me feel flustered and weird.

She unwrapped items one by one. "Egg and lettuce, light on

the mayo. Cucumber slices with cheese, and my peanut butter cookies."

I could feel my cheeks grow warm. "You can't bring things with nuts to school, Bug eyes."

Willa, embarrassed, stood and attempted to rewrap the cookies.

Dash stole them. "Better get rid of them quickly then."

I laughed, if anything, to hide the mortification that was reddening my face and tensing my limbs as Dash shoved the three cookies into his mouth.

I laughed even though I wanted them.

And I laughed even though I saw Willa backing up a step, her lip pinched between her teeth.

"God, Willa." A sinking weight pressed into my stomach, and I snapped, "You're not my mom. Get lost already and quit making lunches for me."

Willa's shoulders curled in.

I didn't care. She knew better than to make a fuss over me in public, and usually, she would ensure I'd have my lunch before I left the house. My best guess was she wanted to see if things would be, or could be, different at school now. If they could be like they were at home.

If we could show people we were friends.

She raced off toward the girls' bathrooms, and Peggy left her lunch behind to chase after her.

"She always play mommy for you?"

I scoffed. "No, she just likes to make stuff."

Dash pondered that, licking his fingers. "Well, I wouldn't look so sad about it. Those cookies were awesome."

My gaze fell to the rest of my lunch, and I picked up half of my perfectly sliced sandwich, but I couldn't taste anything as I stared at the bench seat below where Willa had sat.

She didn't look at me during class, or on the bus ride home, and when we walked inside, she locked herself in her room.

I didn't care. *Let her have her stupid tantrum,* I thought. She needed to learn not to mess with me when she knew I didn't want her to.

I kicked my feet up on the coffee table and switched the TV on to sneak in some time on the Xbox before Mom and Dad finished work.

Later that night, as Willa stabbed at her peas and corn across from me at the dinner table and hardly answered Mom's questions about her day at school, I began to grow tired of it.

I followed her upstairs, took a shower, then knocked on her door, ready to berate her for acting like a brat when I'd done nothing wrong.

When Willa cried, she did it in a way that would never give her away unless you were staring right at her face. You'd never hear it, never guess at it until you saw water overflowing from those huge eyes and trickling down her rosy cheeks.

I closed the door behind me, swallowing every scathing word I'd been about to hurl at her, and choked on them as they swelled in my throat. "Bug…"

"Go away, you toad."

I wouldn't, and she couldn't make me.

I took a seat beside her on the bed, eyeing the tissues stuffed inside her clenched fist. "Don't cry."

"You can't just tell someone not to cry," she rasped, sniffing. "Just like you can't tell someone not to care about you in front of your friends. You're not the boss of everything."

Her words slapped me twice across the face, and I closed my eyes for a moment to keep from sinking to the floor.

Reaching out, I tucked some of her hair behind her ear, revealing a beautiful puffy hazel eye. "I'm sorry."

She squeezed her eyes shut, but I saw the tears push their way out anyway, and I lost it.

Grabbing her, I wrapped my arms around her, holding her tight and inhaling the jasmine scent of her shampoo. "I really am sorry," I whispered.

"Don't be sorry. Just don't ignore me anymore." Her voice was soft and cracking. "Why do you need to do that?"

I didn't have an answer. Nothing that was good enough. Nothing could really explain why I was embarrassed to have my sister care about me, to show it so openly, and that didn't make any sense. I couldn't even make sense of it myself.

"None of the other guys hang out with their sisters," I tried to explain, sitting back. But that wasn't exactly true. I knew some who did.

Beneath sooty lashes, she glowered at me, angry eyes searching mine. "But I'm not just your sister. I'm your best friend."

I smiled, feeling that weight begin to dissipate. "Yeah, I guess I just need to remember that."

"You care too much about what other people think, Jackson James Thorn." She pushed away. "So until you don't, there's no point in apologizing, because nothing's going to change."

I scowled, about to bite, but then paused.

She was right.

"I want to hang out with you." I always wanted to hang out with her; that was the problem. "But I need to hang out with my other friends too. Meet me in the middle here, Bug. Come on."

After a moment, she wiped her face, then got up to toss the tissues in the purple trash can under her white desk. "You're right." She nodded. "I didn't think of it like that. I'll..." She blew out a breath, then offered a cautious smile. "I'll back off."

I nodded even though I wasn't sure I wanted her to do that, and then I left her room.

Two days later, things were back to normal.

Well, as normal as things could be given that Willa was hesitant to even look at me at school.

It irked and ate at me, a sickness I couldn't recover from because I'd gone and infected myself.

"If you look any more glum, your face will be mistaken for a bum," Dash said, causing Cad and Raven to double over with laughter.

"Who even says *bum?*" I shot back.

Dash licked his teeth, sorting through his card collection with a keen eye. "I do, when it calls for it. Obviously glum doesn't rhyme with ass."

"Mr. Thane, what did you just say?" Mrs. Marelle neared the table, purple glasses lining her frosted blue eyes.

"I said glum rhymes with bum." Dash peered up at her then, offering a smile. "And rhyming is fun."

She eyed him with a perked brow for a moment, then shook her head. "Such words are unbecoming, Mr. Thane. Your vocabulary is vaster than that."

Dash waited until she'd strolled off before mimicking her, which caused more snorts and laughter to erupt from the idiots beside us.

Sighing, I finished my apple from the lunch I'd prepared myself, wishing it was sliced.

Trying to find Willa on the playground, I squinted toward the swings, where I'd last seen her making daisy chains with Peggy to thread into their ponytails.

Except Peggy was walking over here, and Willa was no longer on the swing.

Before I knew I was moving, I was halfway across the school-yard, searching the groups of kids and clusters of trees.

Behind the far side of the school building, in an area that was out of bounds during recess and lunch, I found her plastered to the wall.

"Just one, yeah? It'll be fun. I've heard it's loads of fun," Danny said, smiling his huge metal-filled smile. "And I've wanted to with you since I was in the fourth grade."

"The fourth grade?" Willa said, her brows scrunched, and her hands flattened to the brick building behind her. "That's creepy, and I said I don't want to."

Danny huffed, and I relaxed, slowing to a stop when he took a step back. "Fine."

Then he swooped in, and Willa turned her head, her eyes shut tight, just in time to avoid his lips smacking into hers.

Instead, they hit her cheek, and she winced as the impact knocked her head against the brick.

I charged, pulling him to the ground and swinging my fist into his face.

"Yeah! Fight, fight, fight," the kids shouted.

"Jackson," Willa screamed. "He's bleeding."

It was her scream that made me pause, for I could count on one hand the number of times I'd heard her do that in our entire lives.

When a spider appeared while she was on the toilet. When she'd tumbled off her bike on the driveway and sprained her wrist. When I'd jumped out from behind a tombstone in the cemetery and scared her so much she'd fallen back onto her butt. And when I'd flung a grasshopper at her face.

And now, after some shithead tried to kiss her.

I stumbled back as the teacher rounded the corner, then I was being hauled to the principal's office where I waited for Mom to arrive.

"I can't believe it. Suspended?" She threw her hands up at home, pacing the kitchen. "What on earth has gotten into you, Jackson?"

I licked my lips, unsure what to say.

"Well?" she pushed. "An answer would be nice, unless you'd like me to call your father home too."

Staring down at the streaks of blood on my hands from Danny's busted nose, I frowned at them, my heart still racing with adrenaline. "He was pressuring her to do something she didn't want to." There. That should've done it.

It didn't. "Pressuring her to do what?"

I pleaded with my eyes and voice. "Don't make me say it. She'll get upset."

Mom's lips pursed, and then her face paled, as did mine. "Oh, god. No."

I shook my head, knowing what she was thinking, even though I probably shouldn't have. But we'd watched our first porno at Dash's place last summer, and so I knew enough. "Not that."

Her shoulders slackened, and she sucked in a cleansing breath, then paused. "Wait, how did you..." At the sheepish look I offered, she groaned, slapping her hand on the countertop. "You're only twelve, Jackson."

"Don't worry. I've never even kissed a girl." Though two had tried, and I was curious. More and more curious every day.

She smiled then and tucked her hair behind her ears. She had these small ears, like Willa. Seashells, I'd once thought, right before I gave her a wet willy. "Okay. So what was he pressuring her to do?"

"To kiss him."

Mom's lips parted, and she shook her head, laughing softly. After a moment, she stared at me, then rounded the counter and pulled me into a hug.

Unlike my real Mom, who reeked of cheap perfume and annoyance, Victoria smelled nice. Like overbearing love and frosting. Willa smelled like frosting too, and jasmine.

I hugged her back.

"You're a good brother," Mom said, kissing the top of my head. "I'm not happy about this, but I'm proud of you for being there for her."

With that, she fed me cookies and orange juice, then called Dad while I was made to clean my room.

Hearing the bus pull up an hour later, I tossed my gym shorts into the hamper from across the room, pumped my fist, and then stood in the doorway.

Willa walked upstairs and dropped her bag at the top, rushing to me. "Are you okay?"

I nodded. "Yeah, why wouldn't I—"

She shoved me, hissing as I tripped back inside my room, "You beat him up."

My eyes widened, and I laid sprawled beneath her on my bed. "The twerp was trying to kiss you!"

"So you go and get yourself suspended?" She crossed her arms. "I can take care of myself, you know. You kind of gave me no choice when you decided I was the plague and you didn't want to get infected."

I laughed and frowned. "What?"

"You heard me." She left my room, and dumbfounded, I scrambled off the bed after her.

I pushed her door open before she could shut it in my face. "Hang on a damn minute. I was sticking up for you, and you're mad at me?"

She pulled her homework from her bag. "I'm mad because you have double standards, and even though I know you can be mean, I thought you were better than that." All I could do was stare, and when she looked up, a brow raised, I swallowed. "You can leave now."

I did but returned later that night with heated words of my own stretching out over my tongue.

Before I could open my mouth, she said, "Go to bed, Jackson."

"Jackson, now?" I said, scoffing, and refrained from stomping my foot. Just.

"You're not Jack at the moment. When he returns, I'll call you by that name instead."

"Enough," I said, and she turned over to face me, her book hanging between her fingers. "You don't get to be mad at me for sticking up for you. In fact, you don't get to be mad anymore *period.*"

"Period?" she said, smiling.

I nodded. "Because you're not allowed to leave my sight at school now, got it?"

Her eyes bugged out. "Jackson."

"I said," I gritted, "got it?"

After frowning up at me for seconds that threatened to snake around my throat and suffocate me, she nodded. "Yeah, got it." Then she grinned. "Can I borrow your flashlight? Mine's out of batteries, and I want to stay up and finish this tonight."

Relief, stronger than any embarrassment I'd ever felt, rained over me. "Whatever."

Fourteen

"Willa!" I dumped my gear bag in the foyer, taking the stairs two at a time. "Bug, I got second place. I messed up my fender and front wheel, but it doesn't..." I stopped when I found her room empty and dark, the curtains still closed. "Matter."

A tiny clatter sounded, and I spun, moving toward the bathroom. The door was locked. I rattled the handle anyway. "Willa?"

"Go away." Her voice was faint, and I felt the hairs begin to rise on my sweat-painted skin.

She was supposed to come to the race today, but she'd said she wasn't feeling well.

I'd been annoyed, thinking she was lying. I'd been an idiot, I realized, when I jimmied open the door with one of her bobby pins.

She scrambled back, her face pale and her eyes filled with fear as she stared up at me from the floor. "Jackson, get out."

That's when I saw it.

Blood.

All over her sleep shorts.

Sleep shorts that were on the blue tiled floor.

Willa pulled her knees up, and I caught a glimpse of blood between her legs.

My eyes squeezed momentarily, and she sniffed as I backed up to the door.

I clicked the lock in place, then walked over to her.

Horrified, she gazed up at me, shaking a little.

Her boobs were growing, and she wasn't wearing a bra beneath her flimsy pale pink tank. The number of times I noticed when she wasn't was beginning to make me feel like an asshole.

Mainly because it didn't sicken me. Still, the way I'd feel warmth gathering inside me, stirring in places it shouldn't, shamed me.

At times like that, I'd remind myself she wasn't my sister by blood. Like a chant, I'd repeat it over and over, if only to ease the guilt.

We could never go there.

But over the past year, we'd gone there and many different places, all within the confines of my fucked-up imagination.

"You got your period," I stated the obvious.

She nodded, her lip white between her teeth as she gazed down at her scrunching, peach-painted toenails. "I felt so sick all night, and I couldn't sleep."

I frowned. "That's why you didn't come?"

It didn't bother me if she didn't want to watch me race my dirt bike. It bothered me when she said she'd do something and then didn't do it.

I wasn't good enough to go pro. I could've been, but I didn't want to push myself that hard. I'd seen, as had my dad, what it could do to those who loved the sport. For some, passion was swapped for work, and for those who still loved it, disappointment unlike anything I'd seen upon someone's face before.

Willa twisted her fingers together. "I couldn't get up. I was so tired. And when I did"—her nose crinkled toward her thighs—"I found all this."

"When did you wake up?" It was almost one in the afternoon.

"About ten minutes before you got here." Swallowing, she said, so quiet, "I didn't know what to do. It's nothing like I thought it would be."

"It's a massacre," I tried to joke.

Her cheeks caught fire. She reached for her soiled shorts, then thought better of it. "It's okay, I'm going to shower and—"

"I'm messing with you, but yeah, it's gross." I opened the shower door, turning the water on. "So get in and get cleaned up. Mom should be inside by now." She'd been helping Dad unload the car.

"I don't want her to know. I mean, I'll tell her, but not today."

I didn't need to ask why. Victoria was a fusser. She'd give her the talk, another one, and would likely put her on some type of birth control.

Nodding, I walked over and grabbed her hand. I pulled her to her feet, making sure my eyes stayed on her face. "You need anything?"

Slowly, her eyes dragged up my face, colliding with mine. Her bottom lip, indented from her teeth, rubbed her top one, and she shook her head.

When her eyes dropped to our hands, and I felt her thumb brush over mine, I shivered and bounced back, then got out of there.

It'd been a few years since I'd been in her panty drawer. The last time I had, she still had pairs with frogs and cats on them.

Now, they were all purple or pink or black. My fingers shook, hovering over the purple pair, her favorite color. I snatched them and slammed the drawer closed, then opened the next one to get a bra.

Fuck. I began to sweat all over again. "Don't think, just pick one."

It didn't match, but I didn't care. Moving to her closet, I grabbed the orange T-shirt dress she usually wore around the house.

Opening the bathroom door just enough to slide them inside, I heard the slap of suds hitting the shower floor.

Swallowing, I went to shut it when Willa said, "Thank you."

I cleared my throat. "It's fine."

"And I heard you, that you came second," she said before I could close the door. "Congrats."

Smiling, I couldn't help but say, "Congrats to you, too."

Her laughter encouraged my own to burst free.

five

Willa
Fifteen

"**A**ren't you a little old for camping?" Dad said, turning the page in his car magazine.

I pulled the tray of fresh cookies from the oven, setting them on the stovetop. "It's still fun."

"It's her birthday," Jackson said, entering the kitchen and opening the fridge. "If she wants to camp, we'll camp."

"Correction," Dad said, holding up a finger. "You two can camp. I'm staying indoors where there are no mosquitos."

I smiled down at the cookies, pressing one with my finger. "You'll cramp our style, anyway."

Dad scoffed. "Nothing you say will convince me, Wil."

That had been what I'd hoped for. The last thing we wanted was he and Mom squeezing into the four-man tent with us.

Jackson had been setting it up at the very back of the yard. I hadn't had a chance to go out and see it yet, but I knew from the way he was glugging down juice at the fridge from the carton with his back turned that he was done.

"Where's Mom?" Jackson closed the fridge.

"Got caught up with the conference." Dad drained his coffee. "She'll be back in time for tomorrow, don't worry."

After years of studying and raising us, she'd become an attorney when I was seven years old.

Dad owned and ran Thorn Racing, an action sports company that had been in his family for the past two generations.

Already, Jackson wanted to follow in his father's footsteps, and he often tried to get Heath to take him along to board meetings, events, and to let him listen in on Skype conversations. When I'd asked him why, he'd shrugged and said there was just something alluring about running a company with that much importance. That and he loved to ride, both BMX and dirt bikes. The safety, the family name plastered all over people's gear, and the lives it helped protect awed him. Not only did the company rely on our dad to keep it running and turning a profit, but its customers, the sponsors, the athletes, and some of the general population did as well.

It seemed like too much pressure if you asked me, to which he'd said, "Exactly," with a smile that gleamed and caused his green eyes to spark with excitement.

"Make sure you lock up and keep your phones on you." Dad waved his hand, laughing as he scooped up his magazine. "Who am I kidding? You're not kids anymore. You won't last past midnight."

Jackson waited until he was gone before turning to me. "A challenge, Bug. Are we up for it?"

He chuckled at my raised brows, and the deep, abrasive sound of it always caught me off guard, even months after it'd changed.

He was no longer a boy, but a young man, and the changes weren't going unnoticed by just me. He'd been asked to every event and dance since we'd started high school, and he'd accepted most of the invites. Yet as far as I knew, he hadn't had a girlfriend yet.

I cleared my throat, then tied my hair back into a loose braid. "What kind of question is that?"

"A valid one, considering we are indeed not ten anymore."

I'd wanted to camp since then, which was the last time we had. My dad, my real one, had been the only one to oblige me, though, and that was last summer.

"I'm no flake."

Jackson stole a cookie, hissing as it burned his skin. He threw it in his mouth anyway and spoke around it. "No, but you are a girl."

I shoved his shoulder, and he laughed, bits of cookie flying from his mouth and landing on my cheek.

"Ew." I brushed it off, and he laughed some more as he left the kitchen.

"Don't forget the red frogs, or I probably will bail early."

An hour later, cookies in the Tupperware container, the red frogs in a bag with other candy hanging from my wrist, and the mini sandwiches I'd prepared, I headed outside and almost dropped everything once I saw the tent.

Standing beside it, Jackson rubbed the back of his neck. "It was a little mucky from not being used, so I had to spruce it up."

Fairy lights were strung like garland from the front of the canvassed roof to the fence, and flickers of light glowed from inside. The sun was setting, yet Jackson had created this little world of light for our very own.

Moving closer, I barely noticed when he took all the food from me, and I bent low, opening the tent flaps.

Our sleeping bags, mine pink with fairies and his green with spaceships, sat over a huge blow up mattress, and beside it, on an upside-down milk crate that was covered with a white cloth, was a Mason jar filled with fireflies.

"How?" I asked, nearing it and reaching out to run my fingers over the glass.

"I'm a pro, that's how. Did you grab any drinks?" When I

didn't answer, he huffed and walked out, presumably to go get them himself.

The fairy lights were in here, too, I realized, looking up to see a row hanging from the ceiling, snaking through tiny holes at either end of the tent.

Jackson returned with two bottles of water and cans of orange pop. He cracked open a can and plonked the rest, and himself, down on the ground near the door where he'd set the food. "Cool, huh?"

I blinked, then lowered to the mattress. It bounced in time with my heart. "It's amazing."

We ate while he regaled me with tales of how he and Dash had snuck away to set off fireworks during the dance on Friday night.

After he opened the laptop, we settled on the bed to watch *Moulin Rouge*. He hated it, but it was my birthday, and he knew I adored it.

Jackson was staring absently at the screen with an arm tucked behind his head.

The Mason jar, on the side table he'd constructed, was still aglow with the fluttering bugs inside. The flickers of light cast dancing black shapes over the interior of the tent, and my eyelids grew heavy as I watched them.

Jackson bumped my elbow with his. "Not interested in 'Come What May' tonight?"

I slouched down onto my back, puffing out a sigh. "Ainsley likes you."

"I know."

I forced a smile. "You went to the dance with her, but you left her to mess around with fireworks?" I hadn't gone. Brendan Peters had asked me, but my cheeks had burned so hot under his nervous gaze, and thanks to Jackson's presence a few lockers down, that all I could do was shake my head.

Jackson had watched him walk off down the hall, his brows furrowed, then eyed me before turning back to his friends.

"She might like me, but I don't like her."

"That's mean," I said, turning to face him.

He leaned forward and shut the computer down, placing it on the ground before dropping onto his back. "I don't dislike her. I just don't *like*, like her." He cleared his throat, turning his head slightly. "You know?"

I studied his green eyes, the lashes that surrounded them fanning out like dark feathers, and the tiny, faded freckle that nestled the corner of his right eye. "I get it."

Tucking his arm behind his head again, he yawned.

"Who do you like then?" Ainsley was pretty, with her blond hair and blue eyes. If he didn't like her, then did he even like anyone? All the girls were crushing on the boys, and the boys were making idiots of themselves over the girls.

His harsh exhale rolled his lips and brushed my cheek. With his teeth scraping over his bottom lip, he smiled, wane and reproachful. "Someone I shouldn't."

Something hard and heavy fell into my stomach and slowed my breathing. I couldn't keep from frowning if I tried, and so I didn't. "Who?" I demanded.

Laughing, he settled his eyes on mine, bright in the dark and bobbing over my face. His smile drooped as he took a piece of my hair and twirled it around his finger. "You don't need to know, Bug."

I needed to know more than I needed air to breathe, and it was killing me just the same. My lungs were tight, shrinking, and my exhales short.

"Hey," he said, concern marring his brow as his finger released my hair. Warmth hit my skin, startling my eyes to his studying ones, while his hand curved around my cheek. "Don't cry."

"I'm not." I didn't realize I had been.

"Your eyes are wet. Wait…" He bent closer, questions filling his own. "Willa, you…" He didn't finish, just stared for five unbearable beats.

Then he moved, his unsaid words fading into a kiss that would break a thousand rules and promises for years to come.

I gasped against his lips. His warm, gentle lips. Then I pulled away, my breathing more erratic than before. "Jack."

He swallowed loudly, his throat rippling, and shut his eyes. "Shit. I'm sorry."

And then I was leaning forward, my lips searching and finding his, sweet and soft as butter.

His hands wrapped tight around my face as we both carefully pressed and retreated, only to go back again and again, each time more urgent than the last.

Between breaths, he murmured, "Is this your first kiss?" I nodded, and he mumbled, "Me too."

Shock stiffened my limbs, my mouth, but it melted when his bottom lip meshed between mine, and my tongue poked out to touch it.

A groaning sound flooded my ears, and stars burst behind my closed eyes. I fell to my side, his legs intertwined with mine, and his tongue caressed the seam of my lips, asking for entry.

It was warm, wet, and tickled against my hesitant one, but after minutes, or maybe hours, kissing felt as easy as talking to him did.

For that was what we were doing, speaking a different language. A language that tasted of disaster and sin but felt like promise and perfection.

A wrong so wrong that it couldn't be anything other than just right.

The night crawled on, the stars glittering above a world we'd manufactured to harbor a secret that would follow us into every dawn thereafter, yet our mouths refused to part, and our heartbeats refused to slow.

A bird was singing above my head.

Not my head, I realized, my eyes blinking open as my surroundings came into focus.

The tent. I blinked again and felt something warm beneath my hand.

Jackson's stomach.

My cheek.

His chest.

The kiss.

All the kisses.

So many kisses, my lips were chafed, rubbed raw when I licked them.

Fear crashed in like a tidal wave, and I carefully pushed my hair off my face, my braid a distant memory thanks to Jackson's hands.

Sitting upright, I combed my fingers through it, staring at the light that streamed in through the gauzy material of the tent, highlighting the forgotten snacks and the laptop on the floor.

I couldn't look at him.

I couldn't not look at him.

My ears seared as I touched my lips, sitting perfectly still as Jackson's eyelids twitched, his lashes tiny curtains over his cheeks. They looked more angular in the harsh light of day, his lips more symmetrical and plumper after kissing mine.

But it was his mussed brown hair, the dark strands in disarray, that crumpled my shaking composure into a breaking ball of dust.

"Guys," Dad's voice sounded.

I jumped, and Jackson snorted, eyes opening and narrowed up at me. "What time is it?" His voice was rough and sleep stained, just as it usually was when he woke up; only now, it sounded different.

Unable to speak, I got up and dragged my hands through my hair as I paced the small space.

"Oh, good. You're up." Dad must have seen my shadow moving and opened the tent. "Mom just called, and she'll be here in time for some brunch. Choc chip pancakes?"

I smiled, then coughed. "Yeah, sounds good."

He smiled, pulling me to his chest to lay a kiss on my messy hair. "Happy Birthday, baby girl." He sighed. "Fifteen. Slow it down, would you? You guys are making me feel old."

I forced a laugh, noticing when I pulled away that Jackson was just staring at me.

"Birthday or not, you guys are cleaning this up." He looked at Jackson. "You look comfortable."

"I told you," Jackson said. "The blow-up bed isn't all that bad."

"My back told me differently last time I used the stupid thing, but whatever." He waved a hand, ducking back outside the tent. "I have some calls to make before we can head out when your mom gets here, so be sure to keep it down if you come inside."

"Okay," I said, watching the flaps of the tent fall and slowly stop moving.

I couldn't bring myself to turn around, but I had to.

He was my brother. Granted, he wasn't my real brother, but we shared the same surname. We'd taken baths together until we were seven years old.

For months, he'd made me listen to jokes he read from his joke book while he was on the toilet.

Fear slithered through my bloodstream and caused my limbs to tremble with guilt.

What had we done?

What we were even thinking, I didn't know.

I mean, I knew what I'd been thinking. I knew what I'd been thinking since I noticed the jade green to his eyes more than a year ago. Since I began to watch his gait, casual and unhurried, as he walked down the school halls when we'd started high school. Since he'd gone to the dance with Ainsley, and I'd felt relieved when I found out he hadn't even danced with her.

I'd noticed specific things about him for a while, and they only grew more specific over the past few months, each one more dangerous than the last.

I just never knew how dangerous until I feared he had feelings for someone.

I didn't think. I never would've guessed that... that someone would be me.

My last thought gave me enough courage to turn around and face the reason for my heartbeat's change of pace.

Jackson was out of bed, folding the blankets. "I'll clean up."

"I'll help," I said, moving for the food.

"No," he said or, rather, snapped. I watched his back, the way it rose, then fell sharply. "Just... forget it, please."

Sensing he was referring to more than the food, I straightened and glared at the back of his head. "What do you mean?"

"You know exactly what I mean." His tone was firm and unyielding.

Retorts, protests, thick and hot, queued to vomit from my mouth, propelled by the raging organ in my chest, but I swallowed them when he turned.

With his brows furrowed, arms tense around the folded blankets tucked to his chest, he said, "We have to."

It wasn't his words that had me nodding, that had me seeing what he was trying to say without saying it, but his eyes.

They pleaded, begged, but they also screamed of the ramifications that would unfold if we couldn't do what he'd said, and forget it.

I could never forget, but it was because I knew he couldn't either that I moved my chin up and down, then walked out.

It was wrong, but it couldn't be undone.

Wrong and stupid.

It was wonderful, but it could never happen again.

Wonderfully stupid.

Six

Willa
Fifteen

Hours of forbidden became months of torment, creating wounds I didn't know how to heal.

Not when Jackson did everything he could to ensure I stayed away from him.

It was for the best, he'd say.

But when I'd stop listening and push harder, he'd snap. *"Willa, back off."*

I'd brought this upon myself, I supposed. I knew he'd been right. That we should've left it well enough alone, and I'd been trying.

But I still wanted to be with him. I didn't need to touch him or to kiss him again. Thoughts of doing so would make me squirm anyway, with both discomfort and something else that tingled in sensitive places.

He was my best friend, my brother, but I was terrified he'd become my biggest regret if we couldn't find a way to salvage what we might've ruined.

Guarded looks and stiff limbs greeted me at every turn during school, daring me to say or do anything. I never did. Begrudgingly, I behaved.

"Willa needs her eyes checked," he'd joked over dinner one night.

"Why?" Dad had asked.

A smirk at me, and then, "She missed the hoop by a foot in gym today."

Dad chuckled, and Mom had shaken her head, trying not to laugh. Meanwhile, I'd smiled down at my plate, feigning embarrassment that for once, I'd wished was real.

It was business as usual in the Thorn household, that is, until Mom and Dad weren't looking or in the same room.

Then it was cold shoulders and cruel silence.

For weeks, it dragged on. For months, I prayed that time would make what we did fade enough for him to forget his new favorite pastime; ignoring me.

I couldn't tell Peggy. I couldn't tell anyone.

I was left to suffocate alone.

Jackson's sixteenth birthday was nearing when I wondered how much longer it'd be before what I felt faded. Crushes, those feelings were supposed to pass. And I was desperate to breathe without the burn.

Lately, Ainsley and Annabeth had been two constant fixtures by Jackson's locker. And usually, he'd offer them that irritating smirk of his before leaving them to blush in his absence.

Today was different.

Today, he turned to Ainsley and leaned his shoulder into his closed locker, his lips moving as she stepped closer, gazing up at him with wonder.

Idly, I wondered if I ever looked at him the same way. The thought didn't stand a chance at lingering as a tightening sensation exploded through my chest and worked its way up my throat.

I shouldn't care.

I wasn't sure I wanted to care.

But I did.

He'd been the one to make the first move. The one to propel us into this dark space where we were left to find the sun on our own.

I couldn't watch, but I still did, as he said something that made Ainsley giggle and sway even closer. She'd taken to wearing heels to school, her knee-high black socks covering her knees.

I looked down at my own that wrapped snug around the tops of my shins, my toes scrunching inside my black ballet flats, and sighed, blowing hair off my face as I forced my feet to class.

"But I told Mom I didn't like them, and she gave me the angry eyes," Peggy was saying. "Can you believe it? Like, it's been years, lady. Lay off already."

I smiled at Peggy and nodded even though I wasn't listening.

Jackson and Ainsley walked outside, and I stood. "Jack, I brought some pudding cups."

Jackson stopped, grinned at Ainsley, whose brows were puckering as she gazed back and forth between us. "Cool story, Wil. Better watch it doesn't add another member to the family of zits on your chin."

My stomach turned to lava, bubbling and roaring, rising to flood my face and ears.

I fell to the bench seat as he and Ainsley walked through the doors to sit outside.

Dash sauntered over and snatched one of the pudding cups. "His loss." He winked, then tore the lid off on the way to Lars and Raven, who were sitting on the other side of the cafeteria.

One of the cheerleaders, Daphne, was watching me, and for some reason, that only made it worse. Tears pushed and demanded to be set free.

It's only pudding, I berated myself. *Don't be such a baby.*

Peggy's hand fell over mine. "Hey, he'll stop being a dick eventually. That's just what brothers do, you know?"

I nodded, forcing a smile that barely moved my lips. Peggy had witnessed a few of Jackson's snubbings. She'd also witnessed most of our relationship, so I knew she could understand, as much as anyone could without knowing everything, why it wasn't so easy to shake off.

I wanted to tell her that he'd kissed me. That almost nine months ago, beneath a fairy lit sky, I'd kissed him back. I needed to tell someone, and he wouldn't dare let me utter a word about it to him.

Hysteria sparked and pricked at my chest, pushing out a rough laugh. "I know. I don't even know why I bother. It's stupid. *He's* stupid."

Peggy took her hand back and opened a snickerdoodle. "Not stupid. You guys were like best friends. I'd be sad if Dash never wanted to hang with me, especially in public."

Dash and Peggy had been best friends since they were toddlers, maybe earlier than that. So if anyone knew how I might be feeling, it'd be her.

And still, I said nothing.

It was too bad, really. Too bad that I had to deal with this alone. Too bad that I had to watch Ainsley flirt and follow Jackson around.

Too bad that I had to get over something that didn't feel wrong at all, but every shade of right. For I knew I did. I just wasn't sure how to.

As if he knew exactly what I needed, Jackson fixed that for me the following week.

It didn't matter that I'd been his first. Not when I wanted to be all the in-betweens and his last too.

And where were the teachers when you actually wanted them to be around? Nowhere to be seen from my vantage point by the drop-off zone outside school.

They were kissing in plain sight. Ainsley's head tipped back and Jackson's angled down as his hand cradled her face the same way it had cradled mine.

Even as my stomach churned and my heartbeat slowed to a painful thump, I wondered if his hold was just as gentle, if his lips were as curious and hungry, and if his heart was racing or merely beating.

And I wondered why, out of all the places he could've picked, he chose to kiss her there. Mere feet away from where our driver would pull up to take us home.

When he'd eventually climbed inside the black Town Car, Lynne giving us small smiles in greeting, I decided I was through with wondering.

I knew too much to keep wondering. I had cold hard facts.

We were stepsiblings who never should've touched, let alone kissed until our lips were cracked and swollen.

Until my heart was cracked and swollen.

I should've felt sickened. I should've struggled with what we'd done. But I hadn't. I didn't. I hadn't felt anything but desperate longing for a long time.

But now, it was painfully clear he felt differently.

Home was unable to provide reprieve. Everywhere I went, he went too. That was the crux of it really. What we'd done was as inescapable as ourselves.

The anger and injustice brewed throughout dinner, no longer a steady simmer but a boiling mess that couldn't be unleashed.

Mom and Dad chattered, a few times trying to coax me into conversation, to which I just smiled and kept scratching at the food on my plate.

Jackson was all carefree attitude and smiles as though he couldn't see the tension or feel it rolling off me from where I sat across from him.

Mom eyed me as she finished her wine, and I excused myself, blaming an unsettled stomach.

No lie, but only partial truth. Each step was weighted as I went upstairs and fell back against the closed door.

I stood there, eyes shut and my chest heaving, for untold seconds or minutes, and then I was storming across my room, unable to feel anything but this energy that was strangling every breath I drew.

Pasta jewelry and art cracked as it smacked to the floor. The framed photo I had of us on my dresser, where he was smiling, a fish hanging from the rod in his hand, and I was pointing at it, dented the wall before meeting the floor, the frame splitting and the picture tilting.

"Willa." His voice penetrated.

But I wasn't done. I was so far from done as I opened my desk drawer and threw the scrapbook album I'd made for us across the room.

Jackson moved in time to avoid having it hit his stomach, his mouth agape. "Bug, stop."

I stabbed a finger at him, growling, "Get out."

Biting his lips, his face pale with apprehension, he ignored me and came closer.

"Don't," I said. "Just don't. I love you, and you, and you…" My voice cracked. "You treat me like that doesn't mean anything. As if we were never friends at all, let alone more. You just keep throwing it back in my face. All the freaking time."

His head was shaking. "Will—"

"Get. Out."

He reached for me, eyes soft and glossy. "Bug."

My heart seized and splattered.

"Jackson," Mom interrupted.

He stepped back, his gaze remaining on me.

My chest was going to explode, my fingers curling and uncurling, nails scoring into my palms.

"You two haven't been getting along for some time now," she said, her eyes flicking back and forth between us. "Dad and I spoke about it. We think you'd be better off with some time apart."

No.

I began to protest, but Mom raised a hand, taking Jackson by the elbow.

He didn't move, his expression of shattering steel still on my face, until Mom said, "There's only one other alternative if you can't agree to this."

Jackson relented then, and horrified, I widened my eyes at her. "What?"

Dad, my real one, was on his last tour, and then he was taking a job close to where he'd bought a house on the outskirts of town.

Mom sighed. "You aren't yourself, Willa. Don't think I haven't noticed. I've been patient, but enough is enough." Her eyes roamed my bedroom, creasing with displeasure. "It's time to make some changes. No arguments."

Jackson stared at me over his shoulder as she encouraged him from my room, then helped him pack up his own.

Unable to understand how I could feel so angry yet feel so guilty, I found myself stuck in the threshold of my doorway at midnight.

Sleep refused to arrive, and rather than tossing and turning,

I got up to get a drink, but I couldn't force myself down the stairs.

Jackson was still in his room and remained there until his bed was set up in the basement. The basement wasn't as cold and dreary as it once had been. It was carpeted, air conditioned, and even had a window looking up into the side of our yard.

Still, I'd done this. I'd had him moved as if he were some troublesome child who needed an intervention.

He wasn't doing anything wrong.

It took some time, but a few nights later, sleep still a distant memory, I drained a glass of water and watched my hand shake as I set it down in the sink, knowing it was me.

I was the troublesome child with feelings and thoughts that shouldn't exist. The one who kept getting away with being a nuisance.

Exist they might, but it was past time I locked them away. If Jackson had any, then he'd clearly done the same thing months ago.

"Hey," he said.

It was almost midnight, but I wasn't all that surprised he was still awake.

Turning around, I tucked some hair behind my ear, trying to say what I needed to. I refused to look at him as I did. "I'm sorry, Jack."

His bare feet carried him closer, too close. Tipping my chin up, he forced my eyes to his. The touch alone was enough to make my heart kick. "Don't cry."

I sniffed, laughing a little. "So bossy."

He smirked, but it fell after a second, swept away by the stark lines of his cheekbones and the shifting of his squaring jaw. "You don't need to be sorry. I've been asking Dad if I could move down there for months."

Months. I swallowed, backing into the counter to force his fingers off my skin. "You wanted to be away from me?" My voice was meek and accusing, but I didn't have the strength to care.

Jackson's brows lowered over his vivid eyes. "No. I wanted away from them. My room is next to theirs."

"Oh," I said, the word rushing out on a relieved breath while I dragged my eyes to the floor.

"You said something that's been bothering me," he said after a moment of crushing silence.

My head snapped up. "What?"

Looking uncomfortable, he scratched his head, chewing on his lip. "Um, in your room. The other night."

Alarm sprinkled like rain, followed closely by devastating pain. He was talking about when I'd said I loved him. In many ways, I did, but it was in all the wrong ways that I felt it the most.

He didn't need to know that.

And I didn't need to feel it.

It should've been fleeting, the constant sensation of falling, but it wasn't. That didn't mean I couldn't do my best to ignore it.

"Wil…" His voice was strained. A long sweep of his broadening frame showed tension. "I…" His lips shut, unsaid words clamped behind them, threatening to make something out of a force too big for us both.

He couldn't do this. If I was being honest, I didn't think I could either. His eyes implored, screaming that what he needed was anything but this.

What I felt was wrong, which was why he would never know. And how I felt didn't allow the strength to hurt him.

I never wanted to hurt him.

"You're like a brother to me." The words were thick and sour, protesting as I pushed them out. Forcing a memory of when he'd eaten pumpkin stew as a dare, then spat it all over the kitchen floor, I was able to smile genuinely while I shrugged. "My best friend. Or, at least, you were. So, of course, I love you, if that's what you mean."

He stared, expression unreadable, and his body still tense for drawn-out seconds.

Then he licked his lips and sighed. "I've been a dick. I know I have. I'm sorry."

I nodded, folding my arms across my chest and straightening from the counter. "Why?"

He took his time to answer, those eyes of his traveling over my face, dipping to my chest, then to the fridge. "I guess I thought something bad would happen if I didn't keep you away."

I didn't need to mention that something bad had happened because he had. Instead, I went to leave.

Moving by him, he bumped my shoulder with his, jerking his head to the window as rain began to splatter against it. "Just a bad day."

Smiling up at him, I murmured, "So it is."

His smile faded, his throat rippling as his lashes lowered. "Can someone have a bad couple of months?"

My smile faded too, and I forced myself to look away. To move away. It was surprisingly easy when it hurt to be too close. To have his cedarwood and mint scent and voice caress my skin.

"Yes," I finally said, throwing a hint of a smile over my shoulder. "I guess they can."

The news played in the background, a gentle hum to accompany the ever-present one I still felt in Jackson's presence.

It was nice, being able to hang out with him like we once did, though it wasn't the same. Gone were the days when we'd fish in the creek, explore the cemetery, or go camping. Now, we'd do the quieter things. Things less likely to lead to trouble we couldn't escape from.

"Got any fives?" I asked.

Jackson shook his head. "Go fish."

I peered at my new card, licking my teeth to make sure the apple pie I'd made for dessert hadn't hung around. "So, how are things with Ainsley?"

They'd been seeing one another for a while now, and although it never got any easier to see them together, I was able to numb myself to it after watching them enough.

Jackson stilled, then casually threw a glance over his shoulder to the living room.

Mom had been playing with us, but she'd left a few minutes ago to take a call, saying she'd be right back.

"Willa." It was a warning, the firm use of my name.

"It's just a question," I said, smiling a little. "You don't need to answer if you don't want to."

He stared at me for a moment, and I feared if he kept doing that for too long, I might climb over the table and beg for his lips to touch mine. Soft, plumper on the bottom, and perfectly curved at the top, they parted when he blew out a breath.

She got to kiss those lips.

"Things are good." His mouth had moved, and his voice sang with truth, but his eyes were downcast, focused on his cards.

I let it go with a slow nod. "That's good. I heard she left the cheerleading squad."

"Yeah, she wants to focus on dance now."

"She's a great dancer," I said. "Good for her." I meant it, even if it hurt to line myself up next to her. I had my strengths, but I didn't think a strong eye for detail and baking inspired awe next to the likes of Ainsley Brown.

"Yeah." Jackson cleared his throat. "She's great."

My next question was likely a terrible idea, but it was too late to stop it. "Why don't you ever invite her over?"

Jackson looked up, his hands lowering to the table as his eyes scrutinized mine. "What?"

I tipped a shoulder, taking a sip of lemonade. "I just never see her here, that's all. I was wondering why." He was turning seventeen next month. I'd be seventeen before junior year began. We were at the age when boyfriends and girlfriends were starting to get serious, meet parents, and visit one another's houses.

Another quick glance over his shoulder, and then he said, "Things are normal again."

"With us," I said, smiling. "You mean."

His brows almost met. "Exactly." After a few restless beats, he groaned and scrubbed a hand down his face. "Don't do this, Bug."

The use of the nickname warmed me in wicked ways. "Sorry." I wasn't sorry, but I wasn't interested in digging at what solid ground we'd managed to lay over our transgressions either.

Anger laced his low tone. "Doesn't it get hard enough?"

I blinked. "What?"

"Do you still think about it?" The anger drifted before he'd finished asking that question, leaving his voice rasped.

I couldn't say a word. Paralyzed by fear and untamed desire, I felt my cheeks heat.

That answered his question, and after a minute of staring down at his cards, his jaw tight and shifting, he mumbled, "Sorry."

I had to let it go. I had my answers. More than I thought I'd need.

He wouldn't invite her over because of me.

Best of all, he still thought about kissing me.

I forced back a smile that would surely give what little joy I'd found away. "Got any sixes?"

Sighing, he muttered, "Go fish."

Seven

Willa
Sixteen

"**A**re you going to drop that thing or not?" Peggy called. Shifting out of my flip-flops, I kept the towel wrapped around me as I bent low to carefully situate them next to my bag.

Peggy groaned. "Willa, quit stalling."

That was easy for her to say. The object of her every fascination wasn't present and wading in the deep end of the salt water pool with another girl.

Dash swam over, his expression strained, and when he neared Peggy, he sprayed a mouthful of water into her face. She screamed, laughing and splashing him. "You're disgusting, oh my god."

Maybe I could just sit down, I thought. Read the book or magazine I'd packed.

"Do those legs match your name?" a rough voice asked.

I didn't realize they were talking to me until I looked up and caught Raven grinning at me.

"W-what?" I clenched the towel tighter around me.

Dash chuckled. "Her name isn't Willow, you fucking idiot."

Raven wasn't deterred and swam to the side of the pool, his long hair slicked back, revealing bright blue eyes on a sculpted, sun-kissed face.

His strong jaw worked as his eyes appraised my towel-clad form. "I know what your name is. I was just trying to make light of"—he scrunched his nose, gesturing at me—"whatever the hell it is you're doing."

I appreciated that he'd kept his voice low, yet heat still glazed my cheeks. "I'm…" I had no idea what to say.

"Coming in?" he offered, Peggy splashing and shoving Dash farther out in the pool now. Raven scratched his cheek. "Could you bring me some lotion when you do?"

Swallowing hard, I bent and dug through my bag, and when I rose, I left the towel behind.

I wasn't sure if anyone was looking at me, or if I could just feel eyes on my body due to paranoia. With my next breath trapped tight in my lungs, I kept walking, dunking my legs into the water as I took a seat on the side of the pool and handed Raven the sunscreen.

He blinked at it, then up at me. "I've never seen a one-piece look so good."

I bit my smile and ducked my head. "Thank you," I said, knowing in some backward way, he'd helped make an awkward situation less so.

Taking the tube, he squirted a heaping dollop into his palm, then handed it back. "You can repay me by doing my back."

It wasn't a question. He turned, rubbing the cream into his tanned arms, chest, and face while I stared mute at the broad expanse of his back.

"You've got admirers," he murmured so quietly I almost didn't catch it.

With a slight shake to my hands, I smeared sunscreen over the warm skin of his shoulders and upper back, and then rubbed it in. "What do you mean?"

"Two o'clock. Green-eyed monster."

I snorted a giggle at the double meaning, then stilled when I glanced up to find Jackson staring at us. The sun bounced off the lapping water of the pools, making it hard to catch his expression. An unwavering hardness seemed to have overrun his features, though.

When Ainsley bobbed closer to him and clung to his arm, smiling, I gave my attention back to Raven, unsure what to say.

Thankfully, he didn't push, and I had to wonder how much he knew, or thought he knew. I wasn't sure there was anything for anyone to know.

I thought all our filthy secrets were mine and his alone.

"Stepsiblings, am I right?" I said nothing, and Raven hummed. "Don't worry, it's not overly obvious."

"What isn't?" I tried to infuse as much confusion as I could into the question.

Raven's back vibrated with his rumbling chuckle. "That he's obsessed with you."

Before I could ask him why he thought that, he pushed off the wall and disappeared underwater.

I watched his long frame shift and sway beneath the surface until he appeared before a girl sitting with her friends at the other end. She laughed, her hand at her chest when Raven broke through the water.

"He's so gross," Peggy said, pulling herself up to sit beside me a minute later.

No longer did I worry about my blue and white modest, floral one-piece, and how my burgeoning chest might appear. No one else seemed to care, so I stopped too, and I even kicked my legs in the cool depths below. "What did he do now?"

"Seaweed," she said with a scoff. "He threw a wad of seaweed at my face. Ugh, I hate him."

Turning to her, I smirked. "Sure you do."

She scowled, her damp curls clinging to her cheeks, then screamed when Dash, from behind us, grabbed her and sent them both tumbling into the pool.

When they emerged laughing and splashing, I felt like too much of an observer, so I pushed off the wall and slipped into the water.

Cool warmth enveloped me, and as soon as I bobbed to the surface, I pushed my hair back off my face, wishing I'd brought a hair tie.

Treading water near the edge, I let my gaze roam over all the people in the pool, but I couldn't find Peggy or Dash. The only person I could see was Jackson, who was grinning down at Ainsley.

A throbbing sensation wracked my chest, spreading to my head and eyes when she wrapped her arms around his shoulders to meld her lips to his.

I looked away before I could see it and tried to be content with bobbing about on my own, but I wasn't. After a few minutes had passed with no sign of Peggy, I waded to the stairs and climbed out.

Taking my time, I wrapped the towel around me, then grabbed my things and headed for the bathrooms. They sat atop the beach, and I was thankful they seemed to be empty when I entered them.

I was used to it. I was. Seeing Jackson with Ainsley, watching him flirt with other girls, was nothing new even though the old ache didn't fade. It grew new thorns that protruded every time I saw something I'd rather not. I'd grown accustomed to the pain.

Sighing out a heavy breath, I went to close the stall door and then stumbled back, almost falling into the toilet, when it was pushed open and slammed closed.

Jackson, dripping wet and clad in only a pair of black board shorts, loomed over me.

His presence, his sea-salted scent, the heavy look in his eyes, swallowed the air and rendered me speechless when I attempted to open my mouth. "Jack—"

"Don't," he said, nostrils flaring. "Raven?"

I felt my brows pull. "Huh?"

"Don't play innocent, Willa. I saw you. Everyone fucking saw you rubbing all over him."

With my eyes rounding, I gasped out a shocked laugh. "Excuse me?"

I backed up into the wall, its cool peeling paint pressing into my damp back, as Jackson took my chin in his stiff fingers. "Did you do it to make me mad?"

"I did it because he needed help, and he asked me to."

Beads of water slid from his hair down his neck to his heaving chest. After staring, those green eyes sharp and studying, for the longest ten heartbeats of my life, he moved.

His lips crashed into mine, his hand meeting the side of my face to keep them there while he pried my mouth open with his. "Jesus, this fucking swimsuit..."

It was hard to draw a breath, to gather enough oxygen to fuel the riot in my brain. I shut it down. My hands found his strong forearms, gliding over muscle and smooth skin, making him groan as his tongue coaxed mine into stroking his.

Velvet soft fingers skidded from my cheek to my chest, fire crawling everywhere they touched until he reached my lower stomach and stroked.

Sensing his hesitation, my hands slipped into his hair, and I tilted my head to kiss him deeper, my thighs parting slightly on impulse.

His fingers remained on my stomach a minute longer, rubbing and tickling over the thin barrier of damp polyester.

Then they dipped lower, and a harsh breath fled me when they roamed to where it grew more damp between my legs.

A gravel-coated groan vibrated up his throat, his fingers soft in their torturous game. Back and forth they slid, with only the slightest pressure, exactly where I needed them.

Gull shrieks pierced the air, and flip-flop-covered feet scuffed over the floor of the bathroom, voices accompanying the sounds.

Still, we didn't stop, and I knew he wouldn't until it happened.

Dizziness swamped me, feeling his skin beneath my fingers, touching and tasting him... his mouth clamped hard over mine when a moan almost thundered out.

When the voices left, his fingers pressed harder, digging into the fabric while his lips shifted from mine to my ear. "You're soaking this swimsuit, Bug."

I could hardly breathe, let alone talk.

His low voice rumbled into my ear, his finger flicking now, harsh strokes that caused stars to dance behind my fluttering eyelids. "He couldn't do this to you. With just a touch. No one else could."

Kissing my cheek, he cupped me, hard, and I splintered. His other hand clapped over my mouth, his eyes boring into mine as I struggled to keep them open, and I shook against him.

Sadistic, he smiled. "Don't bring this up. Don't say a word. It never happened."

My breathing slowed, and I nodded, trying to pull his hand from my mouth.

"Say it, Willa."

"It..." I stopped and swallowed. "It never happened."

"Good." Cold rushed in, blanketing me in waves of ice when he stepped back. Before he opened the door, he said, "Remember what no one else can do next time you think you're helping someone."

The door shut with a bang, and disorientated, I peeled myself off the wall.

I removed my swimsuit and dried off. Then, after throwing my blue checkered sundress on, I headed outside.

Deciding I'd pretend to read in the sun rather than try to hide what Jackson had just done to me, I sat on a small patch of grass atop the hill that overlooked the ocean and pools.

The heat was no match for the goose bumps pebbling my arms. The words on the page were no match for the constant replay swimming laps through my mind.

A half an hour later, Dash, Raven, Cad, and Peggy all lumbered up the concrete path.

"There you are," Peggy said. "I was worried until Raven said you'd gone to the bathroom."

I smiled, then looked behind her. "Where's Jackson?"

"He's heading out with Ains," Cad said. "We said we'd take you home."

Bookmarking the page, I closed my book with a thud that matched the stalled beat inside my chest.

Clouds filled my head. I squinted at the bottle in my hand, trying to make out the words.

I said the name slowly, dragging it out. "Chardonnay." Then I laughed to myself, took another sip, and decided I didn't hate it enough to quit drinking.

Mom and Dad were out of town for a Thorn Racing event. Jackson turned seventeen last weekend and had decided to throw his first party.

I'd warned him it was a bad idea.

Bad ideas always make for good times, he'd replied.

I'd raised a brow at that, to which he'd laughed, then chucked me under the chin like I was seven years old again before wandering off. I'd taken that touch and stored it away with the forbidden moments he still refused to acknowledge.

Two weeks had passed since he'd followed me into the bathrooms at the beach. Two weeks of lingering in rooms too long, hoping he might stay or follow me someplace else.

He never did. He'd have to be home more for that to happen, and most evenings, he'd retire to his room as soon as he did get home or until dinner was ready.

The thudding music matched the sluggish tempo of my heart as I did my best to avoid being in any room Jackson and Ainsley occupied.

In the kitchen, as I scrambled for some water to rid the dizziness that'd taken hold, I almost choked when Ainsley sauntered in, a bottle of something pink in her hand.

"Hey, Willa."

I wanted to spit at her. I swallowed, then smiled instead. "Hi." I peered around her, noticing she was thankfully alone. "Having fun?"

She grinned. "Yeah, I can't believe how nice your house is." She half rolled her eyes. "He's never once let me inside before."

I pursed my lips. "Our parents are kind of strict." Why the hell I was lying for him—well, kind of lying—I didn't know.

She sipped from a white straw, her pink-stained lips large and bee-stung looking. "Right? I heard. Such a buzzkill. I want to meet them and hopefully win them over." Another grin, and then she stepped closer. "But hey, at least I get to hang with you."

She'd never once tried to hang out with me at school. I didn't fool myself into thinking it was because she spent most of her time chasing after Jackson's whereabouts. No, she hung out with Kayla, Annabeth, Annika, Daphne, and the rest of the squad.

Daphne seemed okay from the brief encounters I'd had with her, if not kind of cold and closed off, but the rest were mean and didn't hesitate in displaying as much.

Ainsley was hard to peg. Though I knew if it weren't for Jackson, she'd likely not be standing here, trying to rope me into conversation.

I needed more of that chardonnay. "Yeah, so cool," I said, wanting to cringe at my forced words.

She didn't seem to notice and swayed forward, her hand reaching for my hair. "I'd kill for curls like this. The way your hair just falls into them, like a damn waterfall or something."

I wanted to cry. To slap her hands off me and run away.

I did neither as Jackson halted in the kitchen, his eyes narrowing on what I was positive was my panicked expression. "Ains," he said, still staring at me. "Wanna help me start to clear everyone out?"

She bounded over to him, slinking her arm through his. "Not yet," she whined, batting her lashes.

Removing his unreadable eyes from me, he directed them to her and grinned, saying something too quiet for me to hear above the music.

But I didn't have to hear. The way Ainsley bit her lip suggestively and pressed herself into him told me all I needed to know.

Inside the small downstairs bathroom, I locked the door and leaned over the sink, blinking over and over to keep the sorrow and breaking pieces from rattling loose.

Sniffing it back, I closed my eyes.

He wanted everyone gone so they didn't wreck the place while he was downstairs, doing whatever he'd planned to do with Ainsley.

All this time, I'd kidded myself into thinking that he wasn't that serious about her. Yeah, they'd kissed, but I thought that was it. I hadn't dared to even contemplate the idea of anything else.

Then the memory of his expert fingers, his purpose-filled touch, seared.

They couldn't do anything else.

They just couldn't.

I had minutes, maybe ten, to fix myself up, as the noise in the house began to fade, and cars came and went out front.

I used them to freshen up, wiping the few smears of mascara from beneath my eyes and righting my hair. I was wearing an ice blue dress with capped sleeves and a short, frilled hem and no shoes.

I didn't need shoes for where I was going.

Peering into the hall, Dash and Raven shoving each other on the way to the door, I waited, then I took the stairs near the garage. The stairs that led down to the basement where Jackson's room was.

Curled on the foot of his navy blue and brown bed, I waited again.

Posters of bands were stuck to the brick walls, and he'd taken the old furniture Mom and Dad stored down here and used it for his own.

A little sitting area was tucked into the far-right corner, an antique coffee table covered in dirt bike magazines and textbooks. An old refrigerator was plugged into the outlet near the sitting area, and inside it, I knew there were bottles of water, juice, and milk for the box of cereal that he kept above the fridge.

His desk was organized with pens tucked neatly in jars and books stacked to the right and in the center. His lamp was off, and I reached over to turn it on just as I heard the door above creak open.

My pulse screamed and almost drowned out the sound of Jackson's and Ainsley's laughter and their descending footsteps.

I scrambled for the book on his nightstand, a Stephen King novel that would scare the hair right off my head, and opened it to appear as if it was normal for me to be hanging out in my brother's room.

I suppose it could have been, but we rarely hung out alone anymore, especially not at nighttime.

At what I assumed was the glow of his lamp, Jackson's steps slowed near the base of the stairs before he rounded the corner.

When he did, his face was blanker than a sheet of white paper. "Willa?"

I lifted both brows. "Great party."

Ainsley wrapped her arms around his midsection, smiling at me. "It was awesome." She frowned then, as if sensing I shouldn't be in here.

"Willa," Jackson said, then mouthed the words, "don't do this."

Ainsley shifted. "So, whatcha doing in here, Willa?"

Jackson smirked. "Good question."

Betrayal came in many forms. I felt it then, a new version. The type that came with feeling replaced, and like I'd become some type of burden—a pest.

It only spiked my determination higher. I wouldn't be cowed or told to go away. All this time, I'd let him make every decision that concerned the two of us, but I wouldn't let him do this. "I feel sick." I tossed the book aside. "And we're out of Tylenol."

Ainsley pursed her lips. "I might have some in my car."

Jackson said nothing, only stared for sweltering seconds with an intensity that raised every hair on my body.

My trapped breath flew out of me when his stiff shoulders slumped, and he took Ainsley upstairs, murmuring words I could no longer hear.

I watched the clock above his desk, counting the ticks, hating that they crawled into a full four minutes before he returned.

His footsteps thundered down the steps. He raked a hand through his hair, pacing the floor beside his bed.

I didn't wait. I didn't bother with any more false pretenses. It was pointless. "I know what you were going to do."

"That's none of your fucking business. How much have you had to drink?"

"Not enough to lose my mind because it is," I breathed, emphatic. I might not have been drunk, but there was enough liquid courage still with me to see this through. "Isn't it? It *is* my business."

He stopped, staring straight ahead to the flat screen mounted on the wall. "You should've let me."

"No."

"Why, Willa?" He leveled me with a cold smile as he swung his feet forward, slow and calculated, nearing where I sat. "Why fucking not?"

Uncaring that it would ruin what we'd tried to rebuild, I said, "You know why." Because the alternative, having him be with someone who wasn't me, wasn't something I was okay with. I could never be okay with that, and I was sick of trying to be.

"I don't know if I do." His tone was too aloof, eyes too hard, for me to read.

That didn't matter. "Because if I can't, then you can't either."

His entire body stiffened, his face scrunching with annoyance and something else. "You mean to tell me you've tried?"

I swallowed. "Well, not exactly, but I… I don't want to."

He groaned. "For fuck's sake, this is so vague we're practically speaking in code. Which is exactly why you should've stayed out of my room."

I nodded, knowing he was right. What were we even thinking all those months ago? How could one kiss change things so much? The answer was complicatedly simple. We hadn't been thinking then, we hadn't been thinking last month at the beach, but all we did now—all I did now—was fucking think.

I watched him take a step back, and the moisture in my eyes misted further as I wondered if maybe I'd read this all wrong. If maybe, he'd never wanted more than to see how my lips felt moving over his.

If maybe, I could call his bluff by leaving.

"You're right." Climbing off the bed, I tugged at the hem of my dress, and went to pass him. "I won't interrupt next time."

Jackson's laughter was abrasive and dark as he grabbed my arm. "Next time? No. I don't think so."

Scowling, I pulled my arm away but not hard enough to do much of anything. "Let go."

Through gritted teeth, he rasped, "I've been trying to let go for years, and you don't seem to care. You're happy to let me do all the work, all the hard things, while you continue to dream."

I frowned, and then it all crystalized.

He'd been pushing me away, I'd known that, but he was still doing it.

"There they are." Soft and decadent, his tone changed. "Bug eyes." His finger drifted beneath one. "Beautiful fucking eyes."

"Jack, I—"

"No, you brought this upon yourself when you came down here." A gleam brightened his eyes. "You don't want me to see other girls? To touch another girl?"

I shook my head because the thought alone made my stomach protest.

His head dropped. "Then this time, there's no pussyfooting, no running away from this." He paused, waited. "This is your last chance before we probably ruin everything. Five."

He was right.

"Four."

We would ruin everything.

"Three."

But only if we weren't careful.

"Two."

"I never ran away from anything," I whispered, rising to my toes to skim my lips over his. "That was all you." His hands were bands of steel clamping around my waist as my lips closed over his, and we fell into the wall behind me, exploring each other's mouths.

Monday morning, with my books tucked to my chest, I watched Ainsley fly past me down the hall and disappear around the corner, her head lowered to hide her tears.

I blinked, then dragged my gaze to Jackson, who was looking straight at me.

Raven thumped him on the back, laughter in his eyes, and then they walked on to class.

My heart was singing, stretching and pounding and humming as I bit back my smile and did the same.

"You dumped her," my first words to Jackson at lunch when he met me at my locker.

He grabbed my food and closed the door. "I've continuously told her she wasn't my girlfriend."

I tried to match my steps with his as we walked down the hall. "She thinks different."

"That's not my fault." He peered around, then opened the door to an empty room and pulled me inside. "And it's definitely not yours, so don't worry about it."

Taking my hand from his, I shuffled a few steps back, nodding.

"Seriously, Wil?" He laughed, dry and disbelieving. "You backed me into this corner, and now you're just leaving me there?"

I hit the lock on the door, dropped my food to the closest desk, then pulled down the blinds before turning to him with a brow raised.

His lips shaped around the word, "Oh."

Our smiles grew at the same time, and then I was against his chest, his hands traveling up and down my back in deliciously slow sweeps. "I'm fucking dying to kiss you again."

"You kissed me last night," I reminded him yet felt my mouth floating closer to his, my head tilting back when his hand threaded into my hair and gently tugged.

He had kissed me last night. It wasn't the make-out fest we'd fallen into in his bedroom on the night of his party, thanks to our parents arriving home, but he'd come to me after they'd fallen asleep and spent a solid ten minutes devouring my mouth.

It ended when our sighs and heated whispers turned to groans and tiny pleas, our hands getting too excited.

But the promise of it never having to end if we played our

cards right had my kiss-bruised lips tilting as I'd watched him leave.

His thumb ghosted over my chin, skimming beneath my bottom lip. "I want you to feel how hard I am, and that should make me sick."

I licked at his finger and his pupils dilated, then I reached between us and, tentatively, felt how much he wanted me, how thick and long he was, and my stomach jumped into my chest.

His deep groan rumbled, and I wanted to hear it again, to rub my nose against the column of his throat and feel it leave him.

So I did, then licked his skin as I moved my fingers over him.

"We're going straight to hell," he wheezed, but when I pulled back, I saw his lips were curling.

"I don't think so," I said.

"No?"

"No. This"—I pressed my mouth to his thumb, then brushed my nose against the stubble on his chin—"whatever it is, could never be considered anything but good."

"You're too sweet for this world, Wil."

Grabbing his hand, I laid it over my chest. "Feel it beating?" I didn't wait for him to answer. "Now feel it beat harder when I move it a little..." He swallowed, his hand covering the swell of my breast. I grinned. "Maybe I'm not so sweet after all."

"You'll never be anything but even though you are a temptress." Delicious and wicked, his words hit my cheek, his fingers squeezing, his length pushing into my hand. "We shouldn't be doing this."

Hurt threatened to storm in, but I refused to let it and smirked against his cheek. "But you won't let go."

"And neither will you."

"Never," I said, then stole his lips in a kiss that damned and awakened.

He pulled back after a moment, breathing hard. "I didn't mean this." His frown tugged at my heart, and I released him to wrap my arms around his waist. He did the same. "I meant we should be dating, having fun, all that kind of shit before we step straight into the flames."

"That's the beauty of this," I said. "We don't need to because we've already done all that. And really," I said, smiling up into his curious face, "we've been dodging the flames for long enough, don't you think?"

He gazed at the closed door behind me, then dropped his forehead to mine. "I think you deserve better, something normal. That's what I think."

I began to pull away, sinking. "If I wanted something normal, I would've—"

"I wouldn't have let you have it," he said, tone hard but his eyes playful. "Let me finish." He kissed my forehead, sighing against my skin as he held me tighter. "I don't want normal, Bug, and I know I'll never find another you." He tipped my chin up when I failed to respond, then chuckled. "Fucking hell, don't cry." His hands cupped my face, thumbs swiping beneath my eyes.

"Shut up," I said, sniffing.

He did, forcing my mouth to his, where it stayed until the bell rang.

eight

Jackson
Seventeen

D irt sprayed, pelting the bikes beside me as we raced toward the midday sun.

Raven flipped us off from where he stood by a jump he was trying to fix, and it almost collapsed beneath the weight of our bikes.

While I enjoyed tearing up the track we'd built at Dash's place, I missed racing. If he wasn't working, Dad would make sure I made every race, but lately, I scarcely made time for it myself. It'd been months since I'd last felt my adrenaline spike like this. Since I'd felt my body heat beneath the gear I had on. Since I'd smiled over something that wasn't Willa.

Her dimpled smile flashed before me.

I eased off, heading into a tree-strewn corner, then smacked it when it cleared into a long run of pocketed dirt. Dash's two stroke screamed ahead, Lars standing atop it as he neared what we'd marked as the finish line.

Dash kept neck in neck with me until we'd reached him. I rolled over the small boulders and crests in the ground, my breath clouding my helmet, then turned to a stop where they were standing by the trees, yanking off helmets and goggles.

I did the same, then guzzled water from my hydration pack.

"Scale of one to ten, how pissed is Rave going to be?" Dash said through his shit-eating smile.

"Four," I said, dropping the mouthpiece and climbing off my bike.

I leaned it against the tree, then took a seat against the trunk, running my hands through my sweat-soaked hair.

"Four?" Dash scoffed.

Lars chuckled. "It's Raven. He couldn't stay pissed at anyone for longer than five minutes."

Dash lit a cigarette, scowling.

I shook my head, sweat droplets splashing to the dirt.

Lars was right.

"Ainsley's still pissed about your sudden breakup," Raven said an hour later as I was loading my bike into the back of my truck.

I tightened the tie-downs, then slid the ramp in before taking a seat on the tailgate. "Is she?" I knew she was. I'd received numerous texts and DMs in the weeks after, begging for a reason, and even one saying she thought she was in love with me.

After apologizing once, I didn't respond to any more. Not because I felt like being a dick, but because there was little point. It wouldn't help, and although she deserved some type of explanation, I couldn't give her one.

"You know damn well she is," Raven said, kicking at a cluster of weeds with the toe of his boot. "You haven't been with anyone else since, though."

"Your point?" I said, growing impatient.

He smirked. "There is none. I just find it bizarre. You seemed into her enough, but you're not with anyone else after dumping her."

"She was never my girlfriend." Yeah, I liked her, but like

wasn't enough to smother what I felt for Willa. Ainsley was cool, but she wasn't Willa.

"Don't think she got that memo." Raven lit a blunt, taking a deep drag.

"Why do you care?" Dash said, coming around the side of my truck. "Got a hard-on for Jack-Jack now?"

Raven narrowed his eyes, grinning as he exhaled smoke. "Nah, baby. I wouldn't betray you like that."

Dash scowled, then stole his blunt.

"And I care because she asked me to fuck her," Raven said.

My brows shot up. "She did?"

Rave shrugged. "Don't look so surprised. Word has it that I'm a great lay."

Lars snorted, slumping to the grass-flecked dirt and lighting a cigarette. "Who'd you fuck?"

"Ainsley," I said without an ounce of feeling. It bothered me my friend would do that but not enough to say it did. She could do whatever she wanted. In fact, what I wanted was for Ainsley to be happy.

She could be reckless and a little mean like the rest of her crew—Kayla, Daphne, Annabeth, and so on—but when she was on her own, she was different.

Lars hooted. "Breaking bro code." He nodded, sarcasm dripping from his tone. "Nice."

"I didn't fuck her. I said she asked me to," Rave said. "Read between the lines, motherfuckers."

"And what, you just said no to those tits?" Dash passed the blunt back.

Raven was a boob guy, and everyone knew it. "Sure did. I already had a ride lined up."

Laughing silently, I swiped my hand over my cheek, then stood. "Good for you. I'm out."

"You coming to Summer's tonight?" Lars called.

Rave moved away from my truck as I climbed inside and tore my boots off. "Nah, got that bio paper due." I threw my boots into the back, then grabbed my Vans. "You already finished, oh smart one?"

Lars shrugged, which meant yes. "Give me a ride?"

I jerked my head to the passenger side in answer, then flipped off the other two before peeling out the side entrance that led to the wooded area behind Dash's house.

"I can't believe she asked your friend to fuck her," Lars said, flicking ash out the window. "How are you not pissed?"

"I ended shit with her for a reason," I said, wishing everyone would leave it well enough alone already.

"Cold, man, cold."

"And what you do with chicks is any better?" The guy had been following every move Daphne Morris made since he'd been accepted into Magnolia Cove Prep via a full scholarship, the likes of which were only handed out to one student each year. Meanwhile, he fucked anything in sight and never committed. He could pine all he wanted; Daphne was the cold one. And she wasn't interested in him or any of the assholes who attended school.

"Love and leave them, just leave them nicely enough to make sure they don't spit fire at you in the school halls."

I chuckled, nodding. "You've got a point."

"So," he said after he'd finished his cigarette, "you're really not hooking up with someone else?"

Lying was becoming an overused pastime, one that shouldn't have come so easily. It had to. The alternatives were nothing we could ever contend with. Ignoring how we felt was something that couldn't be done.

I'd lie forever if I had to. As long as she was willing to lie with me. "Nah, dude. No one."

The stars, moon, headlights, and blazing bonfire were the only sources of light as far as the eye could see in the barren fields of Danny Vestin's property.

His family owned a ranch near the edge of town, but they were currently enjoying a two-week stay in the Bahamas to escape the frigid winter that'd swept through the cove and had decided to stay a while longer than what was normal.

By March, things would usually begin to thaw and warm up, but it was nearing April, and if anything, it was colder now than it was in January.

Parked as far away from the festivities as possible under a cluster of old oaks, I pulled my hooded black jacket tighter around me, itching to do the same for Willa.

I couldn't, not only because it'd look strange to have her brother fussing over her in that way, but also because she was stalking across the grass toward the bonfire, hands tucked in her denim jacket pockets. It was fur lined, and her cream dress fluttered around her black tight-covered thighs, the knee-high weeds caressing what my fingers longed to.

"Jack-Jack," Dash shouted, racing over with a bottle of Jack. "Fucking thought I saw you pull in."

I took the bottle, taking a few sips as Daphne walked over to Willa, greeting her with a blinding smile that I could make out even from my vantage point.

I handed it back, and Dash drank greedily before plonking onto my tailgate and lighting a blunt. "Don't suppose you've got some cups back here under all those blankets, do you?"

"I don't," I said, eyes tracking Willa as Daphne handed her a bottle of something, and Willa took a sip and a seat next to her by the fire.

"You devil, you." Dash laughed. "Planning on getting some pussy under the blankets tonight?"

I didn't see the point in lying because he'd see right through it. "That's the plan."

"Don't sound too excited or anything, fuck." He scooted forward, legs hanging over the gate. "You get more somber and shit as you get older, know that?"

"Fuck off, then."

He laughed. "Nah, luckily for you, I like somber. Makes me feel good about myself."

I took an offered blunt, lighting it when he passed me the lighter, then handed it back. "Where's Lars?" I knew they'd planned to ride together.

"Probably in the trees fucking some cheerleader."

"Rave?" I sucked in a drag, held it within my lungs as Danny and Byron neared Willa and Daphne, and Kayla stared daggers at the lot of them.

"Grandma needs babysitting again," he said. "If you ask me, the old bird just wants someone to baby instead of being babied."

I smirked, exhaling. "No wonder Raven drops anything for her." The guy was a sucker for being taken care of.

"What's Daphne want with Willa?"

Good question. Daphne had been the one to invite Willa, and Peggy, being Peggy, wasn't all that interested in parties just yet. Even if she'd accompanied, I'd still have come. Willa wasn't used to parties, and she needed to be looked out for until she was.

"She invited her." I took another drag. "Got no idea why."

Dash hummed around the lip of the bottle. "She's cold as ice, that chick. Maybe she wants some of Willa's sunshine to warm her up."

My teeth gritted. That he'd noticed enough of Willa... I shifted, telling myself to curb the bullshit. He'd known Willa for as long as he'd known me. Since elementary school.

He didn't want her. He just knew her.

My shoulders loosened somewhat, and I finished the blunt before stomping on it, desperate for the rest of my body to relax.

"So are you a chaperone, or did you come to party?" Dash pushed some more. "Because from where I'm sitting, you don't look like either."

"It's Daphne. She's friends with the worst of the best." I scoffed and folded my arms over my chest. "Of course I need to keep an eye on this shit. Mom and Dad will kill me if Willa gets hurt."

They didn't even know she was here. They bought the excuse of a movie trip with her friends. I'd said I'd take them and hang out with my own friends until they were done.

I didn't think Daphne would hurt her in any way. But even though I'd attended school with the girl for years, I didn't know much of anything about her. She'd always kept to herself, even among the posse of hyenas she hung out with, and I couldn't get a read on her.

"Daphne will be fine," Dash said. "It's the others who don't know how to play nice. So let's get wasted and wake up wondering where the hell we are."

"Can't. Mom and Dad know I drove." And I wasn't about to ditch Willa to drink with friends. It was too dark, too crazy, and I wanted, needed to be exactly where she was.

The crowds grew thicker as the night wore on, and Lars soon joined us, zipping his fly and groaning at the rip in his T-shirt.

Girls were dancing in the back of trucks, some even on top of cars, and at least three different songs vied for attention from all the speakers.

"How is Stacia?" Dash asked.

"I don't kiss and tell," Lars mumbled, sighing as he plucked the cigarette from behind his ear and stuck it between his teeth. "Mom's gonna kill me. This was a Christmas present."

Dash handed him a light. "Still a screamer? Not your mom." He winked. "We already know she probably is."

The smoke almost fell from Lars's mouth as he fumbled to hand the lighter back, laughing. "You sick fuck."

Dash sipped from the bottle of Jack, shrugging.

I smothered my laughter by scrubbing the stubble growing in around my mouth and looked back at the bonfire.

My chest constricted. I couldn't see Willa.

Trying not to let the apprehension show, I feigned leaning down to tie my already tied laces and squinted through the growing darkness to the shadowed figures, searching for hers.

Over by a truck, she and Daphne were crowded against it by Danny and Hennessy.

She'd said she didn't know Daphne well, that they'd only really hung out during art class, but she'd wanted to at least come and say hello.

Well, she'd said hello. Time to say goodbye.

Dash chuckled when I rose. "Looks like Willa's about to get in that trouble you were worried about."

Lars peered over, smoke clouding his scrunched expression. He grinned, waggling his brows at me. "Want me to rescue her? Might be less embarrassing."

Over my dead fucking body. He laughed at whatever look was on my face, and when I muttered, "She deserves to be embarrassed if she's hanging with those dickweeds."

He chuckled, and I stalked over. They followed, thankfully dispersing into a herd of senior girls.

Willa's drink was still half full, her posture stiff as Hennessy leaned close to bump her arm with his, laughing over something.

She forced a smile that came to life when her gaze found me, but it slowly fell at whatever expression she saw on my face.

"What's up, Jack? Got any green?"

I was sick and tired of people thinking I was always the one who bought the shit. I smoked it, sure, but not as much as my friends did. "No. Got a clue? Because it sure as shit doesn't seem like it."

Hennessy sputtered out a laugh, his brows creasing when he realized I was being dead serious. "We were just hanging out."

Danny licked his lips, grinning broadly. "It's all good, man. Seriously, we were just saying hey."

My nostrils flared as my gaze flicked back and forth between them. Danny was fidgeting, shifting from foot to foot and glancing around while Hennessy stood his ground, that smug smile still on his stupid face.

I turned to Willa, who was chewing her bottom lip and peeling the label on the glass bottle. "We need to head out soon."

Daphne eyed me a moment, then smiled at Willa. "I'll DM you when I get home."

Willa nodded, then followed me when I jerked my head toward the trees where the truck was parked.

"Are we really going?" she asked once we'd escaped most of the people and noise.

"No," I said. "But if I have to watch you being treated like prey for another minute, I'll end up breaking someone's nose."

"Prey?" She laughed. "I was fine."

"You were uncomfortable."

She took a sip from the bottle, smacking her lips together. "Fine, but only when he kept bumping into me."

I snatched the drink and tossed it into the bushes when we'd reached the trees.

"Hey!"

Peeking over my shoulder, I made sure no one was close enough to see as I took her hand and hauled her to the truck. I opened the door and picked her up, leaning close as I said, "I don't want you drunk."

Her brow rose. "It was only one drink." Her cheeks bloomed when my meaning dawned on her, and she ducked her head. "Here?"

Without giving her an answer, I jogged around to the driver's side and climbed in.

We crawled forward, enough for people to think I might've been leaving if they were watching, but only enough to be farther out of view.

Willa climbed out a second later, and I followed. Jumping into the back of the truck, I helped her arrange the blankets before we settled over and beneath them.

Melon rolled off her breath as she whispered close to my mouth, "Did you just stand over here all this time?"

I pulled the blanket higher over our heads, hating that it was too dark to see the green flecks in her hazel eyes but loving the way every part of me began to heat when her leg moved between mine.

I kicked my shoes off and felt her do the same. "Yeah."

She stared at me for a minute, then reached out and ran her finger over the crest of my cheekbone. "I missed you."

"It was only an hour or two," I said, wanting her lips.

"I still missed you."

I smiled, my nose nudging hers as my words floated over her parted lips. "Show me then."

Her hand moved to the side of my face, forcing it down for her mouth to close over mine. For long seconds, she held us there, unmoving and just breathing, her grip tight.

I flew and sank, holding her waist, submerged in the

familiar curve of her lips, the way they fit with mine, and murmured, "I feel like I need you to breathe properly."

Her breathy exhale warmed my tongue. "Me too."

Then I parted her lips, my tongue caressing hers, and my hands going crazy, touching every curving space of her body.

Our breathing grew labored, the air beneath the blanket hot and damp. And when she grabbed the hand that'd been toying with her stomach and hip, guiding it lower, my eyes opened.

Hers did too, luminous with the question, dare, and plea swimming within.

I hadn't touched her there yet. Not skin on skin. Heavy petting over clothes and a fuck ton of kissing was all we'd done; all we'd dared to do.

Some tiny part of me worried that what I felt for her wouldn't be enough to mask the memories I'd had of us as kids running naked through the sprinkler, the dual toilet training, and the time she laughed at my first ever boner. I'd been so mortified, so freaked out by what my body was doing, that I'd snapped, and said, "Laugh it up. I'd rather this than that weird taco any day."

That part and the memories were obliterated when her tights and panties disappeared, and my hand slid lower over her mound, encountering silken skin.

Silken skin that unfolded into warm, wet want. "Holy shit," I croaked. "Willa. Shit."

I was going to come in my briefs, but I didn't care. I leaned over her, absorbing her shocked delight as my finger stroked up and down, familiarizing itself with her. "It's so wet."

"Is that bad?"

"No." I laughed against her mouth. "No fucking way."

When she said nothing, and I found her entrance, thick

with need and so fucking tiny, fear began to trickle in, and I met her eyes, checking to see if she was still enjoying it.

Her heaving tits and the lazy glint to those orbs said she was, but the tense line in her forehead said something was wrong.

My finger stilled, my hand resting over her. "What's wrong? Is it…" I couldn't even bring myself to finish that sentence. Any fear or worry I'd had was completely unfounded. If anything, my hunger and feelings for her were only growing. Yet it was possible that even if she liked what I was doing, those concerns, the wrongs, might still be there for her.

I tried to swallow over the terror that lodged in my throat like a boulder, rasping, "Bug?"

She smiled, soft but not reassuring. "It's nothing. I'm be-ing…" She sighed. "I'm just being stupid."

"If you're feeling it, I need to know it. Spill already," I urged, my heart slowing to a bruising pound.

Her lashes fluttered as she seemed to battle with herself. "It shouldn't matter."

"But it does, or you wouldn't be thinking it. You'd just be thinking about what it might be like to orgasm from my fingers."

She laughed, pressing her finger to my mouth. "Shhh." I nipped it, and she giggled that giggle that would forever be the death of me. "I just, well, have you…?" She stopped, groaning a little.

But I knew exactly what she was asking and bit my lips in relief.

"Don't laugh," she said, slapping at my chest.

I grabbed her hand, my laughter soft as I kissed her fingers. "You can't say it."

"I don't need to." She rolled her eyes. "Which just answers the stupid question I couldn't ask." Pulling her hand back, she shifted, her thighs trying to move my hand. "Sorry. I guess I just feel kind of jealous."

"Kind of?" I scowled, then wiggled my middle finger, causing her thighs to clench.

A small moan left her. "Extremely."

"Better," I whispered, lowering my mouth to hers. "But you're jealous for no reason. I've never touched a girl like this." Her mouth refused to move as I tried to love it with mine, and I lifted my head. "Willa?"

Her eyes were glassing, and she sniffed. "Sorry."

"Jesus." I laughed. "Don't fucking cry."

"Don't tell me what to do."

I laughed harder, kissing every bit of her face until she was laughing too. "I'm relieved. I mean, I would've been okay if you had. I thought you had, but—"

"But nothing," I said. "Only you, so open your legs and let me play."

She clutched my head to hers, her teeth and lips ferocious. But as my fingers continued to explore her softest, warmest part, she failed to keep up.

My blood became a thundering roar, whooshing and drowning out every sound that wasn't her small cries of pleasure.

"Touch yourself," she whispered. "Touch yourself while you make me come."

I quickly shucked off my jeans enough to fist my cock and rolled to my side. Willa turned so I could play with her and pump myself, her tongue and lips sliding over mine and my jaw.

The blanket began to slip, but it didn't matter. We were too lost to save ourselves.

"I think it's happening," she panted out, as I continuously circled the swollen nub, her body and breath trembling more every time.

"Can I push one in?"

"Please," she said.

My pinky finger moved to her entrance, dipping inside just a little, as my thumb kept rubbing her.

Her eyes widened, then her lashes lowered as a slow whine vacated her lips. I was coming without any warning whatsoever, so caught up in the sight of her shocked, then sated expression.

Cum spirted out of my swollen cock, landing on her thigh in thick ribbons, and I cursed, desperately seeking her mouth. She gave it to me, her tongue laving at mine and her thumb stroking my cheek.

"Whoo, yeah buddy! Rock that truck."

The male voice sent ice dripping through every vein. We both stopped, our foreheads touching as we stared wide-eyed at each other, waiting for the crunching footsteps outside the truck bed to pass.

"Should we see who's under there?" That sounded like Ross, one of the seniors.

"That's Jackson's truck. He'll lose his shit."

They laughed, wandering off, and Willa breathed a huge sigh of relief, a tiny laugh hitting my chest when her head did.

I didn't laugh or feel any relief.

The whole drive home, her hand in mine, mine still sticky with her, it was all I could do to remember where we lived, I was so shaken.

The lights were out when I pulled in the drive and put the truck in park.

Willa unclipped her seat belt, her eyes burning into my rigid profile. "Talk to me."

How she knew even though I hadn't said a word made my lips hitch.

Turning to face her, I studied the bow to her upper lip, the tiny dimple that appeared as she munched on it, and those green sprinkles in her eyes. "You're beautiful."

Her lashes lowered, then rose with a flutter. "You're upset." I was, but I didn't want to upset her by talking about it. I went to open the door, and she grabbed my arm. "Don't."

Sighing, I slumped back against the seat. "That was close, Wil. Too fucking close."

Her hand reached out, satin fingers against my cheek. "So we'll be more careful. It was risky. We know better."

My eyes closed as I laid my hand over hers, moving it to my lips to kiss.

That was the crux of it. We knew better, yet we hadn't cared.

In the days after, I couldn't forget how close we'd come. Or how much I hadn't cared at the time.

We might've just been two crazy kids, but I knew, even then, that I couldn't live without her. And that was what would happen if anyone found out.

Not only would I be forced to do so, but she would be ruined in every way.

nine

Willa
Eighteen

"You can drive," Dad said, tossing me the keys to his truck.

Staring down at them, then at him, I smiled. "I have to warn you, I'm not the best driver."

He chewed his lip, then shrugged. "She's older than you anyway, get in."

I did, setting the cookbooks and gift cards he'd bought me for my birthday in the back seat.

The old beast grumbled to life, and I moved the seat forward so I could reach the pedals, then clipped my seat belt on and adjusted the rearview mirror.

Dad had finished his last tour two months ago, and I'd been hanging out with him every week since school let out.

"So how's the job going? Andrew treating you well?" Andrew was a friend of his he'd met during training. At only twenty-two, he'd lost his hand and almost his arm while overseas. After a few years, he picked himself back up and opened his own truck rental business with the payout he'd received.

"Too well." Dad laughed. "All the bastard wants to do is talk about the good old days and yap my damn ear off."

I smiled at that. "He loves you."

Dad chuckled. "Seems so, because no one else would

handle the fact I hardly get any work done and drain his coffee supply."

His gaze fell on me as I wound through the backstreets toward the old dusty highway that leaked into the cove. "So what'd your mom and Heath get you?"

He might've been accepting of the fact I called Heath Dad, but that didn't mean he would ever do so himself. Understandable. "A new apron, these cute pink baking trays, and…" I crinkled my nose, hesitating, then rushed out, "And a new car."

I'd had my license for a while, but I hadn't asked for a car. I hadn't needed one.

Quiet rained down, and he sniffed, jerking his head. "Nice. What is it? An Audi?"

I blew some hair off my face. "Close. A Volkswagen."

Dad whistled. "How's she drive?"

"No idea. I haven't driven it yet."

Dad boomed with laughter. "That brother of yours waits on you hand and foot, doesn't he?"

My cheeks warmed, and I failed to slow quick enough for the yellow light, wincing as we drove through the red.

Dad's gaze seared into my profile, and I fumbled for something to say. "See? Crappy driver."

"Shitty driver," Dad said. "None of this crap business. If you're going to cuss, do it right. The intention's already there."

I laughed, seeing his point. "Mom would have a conniption."

"Wouldn't be the first or last time, and you're not a shitty driver." He hummed. "Just easily flustered. We can work on that."

I was relieved to hit the highway, knowing we were only ten minutes from home. "I barely passed my test."

He waved his hand, then turned up the radio, but not enough to kill the opportunity for conversation. "But you did pass. So what's the plan now, Miss Eighteen? Are you heading to any raging parties tonight? Need a ride home?"

I frowned as drops of rain began to dot the windshield as the burning sun sank low into the distant hills and cliffs. "You would?"

"I mean, I'd rather you didn't party," he laughed out, "but if you're going to do it, I'd like to make sure you're okay, yeah."

Mom and Dad would never think of it that way, though they weren't naïve enough to think we didn't attend them. They just preferred we hid it to keep it from being a point of contention. Not that I did much partying, and Jackson had toned it down some in recent months.

"Don't worry," I said, offering a quick smile. "I'm staying in. The rain messes with my hair."

Another raucous laugh that made my smile deepen and stay in place as we discussed what courses I was looking to take in college.

College, I thought to myself as I rushed inside, hurrying to escape the rain, was something Jackson and I hadn't spoken much about. The exception being at dinnertime with our parents.

Jackson had his schools picked out as soon as he knew he wanted in on the family business. Me? Well, I didn't really know what I wanted to do. Something with my hands. The thought of sitting at a desk day in and day out made me want to weep.

Jackson was in the living room with Dad, looking over plans for the new winter jersey line. "Hey," Heath said, glancing up. "Good time?"

We'd already celebrated my birthday together with brunch at my favorite pancake parlor in town.

I nodded, swinging the purple gift bag around my waist as Jackson continued to look at papers.

Heath grinned, then returned his attention to them, too.

I'd be worried Jackson hadn't even realized I was home if I hadn't noticed the way his hand tightened around the designs and how his eyes had flicked to the side. To my bare legs.

Brushing my hand over the short peach ruffle skirt I was wearing, I skipped out of the room and bounded upstairs to shower.

Mom was in my room when I exited the bathroom, steam trailing me, my fingers tugging at the messy bun I'd thrown my hair into. "Hi," I said.

She jumped, then smiled. "You scared me." Flicking through the gift cards, she muttered, "He didn't give you a card."

"He did," I said, depositing my clothes into my hamper. I tapped the desk where I'd set it next to the others I'd gotten. One from Daphne, one from Mom and Heath, and one from Dad. "I'm going to scrap them."

Mom eyed the new glossed pearl scrapbook album Jackson had bought me, then the card beneath my nail—the one I would hide as soon as she left—before a smile wriggled into place.

Walking over, she clasped my face within her hands, her eyes growing wet as she stared at me. I was the same height as her now, which she constantly berated me for, saying it wasn't fair. "It feels like just yesterday I was bringing you home from the hospital, and now, you're off driving cars, looking at college applications, and cooking everything yourself."

I smiled. "That last one has been a thing for some years now."

"Shush." She laughed, then sighed and placed a kiss to my brow. "You're making me emotional. Now I need wine." She released me and waved a hand, and I smiled after her as she brushed at her face.

The moon was grazing the cards and the gift bag on my desk when my bedroom door opened, silent and swift, after eleven.

His weight settled over me, the cool tip of his nose nudged my cheek before soft lips dragged over it, searching for mine.

Grabbing his head, I pulled, and pushed my tongue inside his mouth, sighing with relief when his stroked mine.

After only seconds, he drew back, and I frowned. "Don't look at me like that. You'll foil my plans." Tugging me from the bed, he handed me my orange summer robe, helping me into it. "Follow me," he whispered into my ear.

Excitement curved my lips and sent my feet hurtling after him, padding over the floor and down the stairs.

Outside, he stopped me on the patio, closing the door as quietly as possible. "We have to be awake before the sun, but I thought…"

He trailed off as we neared the tent he'd fixed at the back of the yard. There were no lights this time, likely to help avoid detection, but inside, everything else was the same as it had been three years ago.

"Jack," I breathed, blinking back tears when I saw a few fireflies flitting about in a Mason jar atop the makeshift crate table.

His hands settled on my shoulders, sliding up and down my arms as he gave me time to collect myself.

Cupcakes with lopsided, melted frosting sat on pink paper plates with a batch of brownies in my green Tupperware tub beside them. Lemonade sparkled in two glasses with paper polka dotted straws.

Moving to them, I laughed as I picked a cupcake up and sniffed it.

"The sniff test?" he asked. "Really?"

He took a seat beside me, and I scrunched my nose, taking a bite. Chewing, I bobbed my head from side to side.

"It's actually not bad." It wasn't the best I'd had, but it was better because he'd made it. "Did Mom help you?"

He took one and bit into it, frosting sticking to his upper lip. "She told me what to do, then raised her hands and said she wanted no part of disappointing you."

I smothered a laugh, almost choking on the thick fluff in my mouth.

"So how was your dad?"

"Good," I said, swallowing and smiling.

He tilted his head, studying me. "You always look happy after seeing him."

"He's..." I struggled to find the words. I didn't want to compare him to Heath. I loved them both, but they were two totally different men. "He's my dad," I said, soft and quiet.

Jackson nodded in understanding. "He let you drive his pride and joy?"

I snorted. "Yes, and I practically ran a red light."

Jackson laughed. "You shouldn't have passed that test."

About to lick the frosting from my fingers, I thought better of it and crooked my finger at him. "Come here, you've got something..." I gestured to his upper lip, where a tiny bit of frosting had smeared.

He bent forward, rolling his eyes a little.

I leaned in to lick it, then swiped my finger over his cheek.

Laughing, I fell back, bouncing onto the blow-up bed as he grabbed a cupcake and held me down with my hands over my head. Grinning, his eyes never left mine as he smooshed it into my nose, then all over my lips.

We both howled until we remembered we shouldn't, and sobered, staring.

His gaze darkened, and his chest heaved as he blurted, "I'm in love with you."

I forgot all about the frosting stuck to my nose and lips and cheeks, all about the parents who would disown us in the house behind us, and saw only the rise and fall of his chest. The lashes that refused to meet as he stared with an intensity that I'd never seen before.

The pulsing beat of my heart echoed in my ears as he repeated himself. "I'm in love with you. I didn't know what it was or if it would just go away. But it hasn't. It's only deepened, grown fucking roots in every part of me." He swallowed, the sound thick, and then said, "Say something?"

His confidence as he'd confessed, laid everything out into the balmy night air for my ears and heart to catch, made his last words ring with vulnerability.

A vulnerability he shouldn't be feeling, because he knew, he had to know. "I bet I was in love with you first."

Finally, he blinked, then shook his head, silent laughter painting his strong features with strikingly sharp beauty.

Lowering his head, his entire body, he licked the frosting from my nose, then my lips, then my cheeks. "You're still a brat," he murmured. "My brat."

"Always," I promised, forcing his mouth back to mine. Our hands explored, heated touches, and then he was stripping me of my clothes while I was tearing at his.

Naked and sweating, we rolled and tangled together on the bed, laughing whenever it squeaked in protest.

All humor fled when his hand settled between my legs, and then he was kissing a path down my body to where his fingers were driving me mad.

He'd done this to me time and time before, and every single time, I thought I'd combust as soon as his mouth touched me, and his hands gripped my thighs.

His tongue dived and dug deep, his hold relentless as

he forced my thighs around his head and my hips began to rock.

"Jack," I rasped out, delirious as he kept nudging me with his nose and poking my entrance with his tongue.

I splintered apart, but he didn't stop until my body quit quivering, and my legs tried to remove themselves from his bruising hold.

He lifted his head, swiping the back of his hand across his mouth, then climbed over me to let me taste what he'd done.

Hooking my legs around his waist, I rolled us, laughing into his mouth when we almost slipped off the bed, then I tore away and found him hard and wanting.

"Wil," he said, then groaned when my lips descended over the engorged head, and I fed as much of him into my throat as I could. "Fuck. You're getting too good at this."

This, to my dismay, was something he'd let Ainsley do, so I was determined to be better at it. Childish and stupid, probably, but I didn't care. I wanted him writhing and panting beneath me because I made him feel like shouting my name to the heavens.

His neck corded as his head fell back, his hips jutting up and forcing his cock farther inside. I took it for a few seconds, then gagged.

"Shit, shit," he muttered, pulling me off him with desperate hands.

I scowled as he wiped saliva from my chin, and settled over his lower stomach, straddling him. "You were going to come."

He stared up at me, and my stomach became a firework display, rattling and popping as I read what he wanted. "Yes."

I smiled, and he laughed. "I haven't even said anything."

I reached for his jeans, and he squeezed my ass while I fished the condom out of his pocket. "This says enough."

"Brat indeed."

I tore the wrapper with my teeth, then handed it to him.

He put it on with expert precision, with an ease that made me feel a little ill. "I thought you hadn't…"

He pulled me down to the bed, rolled over me, and settled between my damp thighs, then brushed some hair from my face. "I haven't."

I frowned.

He grinned, then ducked his eyes. "Fuck, this is going to sound so stupid."

It clicked then, and I bit my lips to keep from laughing. "You've been practicing."

A nod, then he dragged his teeth over his bottom lip. "Every time I get a hard-on you can't fix."

My arms looped around his neck, his chest meeting mine. "That's quite all right then."

"Is it?" he said, eyes laughing. I nodded, and he kissed each corner of my mouth. "Happy Birthday, Bug."

I kissed him, hard and pleading, taking his bottom lip with mine.

"Are you sure?" he said, his hand caressing the curve of my hip, shifting my leg over his lower back.

"No," I said, and when he paused, I continued. "I'm desperate."

His eyes shut, and I laughed.

I stopped when he reached between us, fumbling for a beat, then felt him enter.

I could do nothing, not even breathe as I watched his eyes and nostrils widen, his breath leaving him in a rush that hit my lips. "Jesus Christ," he wheezed.

My exhale rocketed out as he pushed until he couldn't anymore and then stopped.

With his arms braced beside my head, he kissed me.

Gentle, coaxing sweeps until the pain faded into discomfort, and my fingers sank into his hair, needing him closer. We were closer than we'd ever been, as close as two people could get. Every part of us was touching, connected, yet I wanted more. I wanted him where the rest of him lived, everywhere, to fill the unoccupied spaces of my body that were already owned by him.

My skin pebbled as his tongue stroked mine, then my lips, then my tongue again. "I knew this would feel good, but shit, Bug," he rasped. "I never want to leave, and I'm scared if I move, I'm going to blow."

"Then we'll just do it again," I whispered, voice thick.

He hummed, tilting my head back with his nose so his mouth could make love to my neck. "You'll be sore."

I didn't care. "And it'll be worth it."

He began to move then, sharp hips jerking back and forth, careful and deep, and fire lit me from the inside as everything burned. "You okay?" he said, blowing out a hard breath.

His brows were lowered, his cheekbones and jaw rigid with restraint. I reached up, stroking his jaw, and felt it loosen a little beneath my touch. "Perfect."

"You tell the sweetest lies," he said, kissing my finger when it reached his mouth, all the while his body never stopped moving, never stopped loving mine.

"It's not a lie," I said, cupping his face. "It hurts, but I never want you to leave."

He huffed, his nostrils flaring as he moved faster. "I love you."

"I love you."

Then with a groan, his mouth parted, his eyes stuck to mine while his body seized and jerked as he came.

In a daze, I absorbed every shudder from him, every quick

breath, and every quiet curse, and then he was kissing me, our bodies still fused in every way.

Later, as the sky began to lighten, and Jackson drew lazy circles on my back while I laid sprawled over his chest, he asked, "Will you ever get sick of hiding?"

We were trying not to fall asleep, as we had to pack everything up soon and get back inside before Mom and Dad woke up. It wasn't hard. One kiss too many, and a new game of pleasure chasing began anew.

"No," I said. I'd known before we started this, back when all I could do was dream of this, that I'd be happy as long as I had him. "What about you?"

I both feared and wanted his answer. "If hiding is all we've got, I'll happily hide forever. But we won't have to."

I traced his belly button, and he twitched, ticklish there. "We won't?" I failed to see a day when that would be true.

"College," he said a heavy minute later. Squeezing me to him, he kissed the top of my head. "We can be together for real in college."

"Is this not real?"

"It's real, Bug. It's as real as real can get."

Daphne Morris was popular. Possibly one of the most popular girls in school.

Before my birthday, and before school had let out for the summer, she'd waved to me and Peggy as she and her cheerleading friends had walked by our lunch table.

"I didn't think…" I'd stammered with an unsure scrunch of my nose.

"That she'd acknowledge us now that the art project is

finished?" Peggy nodded, eyeing the direction in which Daphne had gone. "Yeah, same."

I removed the wrap from my ham and cheese sandwich. "Jackson said to be careful."

Peggy's eyes narrowed. "Of Daphne?"

"Yeah," I'd said, taking a bite.

"Huh," she'd said. "Well, it's not like she's our new bestie." With an unconvincing smile, she then added, "She'll probably forget all about our existence once senior year arrives."

But she hadn't. Daphne kept in touch and hung out with us over the summer. Then she shocked not only us, but also most of the student body, when she took a stand—or rather, a seat—at our lunch table on the first day of senior year.

"She said something about not wanting fake friends anymore," I told Jackson that night.

Jackson, an arm tucked behind his head, flicked his eyes from the new anime episodes he'd downloaded to me. "For real?"

I nodded, my eyes tracking the fanning motion of his lashes. "Yep."

After staring up at me for a moment, he murmured, "And she's good to you?"

"She is. A little bossy sometimes, but…" I tried to find the words. "But in a way that shows she cares." Grinning, I flicked his nose. "Kind of like someone else I know."

He grabbed my finger, twisting his around it, and gave it a little tug. Our noses touched, and so did our eyes. "Then I guess that's okay." And then our lips did too.

ten

Jackson
Eighteen

The return of school made things somewhat more bearable after a summer spent trying to ignore how fucking starving I was every time Willa so much as blinked at me.

My dick felt bruised, battered, and exhausted, even when it had been inside her. Now, it grew hard at a simple flick of her hair or just the sound of her in the shower.

It was thankful for the reprieve.

My heart, however, was not.

We took only a few of the same classes, so it was lunchtime before I could even glance at her for longer than a couple of seconds most days.

And I feared my jaw would grind to dust as I noticed the other assholes who took too long a look at her.

"What's eating you, Gilbert?" Dash prodded.

I tore a chunk from the salami and salad wrap Willa had made me. "Just can't believe we need to be here for another year."

"Well," Lars said, wiping his chin. "Technically, it's not a year—"

Dash threw a piece of crust at him. "We know, Einstein."

Lars returned to his food, throwing not very subtle eyes to Daphne.

Which was probably why he didn't notice I was staring at their table too, and Dash, well, he was too self-absorbed to notice much of anything.

Raven didn't miss a beat. "Something in sister dearest's hair?"

I forced a smirk. "Probably. She was up late baking."

Raven wrapped his knuckles on the table. "Queen Cold is sitting with her."

"I know," I said, chewing more of my wrap. I swallowed and took a swig from my water bottle. "I suppose she's ditched her bitch posse."

Dash snorted. "If that putrid look on Kayla's face is anything to go by, then yeah." Okay, so maybe he wasn't as self-absorbed as we sometimes wished he was.

I peered over at the cheerleaders table, regretting it instantly when Ainsley's gaze smacked into mine. Unflinching and unperturbed, she smiled.

Frowning, I didn't even see Kayla and dragged my attention back to the table. I wouldn't put it past Ainsley to follow my line of sight to Willa.

"Wonder what she wants from Peggy Sue and Willa Grace?" Raven mused, stroking his clean-shaven chin.

"Probably to be their friend," Lars said with heavy sarcasm. "She is their friend, after all."

Dash laughed. "Simmer down, Mr. Obsessed."

"Rave's got a point," I said. "She might be friends with them, but she's never sat with them before."

Lars looked exasperated. "Guess she's changed her mind."

I suppose she had. Every day for that first week, Daphne was always with Peggy and Willa and hadn't even been seen talking to her former best friend, Kayla.

Willa seemed happy about it, so I didn't quiz or warn her,

and chose to just keep an ear out whenever Kayla and her friends were nearby.

No one fucked with Willa. No guys and no chicks, either.

Ainsley's eyes seemed to stalk me wherever I went as the first weeks of senior year dragged on, and Peggy's birthday approached.

"She's still so into you," Willa said, getting ready for Peggy's surprise party. Tossing her brush to the dresser, she grabbed a hair pin, dragging pieces of her hair back from her face.

It didn't hold, and after a minute, she grew frustrated and threw the pin to the dresser with a clang.

Laughing, I climbed off her bed, where I'd been reading until she was ready, and checked the hall before I moved in behind her.

My hands glided up her bare arms, goose bumps rising in their wake, and scooped up her long, heavy tresses, dropping them so they'd fall against her back. Leaning down, I pressed a kiss to her bare shoulder. She was wearing some fluffy cocktail dress, black pumps on her feet making the drop for my mouth shorter. "It doesn't matter what she is."

"It doesn't?" she asked, her voice quiet air.

My mouth moved side to side, ghosting over her smooth skin, then pressed. Wrapping my hands around her stomach, I pulled her ass flush with my erection. "Nothing matters but this."

She smirked at me in the mirror, her cheeks tinting. "Nice, Jack. Real sweet."

I chuckled. "I didn't mean that. But yeah"—I grinned, kissing her neck and then the side of her jaw when her head tilted—"that's pretty damn important too."

She turned in my arms, her eyes darting to the empty door-way for a second before her lips visited mine in a brief but firm kiss. "I love you."

"And I you." I kissed her forehead, then stepped back, my hands reluctant to let her go. "Leave your hair loose."

Her cheeks bloomed, and she smiled at the ground as I left the room to get my keys and wallet.

Raven followed a blond chick around the side of Peggy's dad's house, so I went inside in search of Willa even though I couldn't exactly hang with her.

I made it to the kitchen before a hand grabbed mine and a familiar voice whispered, "Meet me upstairs in two minutes."

Then Willa was gone, bounding up the stairs. Dash had warned everyone with not a small amount of grit that we weren't to leave the first floor. Most people would listen.

I wasn't most people, and it wasn't like he'd find out.

I waited outside the kitchen, feigning interest in my phone when a set of blue stilettos appeared in front of my shoes. "Hey, Jack."

I tried not to cringe, being that Willa was the only one who called me that. It sounded too personal and all wrong in someone else's voice.

"Ainsley," I clipped, sliding my phone into my back pocket. "What are you doing here?"

Her lip curled, her hands twisting in front of her. "Dad's friends with Peggy's dad, and well, I like Peggy." She shrugged, the puffy sleeves of her black dress reaching her diamond studded ears. "So I thought I'd stop by for a little while."

That was bullshit, and we both knew it. I was sure she liked Peggy just fine, but I was also sure it wasn't enough to attend her surprise eighteenth birthday bash.

Saying any of that would be futile, and despite the way her eyes gleamed, I still didn't want to hurt her feelings. She'd never done anything to warrant that.

"Cool," I said for lack of anything better. Willa was waiting for me, but if Ainsley saw me head upstairs, I wouldn't put it past her to think she could follow and try something, being that Dash repeatedly told everyone it was a no-go zone. "Well, have fun. I need to use the bathroom."

I headed that way before she could say anything else and waited a full minute, staring at the time on my phone before I washed my hands and made sure the coast was clear.

She'd thankfully moved on, so I didn't waste another moment, racing up the stairs as if my life depended on it.

The frosted glass doors to Peggy's dad's office were cracked open, and I slid inside, quickly shutting and locking them behind me.

Her arms over her chest, seated atop the mahogany, paper-strewn desk, Willa scowled. "What happened?"

She always knew, as if she had some type of sixth sense. Or maybe, like me, she lived her life in a perpetual state of desperation and paranoia.

It wasn't what I wanted for her, but I wanted her more than I wanted anything else in this life, so I was okay with being that selfish.

"Ainsley's here."

Her brows relaxed, but sorrow tensed her delicate jaw. "She saw you."

I nodded, ensuring the doors were indeed locked, then crossed the room. Grabbing her thighs, I wedged myself between them. "Yeah, then I hid in the bathroom until she wandered off." Willa sighed, and I tipped her chin up, grinning down at her. "You don't need to be jealous."

"I can't help it," she whispered. "Even though I know you don't want her, even though I know you only want me, I still freaking am."

"Fucking am." Her head tilted, brows pulling with confusion. I laughed. "Stop saying freaking. Fucking, Bug. Repeat after me..."

She slapped at my chest, then grabbed my shirt, pulling my chest to her nose, and inhaled. "God, you always smell so good."

"So fucking good," I teased.

She gazed up at me, her arms tight around my back, and my heart swelled to three times its usual size, stealing all the air in my lungs. "Can you do what I invited you up here to do now?" She pouted, batting her lashes playfully and then puckering her lips. "Kiss me stupid."

Shaking with quiet laughter, I did just that, then gently eased her back over the desk, papers scrunching and pens rolling beneath her, and tore her panties to the side.

"Jack," she breathed. "Not here."

"You can't say that after I'm already nose deep in your cunt." I ran it over her, inhaling. "I'll tell you what else smells so good," I said, then licked slow, so slow, through her folds. "This."

Giving in, she wrapped her legs around my neck, and I lowered to my knees, gripping the tops of her thighs as my tongue feasted on her.

Her head rocked side to side as her quiet mewls filled the small space, bouncing off the bookshelves and the portraits on the walls. I brought her to the edge, then reveled in the sound of her tiny growl as I rose and unzipped my jeans, shoving them and my briefs over my ass to free my angry cock.

Willa, flushed and with feral eyes, sat up and moved to the edge of the desk, open and waiting for me. "You always get me to the point of no return."

I grinned, my pulse thundering. "You would say no?"

Her teeth scraped over her bottom lip, her thighs opening more in answer. "I should, but I can't."

Without any further preamble, I entered heaven, gripping

the back of her head as I seated myself as deep as I could get, and took her lips.

Her nails scratched at my scalp, her legs vises around me, and her body arched into mine as I began thrusting hard and fast, knowing she was close.

Her cunt quivered and squeezed, tight and unbearably hot, and her velvet tongue lapped at mine, her teeth nipping at my lips if I even dared to draw a breath.

It was insatiable, this feeling of euphoria that always had us seeking more and more and more.

Tearing her dress off, I picked her up, holding her to me so hard, I'd leave bruises. She did the same, struggling to breathe, gasping and gripping at my shirt and hair.

Despite living together, we couldn't be with each other whenever we wanted. We'd sneak into each other's rooms and took daring risks only a few times a week when we couldn't handle it anymore.

Around the room we went, crashing into bookshelves as my hips jutted with little finesse and too much desperation.

Need and love were a force we couldn't contend with and forever lost the battle to. We were nothing but its willing subjects, begging for more even as it was handed to us.

That was how it felt to be with Willa, as though I was swimming ashore after being stuck at sea for years, only to have the coastline move farther out of reach every time I neared it.

We weren't an itch we could scratch. We were fire that would never extinguish, and we'd burn anything in our path to keep getting what we wanted. What we needed.

A hunger like ours didn't leave a lot of room for caution.

Slamming into the rattling doors, I gripped Willa's thigh and face, pounding in and out of her so hard, my name was shaken from her lips.

Together, we moaned into each other's mouths, the flames settling as cold waves of pleasure crashed into me. I shook and grunted her name, filling her completely, thanking god Mom had put her on the pill over the summer.

We ended up on the chaise, where we made out until the noise downstairs began to dissipate, and we were ready to do it again, slower this time.

eleven

Willa
Eighteen

Daphne and Lars were together, I was sure of it, yet she wouldn't confide in Peggy or me. I tried to empathize, to see why she wouldn't, but I guess I just couldn't understand why she wouldn't admit it.

She didn't need to when the rumors began to circulate that Lars had knocked up Annika after they'd supposedly hooked up at a party before summer break. The despair that leeched off Daphne in the days after said everything she was never willing to.

She might not have been with him—or maybe she had—but she had feelings for him.

Peggy and I did our best to comfort someone who refused to admit she was breaking, opting in the end to be silent pillars of support, ready for when she might need us.

"How's Lars?" I asked Jackson.

He turned down the music, scanning the lot for a decent parking space. "As good as any guy who finally landed his dream girl, only to have it ruined, can be, I guess." He pulled into a spot in the back where there were less cars, then turned the truck off. "And the whole dad thing…" He opened the door. "I don't know, Wil. He's not handling that part at all, let alone handling it well."

I waited for him to round the truck and help me down,

knowing he'd be annoyed if I didn't. Lars had gone off the rails, missing classes and showing up high, but maybe he just needed time. I said that as Jackson handed me my purse, then closed the door.

"Yeah," he said, sounding unconvinced. "Maybe."

In Seaside, a tiny town about forty-five minutes from Magnolia Cove, was the French restaurant and patisserie Jackson and I had begun to frequent.

Over oysters, soup, and quiche, we could smile, laugh, touch, and almost forget that a world outside this small town would frown upon us doing so.

"Are your applications filled out?" Jackson asked, offering me a spoonful of soup.

I wrapped my lips around the spoon, letting the fragrant creamy spice sit on my tongue before releasing the silverware and swallowing.

His eyelids lowered, and I dabbed at my chin with a napkin. "Yeah, they're done."

"I'll check them later tonight then," he said, hand in mine, thumb caressing my own.

I nodded even though I knew I'd filled them out correctly. He needed it to help him feel in control of a situation that had the power to obliterate everything we knew and loved beyond each other.

"This time next year, we'll be able to do this all the time." I took a sip of lemonade. "But what if we get accepted into the same school, and one of our friends is there?"

Jackson's knee bounced beneath the table, and he shrugged. "They'll find out sooner or later. I'm not as worried about them knowing now."

That had me frowning. "What?"

Licking his lips, he dropped the spoon into the soup bowl

and leaned forward, squeezing my hand in both of his. "Wil, we'll be living at college. Mom and Dad will likely find out before we're through with college, but by then"—his top lip curled, green eyes dancing—"it'll be too late. They can't stop us, and they can't control us."

"Then," I said. Because although he was right, we still needed to be careful *now*.

A short nod, then he lifted my hand to his mouth, lips brushing over the back of it. "Then."

He paid the bill while I stewed on those thoughts, happiness lighting every speck of doubt I'd been harboring. It wasn't that I'd doubted him. Some part of me had doubted we could pull this off. But we had, and we were, and we only had to wait just a little bit longer before we didn't need to skip towns for meals like this.

Taking my hand, he helped me up, then wrapped his arm around me, curling some hair behind my ear. "Wanna play in the cemetery?" His smile was playful, buoyant, and I couldn't stop myself from rising to my toes to kiss it, and I didn't have to.

"No," I whispered. "That's a little too creepy."

He hummed against my lips, kissing them twice before murmuring, "I'm sure they won't mind."

I laughed, shoving him back. "Stop it. Let's just use the truck."

After walking hand in hand to where it was parked, Jackson pulled over into a secluded wooded clearing on the old highway home, and we did just that.

Once home, I didn't wait for him and slammed the door. "Ew," I groaned. I needed to change my panties, stat.

Jackson chuckled. "You weren't complaining when I put it in there."

"You're supposed to keep more than one napkin in the glove compartment, you toad."

He bumped my shoulder, his hand reaching for me. I dodged it and blinked to the lit-up house. Before I could open the door, he bent low behind me, whispering, "I love knowing I'm still inside you after I've left you."

It was all I could do to open the front door without leaning back into him. I forced myself inside and kicked off my heels. Jackson headed down the hall to the kitchen, cursing when he entered.

Something turned over inside my stomach as I slowly followed.

Seated at the countertop, mugs of coffee in front of them, were our parents. They didn't drink coffee this late at night.

The coffee wasn't the only blaring alarm. No, it was the puffiness beneath Mom's mascara-blackened eyes, and the dejected, disgusted look in Heath's.

"What...?" I started, then stopped.

They knew.

Jackson took a step back, as if to shield me from them, as Dad rumbled, "We've tried, we really have, to come up with something to say for what"—he waved his hand, coughing—"what you've done, what you're... doing."

Mom bit her lips, eyes closing over a fresh wave of tears.

Heath took her hand in his, and that was when I saw them. Photographs, printed out on paper, spread out on the countertop. I couldn't make out the pictures, but I knew they were of us. "How long?"

Jackson and I said nothing.

There was nothing I could think to say. No excuses to be made. No apologies to be said. I wasn't sorry. We weren't sorry. And we couldn't excuse ourselves away.

So we stood there, the room collapsing around us, our hopes and dreams crumbling with each new breath, and we said nothing.

"It's incestuous, you know," Mom spat, sniffing.

That had Jackson stiffening. "It's not."

She laughed, then cried. "Dear god, it's worse than these"—she stabbed her nail at a picture, the acrylic tip flying off—"disgusting things suggest."

Heath scrubbed his chin, his gaze never leaving Jackson.

I longed to plant myself in front of him, to take the brunt of the impact from that disappointment. Never ever had I seen Heath look at Jackson like that. Like he didn't know who he was, or if he even wanted to.

"Where'd you get those?" Jackson said, his tone quiet but unyielding.

Mom's eyes widened. "What?" She stood, the stool behind her screeching over the floor. "You cannot be serious right now. You have tainted this family. Your sister. Our fucking livelihood," she said, her face reddening, her voice turning guttural. "And you dare to ask how we found out?"

The cussing startled me, and then what she'd said enraged me. I stepped forward. "He didn't—"

Jackson grabbed my waist. "Don't, Wil."

Mom blinked, then charged forward. "Get your hands off her, right now." Her nails sank into my arm, tearing skin as she hauled me away from him and out of the kitchen.

I gritted my teeth against the pain, not only from her nails, but from the way Jackson lunged forward, hands raised. "Okay, don't. Just"—his chest rose and fell, and Mom quit moving at the base of the stairs—"just don't fucking hurt her."

Mom screeched, "What?" I tore my arm free when her grip loosened but didn't rub where I felt blood trickling. "You're the one who's hurt her, you," she sputtered as she stepped forward to stab a finger at Jackson, "v-vile, treacherous—"

"I love him," I said, for all the good it would do.

Mom froze, and the air vacated the room, leaving me heaving with fear as she turned back, and hissed, "Get upstairs, or so help me god…"

Heath stood behind Jackson in the doorway to the kitchen, his eyes wet and his fists curling at his sides.

I looked from him to Jackson, and Jackson jerked his head to the stairs, his eyes pleading for me to go.

I shook my head, mouthing a silent, "No."

"Bug," he rasped. "Go."

It seemed to come out of nowhere, the sound ringing everywhere.

Mom slapped him, and I screamed when she went to do it again. "Don't you even look at her, let alone tell her what to do."

"It's not his fault," I cried, rushing to them.

Heath grabbed me around the waist, twisting me back to the stairs. "Go, Willa. Now."

Mom was still screaming at Jackson, shoving him into the wall. He wouldn't fight back by moving away. Despite what she was saying and doing, he knew he deserved her ire.

He'd just take it.

I gazed up at Heath, begging, "Please, it's really not."

His expression remained unmoved, even as he conceded. "I have her," he whispered. "Go."

I did, but only when he made good on his word and gathered Mom to him, taking her back to the kitchen while she cried and cursed like I'd never heard before. "They've ruined everything. Everything, Heath. Oh, god."

I heard the door to the basement shut a minute later and dropped to my bed, tears flooding my cheeks as I sat on my trembling hands. They itched to go to him, to tear open doors and do anything other than sit here.

But I couldn't.

We were trapped.

If I thought we were trapped, I'd thought too soon.

Half an hour later, Mom stormed into my room, and without so much as looking at me, snatched up my purse from the floor by my feet and pulled out my phone.

Protests slithered and writhed over my tongue, but my teeth bit them at bay. It was pointless to argue with her. She'd never been this enraged, this upset, in my entire life.

If she wanted my phone, she could take it.

Jackson and I were always careful about what we'd text each other anyway. Sure, there were emojis or kisses attached but never anything too illicit. Nothing that would lead either of us to more trouble than we needed to wind up in.

"Get up," Mom said, her voice cracked. When I didn't move, still shaking where I sat, she repeated, harsher, "I said get up. Go to the bathroom and ready yourself for bed."

I got up, each step past her anger-swelling frame a slow wade through eternity.

"Be sure to use the toilet."

My feet paused in the doorway, but I didn't turn around. I could barely stomach any of this, let alone look at her if I didn't need to. "Why?"

"We'll be locking your door."

I frowned, unsure what she meant exactly. That is, until I'd used the toilet and showered. Wrapped in nothing but a towel, I was brushing my teeth when the sound of a drill pierced the fogged air of the bathroom.

Almost gagging, I quickly spat into the sink, as what Mom had meant by locking the door sank in with cold, hard clarity.

Quickly wiping the toothpaste from my chin, I pushed my hair back and shut off the water, staring at my reflection while the noise outside droned on a minute longer.

A pale face, almost translucent, stared back at me with huge hazel eyes. So pale, my cheeks looked sunken, and veins colored places my hair didn't.

My stomach roiled and churned. I continued to stare until the sluggish beat of my heart regulated, and some color leeched back into my face.

It would be okay.

They were just furious right now. They'd see how crazy this was come morning.

But they didn't.

They didn't, and not even Jackson's yelling after he'd realized what they'd done, or the way I'd ignored breakfast and stayed inside my chamber, remotely fazed them.

He'd tried to see me, but they watched our every move, and on Sunday afternoon, day two of my new solitude, Mom unlocked the padlock on my door and entered my room.

She dumped a stack of boxes on the floor. "Start packing. Your dad will be here at six."

I scrambled off the bed, my heart in my throat, and stuttered, "What? What do you mean?"

"Kylie's a deadbeat, and Heath refuses to send Jackson there. So you're moving in with Daniel."

With that, she marched out of my room, the lock clinking on the other side of the door.

Moving. They were making me leave.

A small glimmer of relief defused some of the tension in my shoulders because I knew I couldn't live like this. I couldn't stay here when she was acting so insane.

I didn't care that she had a reason to be upset with me. I only cared that she was scaring me, and the future, the one we'd planned so meticulously, was moving farther out of sight with every yelling match Jackson had with them downstairs.

That relief was squashed when I arrived at my shelves and removed books to find the small album I'd hidden behind them. My favorite scrapbook album. The one that was made after our first kiss, during the months of torment and yearning.

Stolen pictures and glances filled the pages, and when we'd succumbed to what we could no longer ignore, happiness, brighter than anything I'd seen, lit his eyes as he'd tried to palm away the camera.

Unable to keep looking, I closed it and tucked it inside a box.

I might've been leaving, but he was still trapped.

We both were.

Dad watched me unpack my clothes from the suitcase and hang them in the small closet by the door, disappointed and quiet. As he had been since he'd picked me up and carried all my things inside.

The room was much smaller than the one I'd grown up in. It had cherry pink walls with white molding and a vintage desk that I rather liked. A light pink twin bed perched in the corner, and a cream and brown circular woven rug laid over the worn wood floor beneath it.

Dad's place was three bedrooms, old but tastefully renovated. All of which he'd done himself. I'd never had the heart
to tell him that I preferred purple over pink when he'd so
proudly showed me my room for the first time after buying the
place and finishing it before he'd even started working on the
kitchen.

"Thank you," I finally said. I wasn't sure what else there
was to say.

His disappointment in me was evident in every stilted,
near-silent move he made, but it was nothing compared to the
wrath that clouded every crevice at home.

Half my things were still in my room back at home, or
what was once called home, but I didn't mind. Besides the vital
piece of my heart, I'd taken everything that mattered. If I had
the courage, maybe one day I'd return for the rest. If they ever
allowed me to.

Mom hadn't even said goodbye, and when I'd passed
Heath's study on the way to the door, he'd looked up from
where he'd been leaning against his desk, then moved to the
door to close it.

"For what?" Dad asked.

I folded a green sweater dress, setting it on the pile on the
rose-gold bedding with the rest. "For, you know…" I sucked
my lips, then turned with a sigh. "Picking me up. Letting me
stay here."

A crease formed between his bent brows. His arms unfolded, and he straightened from the doorway to his full imposing height. "You're my kid. I'm not letting you stay here. You'll
live here, with me, for as long as you want."

Tears burned, but I'd cried so much, nothing gathered,
only threatened and ached. I nodded. "You're upset with me."

"Damn right, I am," he said, rubbing his jaw with a

humorless laugh. "You've been screwing around with your brother."

"*Step*," I said. "Stepbrother," I finished, quiet and turning my eyes to my curling bare toes.

He groaned. "Willa, semantics don't matter too much right now. You guys fucked up, okay? You can't excuse that with meaningless words."

"I'm not trying to," I said.

"But you want to. You want to scream it to the world that you're the victims here, that you're probably in love or some bullshit, and that you're technically adults who can do what you want."

I lifted my eyes, blinking. "Because it's all true." My voice was too soft, and I hated it. I wanted to be resolute, fearless, and unmerciful in this love of ours. "It's all true, but I won't say anything else. So don't worry."

Dad shifted, and I turned back around to finish emptying the clothes from the suitcase.

After a moment, he joined me, folding a pair of jeans with military precision. "Your mom's raging pissed."

"I know," I said. "She…" I paused, knowing I shouldn't say it because it didn't matter now anyway.

"She what?" When I continued with my task, he took my chin, forcing my eyes to his hazel ones. They bounced back and forth between mine, that crease between them deepening. "She what, Willa?"

I swallowed, admitting, "She padlocked my bedroom door."

Horror swept over every feature, wiping them clean of each fine line that etched his shaven face. Slack, his hand fell, and I grabbed the pile of clothes, taking them to the chest of drawers that acted as a nightstand beside the bed.

"That's why she made you do the walk of shame on your own," he said. "Because I'd see."

I closed the drawer, then zipped up the suitcase. "Probably, but it's okay. It's done now."

His laughter raised the hair on my arms. "That fucking woman…" he cursed, then took the suitcase from me, lifting it to the top of the closet with an ease I envied. "And for the record, it's not okay."

I closed the sliding door, traipsing back to the desk to unpack the albums in the box there. It had to be nearing midnight, yet I refused to try to sleep until I'd finished.

"Willa," Dad said from the doorway. "I hope, when the dust has settled, that you don't go back."

He left before I could look at him, and I threw the empty box to the floor with the others. I wished I could've told him I wouldn't go back if Mom asked, but the thought of Jackson being there alone…

The thought of Jackson alone was enough to collapse the remaining strength I had, and I soon found myself on the bed, struggling to stay awake.

twelve

Jackson

I felt like I was coming undone at the seams.

The sound of the lock being drilled into Willa's bedroom door followed me everywhere, my dreams, school—always right there.

How one sound could haunt you more than the events that'd transpired since, I wasn't sure.

"Willa?" Raven asked on Tuesday.

I shook my head. They knew, all my friends did. I'd met them at the skatepark the second I could escape, needing out before I clawed my way through the brick walls.

Willa shouldn't have been the one locked in her room. Willa shouldn't have been the one forced to move out of the home we'd grown up in. And Willa shouldn't have been kicked out of school her senior year, torn away from the few friends she had who weren't me.

Because I knew. I knew I was the reason she'd never cared too much about making any new ones. That, and she was content to hang with Peggy, Daphne now too.

I was under strict instruction to go straight home, and I knew my phone would be tracked, maybe even my car too.

I didn't care. I didn't go straight home, and I only showed in the last class of the day long enough to say I wasn't feeling well and then left for the school nurse.

Faster than I'd ever ran before, I bolted outside the school doors, dived into my truck, and sped out of the lot.

I had to see her. I had to see if she was okay, or that she was as okay as she could be, considering.

The roads were quiet, being that most people were at school or work. I arrived within twenty minutes instead of the usual thirty and parked in the brick paved driveway.

Her dad was at work, but Willa was there. I knew she would be.

Which was proven a second later when the screen door slapped open, and in those damn ruffled shorts, a blue tank, and her hair flying behind her, she bounded off the porch. Over the garden, the grass sinking beneath her bare feet and her lips wobbling, she ran to me, and I unglued my feet to meet her halfway.

"Oh, my god," she breathed, choked and sniffing as she burrowed her nose into my neck.

I held her so tight that I feared she wouldn't be able to breathe, but I couldn't ease up. My hand cradled the back of her head, holding her to me with a shaking despair.

My eyes grew wet, my arms and hands and every part of me trying to swallow her whole. "I'm sorry, Bug. So fucking sorry it's killing me."

"Don't you dare," she wheezed, pushing back just enough to give me those huge eyes. "It's not your fault. None of it is." She clasped my cheek, rubbing at a tear that'd escaped. "Come inside before some busybody sees and tattles to Dad."

"The neighbors know?" I asked, reluctant to let her go even with the promise of more touching inside.

She laughed. "No, but I'm sure Mrs. Greenwell next door will ask about the boy who came to see me if we don't move it."

Right. And Daniel didn't need to be any type of genius to figure out who that boy would be.

Inside, I grabbed her cheeks, my mouth all over hers as I kicked the door shut and pressed her up against it. "I've missed you so much." I kissed her nose, her chin, her neck. "So fucking much."

Her hands sifted through my hair, and I groaned into her skin, then took her mouth again.

When something wet slid down my cheek, meeting our lips, I pulled back. "Fuck, Wil."

She tried to keep kissing me, but I grabbed her arms, gently moving her back.

"Don't you dare tell me not to cry," she said, laughing all the while furiously swiping at the tears leaking from her eyes. "Has she hurt you again? Has Heath done anything?"

"No, I'm fine." My thumbs swept in to finish the job, then I took her hand and led her to the black leather couch in the living room. She climbed sideways onto my lap, and I held her to me as she tucked her head beneath my chin, trembling.

"Your dad's place is nicer than I expected," I said, trying to lighten things up.

She knew what I was doing but humored me. "Did you expect a bachelor pad?"

"I did, actually. Something more…" I pursed my lips, pretending to think about it as I let my gaze travel over the huge red rug and the matching throw pillows on the couches. "Rugged."

She laughed, quiet and clinging to me, but I felt something unclench in my chest knowing she could still do it.

"What are we going to do?" she asked the impossible.

"I don't know, Bug." I sighed, stirring her hair. "I don't know."

"They're sending me to the public school. I start next week."

"I know," I said, trying not to let anger seep into my tone. "I saw Mom filling out the forms last night."

"She hates me. It's my senior year, and she couldn't even let me finish school with my friends. She really hates me."

"She hates me, not you," I said, and I'd never forgive her for punishing me by hurting Willa. "How'd your dad take it?"

Willa yawned, relaxing into me. "Not as bad as them, but he's still not exactly happy with me."

I thought about that for a moment, staring out the front window. I'd have to leave any minute to get home in time to avoid danger. I should've already left. "Think you could convince him to get you a phone?"

Willa stilled, pressing a hand to my chest to peer down at me. "But they'll check yours."

"I'll get a cheap one to use and keep it in my locker or something."

Her eyes brightened. "I'll see what I can do."

The fact we didn't even consider ending this should've troubled me, but we were past the point of changing a damn thing. Nothing about how we felt could be changed or altered; it demanded we endure.

I squeezed her to me. "We'll find out who did this." Those photos. I'd only caught a glimpse of them, but they were taken that night. The same night we'd gone on one of our rare dates out of town.

Her hand slid under my school blazer, and my dick woke up when her arm wrapped around my side. "It won't matter."

"It matters, Wil."

I had to leave. Now. Or I was fucked.

I couldn't. "What do you need?"

She nuzzled closer, her lips drifting over my neck. "Just you."

"You've got me."

"Good, just… please, keep holding me."

And so I did, until five minutes before her dad was due home.

I couldn't remember a time when the house had been so quiet. What was once so alive now barely breathed in Willa's absence. Gone was the sweet scent of her shampoo, the strawberry frosting she always kept in the fridge, the shoes she'd kick off by the door, and the sound of the mixer at night.

All the little things I loved but never knew I'd miss.

Dad and Victoria—in my mind, that was who she now was—seldom spoke to me. Most nights over dinner, Dad was the only one who tried. Innocuous bullshit, usually about new lines, upcoming events, classes and college. After a few weeks, I stopped eating with them and ate in my room instead.

They didn't protest.

The times Victoria did speak to me were to remind me of the rules and to request mundane tasks, like bringing up my washing.

Sure, her own daughter was no longer living under the same roof as her and the rest of her family, but one must ensure the washing routine didn't change.

Her priorities, I'd realized, were so out of whack, I wondered how I'd never noticed it all that much before now. Perhaps that was due to never having much of a relationship at all with my real mom.

There were years I'd longed for it when I was younger. So many hours wasted, hoping she'd arrive on our doorstep, or surprise me at school pickup and look excited to see me. Just as Daniel had done for Willa when he could.

She never did. If I saw Kylie—I stopped bothering long

ago—I was taken to her and mostly ignored. Because of that, Victoria had been more than a stepmother to me.

She'd been the only real mother I had.

Until she hurt the one thing I loved more than anything else.

Defiance in small doses would see me through, would continue to fuel the fire not even distance and absence could suffocate.

In a moment of weakness, I took the cheap phone I'd bought with cash home with me, needing to hear her voice before I slept. So I could sleep maybe, just maybe, through the night.

"What are they saying at school?" Willa asked, sounding tired.

I wouldn't dare tell her that. She didn't need to know we were being dubbed with all sorts of inaccurate, stupid names.

For a couple of weeks, it'd been quiet, and I thought that maybe no one cared. I realized my stupidity when I'd passed Hennessy in the hall one afternoon. It wasn't that they hadn't cared, the rumor mill was just running slow for once. He'd laughed with his stupid jock friends, coughing words like sister fucker, incest obsessed, and dirty big bro. The last one was what made me turn back and throw his ass to the ground.

His dumb friends had pulled me off, and Danny even so much as dared to swing an uppercut to my jaw. I'd blocked it and almost twisted his wrist in two until he'd yelped and the teacher had sent us scattering.

The last thing Willa and I needed was a write-up or phone call home.

"Not much, actually." I hoped I sounded sincere, infusing enough indifference into my tone.

Willa hummed. "That's weird. I thought, at the very least, Kayla and her friends would be having a field day."

They were. Annabeth had even cornered me unawares in

the boys' bathrooms, her fingernail scratching down the fabric of my school shirt as she'd said, "No wonder you never let anyone near you. We thought you might've had a thing for guys, you know. Turns out"—my eyes narrowed as she licked her lips and swayed closer—"you just have a thing for family. Has that changed now?"

In answer, I'd stalked away, my teeth clamped as her sickly sweet laughter followed.

"Lars and Annika are giving them too much to cackle about." Lars seemed to be trying to get his shit together, trying and failing, but trying all the same. "Enough about that. Tell me more about the new school."

She'd started a week ago, but we'd only seen each other once, for maybe ten minutes, since, and we'd spent the entire time making out inside my truck.

"It's fine." I wrapped my hand around myself, stroking slowly. "It's not that different, but everyone already has their own cliques, you know?"

My hand paused, my eyes closing with shame. "Wil, you haven't made any friends?"

"There's this one girl Flo, or Florence but she hates her name, in art class who seems cool. But it's okay; no one's giving me trouble."

I found that hard to believe. Some gorgeous, sweet new girl shows up at school... the guys there would be hungry as fuck. "Don't let anyone mess with you."

"Everyone's been nice enough."

I sighed. "I mean guys, Bug. I'm not stupid. I know they'll try." And it was going to continue to drill an anxious pit of fury inside my stomach until she graduated.

She giggled, and my cock pleaded to be unloaded. "I can handle myself, I'll have you know."

My hand tugged again, my teeth scraping over my bottom lip. "Yeah?"

"Yep," she said.

"How about you handle yourself now, then, while I do the same."

Silence, and then she coughed. "Wait, do you mean…?"

I withheld a laugh. "Fingers in that pretty cunt, Bug. Now. If I can't see you come, then I need to hear you."

Rustling hit my ears. "Okay."

"I love you," I said, squeezing myself when I heard her breath hitch.

"And I love you."

My voice sounded strangled, but I didn't care. "Good, now insert one finger and rub your clit."

thirteen

Willa

After a few brusque phone calls from Dad, Mom and Heath relented and allowed me to have my car.

I'd need it for school, Dad had argued, as I was a senior. Having to transfer schools had already disrupted my education enough.

Still, eyeing the fresh ding in the door of my Golf from an old Honda that was parked next to it, I had to wonder if bringing it here was even a good idea.

"I know a guy who could probably get that out," a deep voice said. "But I must warn you, my favors come with conditions."

I knew that voice, had heard it say hello to me before, and had listened to it talk to other people in class.

Todd Belzine. Star soccer player, six feet of arrogant charm.

Sighing, I opened the back door and tossed my books and bag inside before turning around. "It's okay. It was bound to happen eventually." I offered a small smile, barely meeting his impossibly dark eyes, and went to climb inside my car.

I halted when he spoke. "You know, Clay can be a right asshole, but I'm sure once he knows it's your car he's messed up, he'll probably bend over backward to get it fixed."

Clay Evans, I'd quickly heard, was the same guy who'd deflowered Daphne.

It was among the first words he'd said to me. "Prep, hey? You know Daphne? I fucked her virginity right out of her." Followed by assessing eyes as he'd bent closer. "I'm playing this Friday night. You should come watch."

I'd recoiled and backed away to the sound of his friends' laughter, and I hadn't had the heart to tell Daphne I'd met him.

I supposed it didn't much matter. "It's just a tiny scratch. Really"—I smiled—"it's fine."

"Whatever you say, Dimples."

I felt my eyes grow and stilled.

"You have these faint, adorable as fuck dimples." Todd chuckled, walking backward to an old black BMW that was parked on the other side of Clay's car. "Later."

Florence raced over before I could get inside my car, and I almost screamed, wanting nothing more than to call Jackson before he needed to be home.

"Todd just talk to you?"

I nodded. I could see how Peggy had once kissed the guy at a party, but I was incapable of seeing much else.

Flo nudged me, pulling a cigarette from her pocket. "He's the worst with chicks, but he'll show you a good time."

"I'm in a relationship," I reminded her.

She lit the cigarette and pocketed her lighter. "Yeah, sure. So what's happening there?" Her brows waggled as a huge cloud of smoke left her mouth. "Has brother dearest called you at all to see how life at the cesspit school has been?"

Florence had this way of pulling knowledge out of you before you were even aware it was happening, and so that was how, in art class on my second day at Magnolia Cove High, she'd discovered my dirtiest and most beautiful secret. It was no longer much of a secret at all, so I hadn't exactly regretted telling her.

The other students who'd found out had whispered and thrown scandalized glances my way, but it felt more in jest than malicious, and they'd lost interest after a few days.

I looked around, a habit I couldn't squash yet, and bobbed my head. "Yeah."

"Stop it." She laughed. "No one gives a shit. Shane Allens and Mira Seebun are practically cousins, and they fuck like rabbits." She laughed again at whatever look was on my face, stabbing her cigarette at me. "Exactly. So you doing the mango tango with your stepbrother is only worth a five-minute conversation, really."

"I wish it were that easy."

She offered me a drag of her cigarette, and I scowled, shaking my head. "It is that easy. Your parents have a right to be mad, but they're super uptight. You won't need to worry in a few months."

I thought about that as I drove the fifteen minutes it took to reach my dad's place. Home.

It was home now, and the sooner I made peace with that, the better.

The phone rang out, and the sound of his voicemail was probably the only part of him I'd get, seeing as he usually left the phone in his locker or car.

Our parents had been scrupulous in their determination to keep us apart. They were tracking his cell, and they had been tracking his car until Jackson told them he'd take the bus or have his friends drive him.

After everything, they didn't want other parents wondering why their son no longer had the means to transport himself to school, so they'd relented on that, but nothing else. Even so, he was rarely allowed out unless he could prove it was just to see his friends.

Dad, on the other hand, had arrived home in a blaze of temper a week ago, cursing up a storm.

He wouldn't tell me why he was so angry, and I hadn't dared to ask, but when he'd tossed a box with a cheap smart phone onto my desk the following morning, I found the courage to blurt, "What?"

He ran his hands over his growing hair, some gray sprinkling the edges of his hairline, and shook his head. "You need a phone. I work, and you have school and friends, so if something were to happen, like breaking down on the side of the road, you need to be able to contact someone."

I'd swallowed, understanding what he'd tried to do. "And Mom didn't care."

Sighing, he leaned into the doorframe. "It's not that she doesn't. It's that she's caring about all the wrong things." After staring at the boxed cell, he blinked over at me. "I know you're going to call him. Do I like it?" He straightened and shrugged. "Not particularly, but I can't stop you. I trust you. If you want to speak to him, just be smart about it."

My chest filled with so much air, it came pouring out of me with my next words, drowning them. "Are you sure?"

Frowning, he'd laughed dryly. "No. But you're both eighteen. If you want to keep seeing each other, you'll find ways to do that with or without permission or technology."

All I could manage was, "Thank you."

Dad nodded, turning out of the doorway, then paused. "But Wil?"

"Yeah?"

"He can't come here."

I parked in front of the single garage, trying Jackson one last time.

He didn't answer, and it'd be two days before I heard from him.

Time wasn't kind to those who feel left behind.

The days would collide into each other with little care for what hadn't been accomplished. The weeks would turn my heart into a bird that would only sing when the sun came out once or twice a week in the form of a phone call or quick meetup after school.

Dad wasn't much of a socialite, preferring to spend his weekends at home working on an old Mustang he kept in the garage. I hadn't been brave enough to ask his permission to go to any parties that Jackson might've attended because I knew the answer would likely be no.

Our Christmas together had been quiet, and as if he knew the sad corners of my heart were pinching, Dad had taken me on a long drive until we'd found a restaurant three hours south that was open.

As the Christmas holiday came to a close and the new year rolled in, we decided to take more risks but less often.

I buttoned up my dress, then combed my fingers through my hair before heading into the bathroom to clean up.

Jackson had made good work of smearing my mascara and knotting my hair into tangles that wouldn't relent without brushing, but as I stared at my flushed cheeks and glazed eyes, I couldn't bring myself to care.

It didn't matter. It didn't matter that we were in a dusty hotel we had to pay cash for, and therefore could only use maybe twice a month. We were here, together, and I was making the most of it.

My smile shattered when I entered the room and wrapped my arms around his waist from behind. "What are you doing?"

He had my phone and was scrolling through the texts, probably looking at my social media pages and call history, too.

"Who's Todd?" he asked with a calm that threatened to slice me in two.

Todd had put his number in my phone before Christmas when we'd been paired to work on a history assignment together.

"He's my friend." I went to take my phone from him, but he held his hand higher, and I wasn't going to jump. I had nothing to hide.

"Why is he texting you?" He stopped, then laughed, rough and disbelieving. "At least three times or more a week." He turned to me, his jaw rigid and his eyes storming. "What the fuck, Willa?"

I couldn't keep myself from frowning and silently panicking. "Like I said, he's my friend." I gestured to the phone. "Which you'd know if you read the messages. They're platonic, friendly."

"Platonic?" he repeated, tossing my phone across the room. It landed with a thud on the carpet, and then he was stalking toward me. "What's so fucking platonic about kissing emojis? Huh? Or winking ones? And *dimples?*"

He was looming over me now, his eyes swimming with cruel accusation. "I didn't send those, he did, and it's just a stupid nickname."

"You're encouraging it," he seethed through his teeth. "And a stupid nickname? Like the stupid one I gave you?"

My back hit the wall, and I felt tears arrive with a sting. That he could accuse me of wronging him when I'd done nothing but answer a friend's texts was ridiculous. "What about Ainsley, Jackson?"

His brows lowered and pulled, and he took a step back. "Jackson?"

I nodded even as my hands shook.

"What does she have to do with anything?"

"You think I don't see her always commenting on your pho-tos? Liking every one of them, and saying she'll message you about this new Thai place in town?" I couldn't believe I'd said all that, my chest rising and falling and my shoulders loosening. I didn't doubt him, or us, and I didn't want him thinking I didn't trust him. I removed my gaze from his thinned one and directed it to the stained carpet. "I'm so—"

"Maybe it's because she fucking cares about what I'm do-ing. Instead of spending her spare time with new people, new guys, she still pays attention to me."

Too far, and the violent change in his features said he knew it. My teeth sank into my lower lip so hard, I tasted copper, and I began to gather my things.

"Shit," he hissed, then he was trapping me within his arms. "I'm sorry. I'm sorry, but this… it's killing me."

He knew why I couldn't love him the way other girls did online. He'd always known. And I feared what'd just happened meant he was growing tired. Tired of the fact that even though everyone knew, we were still in hiding.

We would forever be in hiding.

"You meant it," I said. "Or you wouldn't have said it."

"I didn't," he insisted, his hand gripping the back of my head, every part of me touching him as he stuffed his nose into my neck. "I swear I didn't."

My eyes closed, my head turning to rest my lips against his throat. "He's just a friend."

Jackson said nothing, and nothing else was said as our lips collided and we tore our clothes off again.

Stars twinkled above the crack between the rooftops, and I kicked my feet up, sinking into the hammock.

After months of pestering, I'd finally caved to Flo's request of attending a party with her.

Other than the surroundings, the scent of cheaper fragrances, and different types of drinks, it wasn't much different from the parties at Prep.

Dad had taken some convincing, but when I'd promised him Jackson wouldn't be here, and that he didn't even know about it, he'd conceded and said to call him if I needed a ride home.

Having Flo over to get ready for the party felt weird. I felt as if I'd been shoved into a different life once and for all, and it was happening whether I decided to live it or not.

Dad hadn't seemed to approve at first, but naturally, she'd worn him down with her innocuous jokes, smiles that were a little too suggestive, and promises to keep me out of trouble.

Where she was now to hold up her end of the unnecessary bargain, I had no idea. I could guess it was somewhere inside with Green, one of the guys on the soccer team who she'd been seeing since New Year's.

It didn't matter, I thought, taking a sip from the too fruity wine Flo had left me with. I'd walked two steps inside the three-bedroom home in the small residential neighborhood by the creek when I realized I didn't care to socialize one bit. I'd much rather be left alone to wonder and worry what Jackson was doing in private.

It'd been four days since I'd heard anything, since a text that'd said he missed me.

Four days that once seemed like an eternity but had now become our new normal.

"That hammock a two-seater by any chance?"

Todd.

I grinned, my belly warm from the alcohol, and my mind relaxed enough to want his company. I laughed as he climbed on and almost sent me to the pebbles below.

He held the fence the hammock was attached to, and I ducked my head in case I swung into the side of the house.

"Not in the mood?" he asked, tucking his feet close, yet they still touched mine. It was kind of unavoidable.

Taking a sip, I handed him the bottle when he gestured for it, and laughed when he smacked his lips together with a cringe. "Dear god. It's cat piss."

I snatched it back. "Beats nothing."

"You didn't answer my question."

With his dark eyes grabbing mine, I stalled for something to say that didn't make me out to be the love-sick girl I was. "Not really in the mood, but I also don't want to go home yet." I took another sip. "You?"

"Always in the mood to get shitfaced," Todd said. "But your proclivity to hanging on your own, even at a party, has me troubled."

"Is that so?" I smiled.

He sucked his bottom lip into his mouth, grinning. "Yeah. Where's that brother of yours?"

"Probably out," I said. "I'm not sure."

He scratched at the stubble on his chin, then ran a hand over his close-cropped hair. "I see."

"You do, do you?" I could never resist humoring him.

He slouched back, tilting his head to gaze up at the sky. "Been seeing for months, Dimples."

I didn't want to respond. Normally, I would ignore any remarks he'd make that crept too close for comfort. Tonight, though, I was just the right amount of drunk to let him wonder. "What is it exactly you see?"

"How's your mom?"

I frowned, noticing how the scruff on his jaw peppered his throat. Jackson's did the same, but that was only when he didn't shave. He always shaved. "My mom?"

"Yeah." He tucked his arms behind his head, giving me his depthless, glinting eyes.

"You know I wouldn't know that."

His long lashes lowered halfway as he studied me. I stared down at my denim covered knees, wondering what he was playing at. "You miss her, don't you? She's been a total bitch to you, and your dad's been awesome, yet you still can't help but miss her."

I did. With an acute ache that was slow to fade, her betrayal simmered deep. "She won't talk to me." I'd only tried twice since she and Heath had kicked me out, but that was enough to know she wouldn't budge. Not until she was ready, should that day ever arrive. "It doesn't matter, does it?"

I looked back up at him when he said, "Yeah, actually, it matters plenty."

Those words lingered in the following silence, the hammock rocking so slowly, it could've lulled me to sleep.

Eventually, I asked, "How's Jade?" He'd given up his playboy job and had decided to get himself a girlfriend.

"We broke up." He stole the bottle from me, taking a huge gulp that made his throat bulge, then he belched. "Fuck me, that's bad."

I grabbed it and drank. "Don't drink it then."

"Don't ask questions I don't want to answer then."

I laughed, stabbing a finger at him. "You can talk. Why'd you break up? You were doing so well."

"Right? Two weeks with the same chick. New record." He made a noise, then pursed his lips. "And I have my reasons, but it's probably better I don't divulge them." His eyes settled on mine. "Not to you."

I was about to ask why when his gaze dipped to my lips. Clearing my throat, I asked for the time, then cursed and all but threw myself to the ground. "I need to go."

"Whoa." Todd rolled to the pebbles, and I laughed, taking his hand to help him up. "Where do you need to be, Cinderella?"

I released his hand when he tried to pull me to the ground. "Home, and about thirty minutes ago at that."

"I'll take you," he said, catching up with me as I reached the side gate.

"You've been drinking." I plucked out my phone to tell Flo I was going.

"Only those few god-awful drops of cat piss."

Smiling, I tucked my phone away and followed him to his car. It smelled like the apple air freshener hanging from his rear-view mirror, and I felt a textbook digging into my heel.

"Why the tense look, Dimples?"

"You really need to stop calling me that." I'd told him a handful of times before, ever since Jackson and I had argued about it back in our hotel room, but he didn't listen.

"Not going to happen," he said yet again. "Quit evading my questions."

"I'm not," I said, laughing a little. "And I'm not tense. I just hope Dad's asleep so I don't ruin my chances of doing this again."

"You are eighteen."

"But I live under his roof," I countered. "His rules. I need to respect them."

Todd hummed, turning down endless winding streets. Every fourth house was lit, the rest lost to the shadows of slumbering night. "You mean after being tossed aside like a soiled toy, you don't want to wind up homeless, or disappoint anyone else."

Flo and her big mouth.

He'd overheard us talking about my mom and Jackson weeks ago during lunch, and being that he'd heard enough, I'd waved Florence off when she'd looked at me for permission to fill in the gaps for him.

"Something like that," I murmured. Though I knew my dad was worlds apart from my mom, Todd was right. I didn't want to disappoint or alienate the only family member who still wanted anything to do with me. Well, the only member besides Jackson.

Though even that had me losing more and more sleep as our lives continued to race away from us in different lanes.

"Would it help if I introduced myself?" He turned down my street, and I didn't bother asking him how he'd known where I'd lived. He'd been by my place once with Flo to drop off homework when I'd had the flu, but he hadn't come in.

"Absolutely not," I said, unclipping my seat belt when he pulled up to the curb.

Relief, thick and velvet, flooded my veins when I saw all the lights were out save for the porch.

I turned to Todd, smiling. "I think I'll be okay."

His eyes bored into mine, the whites around the black pupils vibrant. "Can I say something?"

I tilted my head. "Nothing good usually follows those words."

He chuckled. "You don't even know what I was going to say."

"Do I want to?"

"You're still in the car." He took my hand, and before I could read his intent, he'd pulled me close, and his mouth was an inch from mine. "You're worth loving, and you could never lose someone who knows that."

Breath fled me on a burning exhale as I absorbed those

words. "Who would've thought one of the school's token players could be so sweet?"

His eyes thinned, but his lips lifted, exposing a taunting flash of teeth.

I moved just in time to avoid it happening and fumbled to open the door. "Willa, wait—"

His words were cut off as his door was yanked open, and he was torn from the car and slammed against the side.

I scrambled out, a scream lodging in my throat as Jackson pulled his fist back. "Jack, no!"

He froze for all of a second, but it was long enough for Todd to shove him off.

I hadn't seen his truck parked two houses down. I hadn't thought he'd be here, let alone thought to look.

Jackson's nostrils flared, his eyes alight with an anger I'd never seen before. "This is how your friend treats you, Bug?" His gaze never left Todd as he pushed him, who probably matched him in weight and height, yet Todd did nothing. "You let them kiss you?"

"She moved away," Todd said, then smirked. "Unfortunately."

Jackson swung, his fist hitting Todd's jaw and sending him stumbling back.

The scream escaped as I came unglued and raced around the car, grabbing Jackson's arm as he prowled to where Todd was hunched over, cursing as he gingerly touched his jaw.

"Let go," he growled.

"No. If you really love me, you'll stop. Dad's asleep, and we can't handle any more trouble, Jackson. Please." He halted, his arm muscles clenching and unclenching beneath my hold. "He's my friend, I swear. He was just messing around."

"Stop," he said, pinning me with those fury burning eyes. "Stop fucking defending him."

"He's right, Dim—Willa." Todd straightened, wincing as he worked his jaw. "I'm good. I'll see you Monday, 'kay?" His eyes asked if I was okay, and I nodded, pleading with my own for him to go.

Jackson cursed and stalked over to his car when Todd got in. But Todd ignored Jackson's threats to keep away from me and took off down the quiet street.

"Jack," I said when he started for his truck. "Jackson!"

He was leaving. He was really going to just leave.

"Jackson, don't you dare," I said. "Wait."

He did, turning and grounding out, "I've been waiting for half an hour, hoping like hell you weren't asleep. You didn't answer your phone, and still, I fucking waited."

I thought back to when I'd last used it and then pulled it out of my pocket. Sure enough, there were three calls from him during the drive home. I tucked it away, chewing my lip. "I'm sorry."

He stared, brows low and eyes flashing, then barked out a laugh. "You know what? Fuck your stupid sorry." Then he was climbing in the truck.

I couldn't think of anything else to say that might make him listen, and so I didn't speak, just acted. Running, I jumped into his truck as he started it, then folded my arms over my chest.

"Willa," he gritted. "Get out."

"No."

"I'll pick you up and remove you myself. Get out." When I smiled at him, he huffed with disbelief, then put the car in drive. "Fine."

We passed street after street and ended up on a leaf-strewn road bordering the woods. Finally, I found the courage to try to calm the rage that still wafted from him. "I didn't think he'd do that. You believe me, right?"

"I saw," he said, somewhat reluctantly. "I saw you pull away and move to get out, but what I don't know"—he scrubbed his chin—"what I don't understand, is why you'd put yourself in that position in the first place."

"Position?" I asked, affronted. "I was hanging out with a friend. A friend I never expected would try to kiss me."

"Where were you hanging out?" he asked. When I didn't answer quick enough, he flashed me an impatient look, brows raised. "Well?"

My arms fell, and I slunk back into the leather seat. "A party."

Jackson cursed. "Since when does your dad let you go to parties?"

"Since I asked if I could," I said.

Jackson pulled off the road, and I grabbed the handle as the truck bounded over ditches and dirt potholes, swerving between the trees.

"Jack, what the hell?"

"Let me get this straight," he said, the vehicle coming to an abrupt halt. There was no one and nothing around, no light save for that of the moon and stars trying to breach the foliage of the towering trees. "You won't ask your dad if you can attend the parties I'm at, but suddenly, you ask to attend one that asshole is going to?"

"I didn't know if you were going out," I said. "You never returned my last two calls." I tried to mask the hurt I felt over that, but it was pointless.

"I couldn't, Willa." Removing his seat belt, he swiped both hands down his face. "Jesus Christ, do you think I want to avoid you?"

I didn't, but I didn't know what to think about how hard it'd become for us to even get in touch anymore. "I've always been the one to try to call," I whispered. "I always need to be free around the time you're on lunch at school, before you start school, or after you finish school even though you don't always answer, and you hardly ever call me."

"We're fighting about phone calls now? Is that why you hung out with that guy?"

"His name is Todd, and no, I hung out with him because, again, he's my fucking friend." I was shaking, my voice and my hands.

At the sound of the curse that left me, Jackson's mouth parted, and then I was in his lap, my sweater torn off and his mouth all over mine.

His hands swept inside the back of my jeans and panties, palming my ass, then moved lower to toy with where I needed him. I whimpered, biting his lip, clawing at his hair, then lifted his shirt to touch his stomach, moving lower to his fly. I undid it, then crawled off him just enough for him to free himself, and I tried to do the same.

We groaned as we removed my jeans, but Jackson wouldn't wait for my panties. He pulled them aside hard enough to ruin the elastic, then shoved himself at my opening.

The horn blared behind me, but if anything in the wooded area stirred, I didn't hear or see it. My eyes slammed closed as my head fell back, Jackson holding my hips down on him as he stretched and filled me, and his teeth scraped down my neck.

His anger was palpable, reaching all the places fear and hurt resided deep inside.

His hands were bruising as he lifted my ass and hips, using me to milk his pleasure, and leaving me to find my own. I did, grinding down and taking what I needed until the stars in the sky painted the backs of my eyelids, and I was free-falling into the kind of bliss that made me feel as if everything was going to be okay.

Through the haze, my eyes cracked open enough to see his nostrils widen, eyes blazing bright green as he came. The rough timbre of his voice and his choppy breathing had my hands gripping his cheeks as I slowly rocked my hips over him.

Minutes, or maybe hours, later, I whispered into his neck as he held me flush to him. "Jack, what's happening to us?"

"Nothing, Bug," he lied. "Nothing will ever happen to us."

My voice cracked. "You're lying."

He shut me up with his lips.

fourteen

Willa

The piece of paper fluttered in my hand as I skipped out of the kitchen to my room to grab my phone.

He didn't answer, but that was to be expected, and it didn't dim the excitement.

"Whoa," Dad said, coming inside with his cooler.

He dropped it when I reached him and wrapped my arms around his neck. "I got accepted. Gray Springs."

"Shit, Wil." Dad laughed, squeezing me to him. He pulled me back by the shoulders, grinning. "Try not to get too excited about leaving me, yeah? Might give a lesser man a complex or something."

I laughed, then let him take the paper from my hand.

"It's really happening," he said, reading over it as he walked farther into the house.

I grabbed his cooler, following him to the kitchen.

I hadn't been accepted for any type of funding, but that didn't matter. Jackson had received his acceptance letter last Friday, so I was just happy, so ecstatic we'd be together.

Once and for all.

Dad and I celebrated over dinner, going over the tuition and less fun details. It wasn't an outrageously expensive college to attend, as far as colleges go, but it was still far from cheap.

"I have some savings," Dad said.

To which I'd immediately said, "No way. I'll take out loans."

"Over my dead body." I wouldn't relent, though, and he sighed, wiping his mouth with a napkin and knocking back the rest of his beer. "Later, let's just... try not to cry like a damn baby over the fact you're leaving me."

I took his hand, squeezing it tight, and whispered, "Love you, Dad." For most of my life, he hadn't been able to be there for me, but this past year, he'd more than made up for it. Through one of the worst and most challenging times of my life, he'd shown me that I could mess up, and he'd still be there.

He blinked, then coughed, swallowing hard before saying, "Love you too, kid. Love you too."

At home, we polished off some cake we'd taken with us for dessert and watched the latest episode of *Game of Thrones*.

When Dad passed out on his recliner, I switched the TV off, draped the gray knitted throw over him, then got ready for bed.

My heart nearly dived into my too full stomach when I saw the missed call on my phone, and I struggled to sit still as I climbed onto my bed and returned his call.

"I got your message," he said over what sounded like music and laughter. "Congrats, Wil."

I frowned. "Where are you?" It was a Wednesday night. We still had a few months of school left to take seriously.

"Out," he said, then hollered at someone in the background. "Fuck off. You'll die, you dickhead."

I didn't care to ask who was being a dickhead. I cared to know why we weren't going over all the plans we'd made in hopes of one day reaching this point. "Where?"

"With friends, is that not allowed?" Female laughter followed. Ainsley's laughter.

"Is that...?" I couldn't say it, my voice so faint and shocked, I feared he hadn't even heard the attempt.

"I'll call you later, okay? When I get home." The line went dead, and I stared at my phone, at the picture of us I'd saved as my background.

I stared, and I stared, and he never called back.

I paced my room, round and round in circles, listening to Peggy prattle on about Dash's latest encounter with a cucumber. "Won't touch them, says they're too phallic looking."

"Sliced?" I said, taking her off speakerphone.

"Nope," she said, crunching on what sounded like chips.

I stopped before my desk, sputtering out a laugh. "Come on. Seriously?"

"Dead serious. And the whole time, I was so shocked I hadn't known that about him, I failed to see how ridiculous it was until I'd left."

Dash and Peggy were now official, not that much had seemed to change. I moved around some of my textbooks, trying to find the to-do list Jackson and I had prepared. He'd promised he'd call in a text he'd sent early this morning, but I was still waiting. I'd wait for as long as I had to if the promise of us was what I'd receive.

"What about bananas? Carrots?"

"He's fine with them," she said. "Carrots are too bumpy and deformed looking while bananas are too curved."

I snorted, checking the doorway for any sign of Dad who was home and cleaning up the kitchen after dinner, then whispered, "He does know some guys are well, you know…"

She cackled. "Probably, but he's perfect, so of course, he doesn't care."

I slipped my hair behind my ear, then checked the hallway.

The TV was on, and Dad's head appeared over the back of the couch.

I wasn't sure why I was nervous. He'd said we could talk on the phone. Okay, so he hadn't exactly permitted it, but he hadn't *not* permitted it either.

He'd just never been awake or at home when Jackson had called before. I feared he'd do it now, when he finally was, but I couldn't and wouldn't be picky.

"Willa?" Peggy called. "Earth to Willa," she sang.

"Here, sorry."

"You're even weirder than you usually are now, you know that?"

I closed my bedroom door, frowning. "I'm offended. You're the weird one."

"True." Peggy laughed. "How's Todd?"

She'd asked me that a few times. "If Dash knew how often you asked about him, he'd be angry as hell."

"Angry? Pissed. Fucking furious," she said. "Say it with me, come on."

"Shut up," I said, laughing.

"You going to tell him?" she asked.

"No way," I all but yelled.

"I'm not asking because I like the guy. I'm asking because I know the guy likes you."

I groaned, regretting that I'd told her about the almost kiss. Daphne didn't know. After all that'd happened with her and Lars, and Annika's pregnancy, I refused to call her and saddle her with any of my average problems.

"He doesn't. He's just testing me because I'm taken."

"Sure, sure. I'm also annoyed because you never told me if you apologized for me about that party." She chewed more chips. "You know, where Dash hauled me away from him like an ape."

I took a seat on my bed. "He doesn't care," I said. Which was true. At the mention of Peggy, he'd looked confused. I'd had to describe her for recognition to light his features.

"He said it was a little nuts, but he hooked up with Celeste after anyway."

"Nice. Who's Celeste?"

"Girl from school," I muttered, checking the time on my phone. It was almost nine.

"So, are things with Jackson okay?"

An incoming call chirped as soon as she'd finished asking, and I hurried out, "Gotta go, I'll call you next week or something," then hung up before she could respond.

My hand tunneled into my hair, and I stood, pacing again. "It's been six days, Jack."

"I know, I'm sorry." He didn't sound it, though. He sounded rushed, flippant. I forgot about that when he said, "Got a pen? We need to add some more shit to our apartment list."

He'd be getting an apartment, and I'd be staying in the dorms. But really, the dorm would just be a place to keep my things. We already knew I'd be spending most of my time with him.

My annoyance vanished in the face of excitement. Maybe he hadn't lost his own; maybe he was just struggling to make it to the finish line. But we were almost there.

"Okay." I grabbed a pen and the list from my desk.

The finish line was in sight, and we could make it.

fifteen

Willa

Todd plonked himself down on the grass next to me. "I'm sorry I tried to kiss you, okay?"

"Did you purposely wait until Flo left before you decided to grace me with your presence?" I asked, licking the mandarin from my finger. "Because she's not stupid. She already knows something is up." Being that he hadn't sat with us in the weeks since.

He bobbed his head side to side. "Maybe."

I lifted a brow.

"Okay, yes. But I didn't really feel like getting my ass reamed twice, ya know?"

I tugged my maxi skirt over my crossed legs, my mandarin peels piled in the brown and red rayon. "I'm not mad." I'd been annoyed, but enough time had passed, and his silence had made it wane.

"Really?" he asked, sounding shocked.

I peered over at him, the sunlight bouncing off his strong nose. "Really. Just don't do it again."

I returned my attention to my fruit, popping another piece in my mouth.

The guys on the team were tossing a football back and forth on the field in front of me. From my vantage point in the shade beneath the trees, I saw Green lean down to whisper something to Flo that had her head falling back with laughter.

"So," Todd said, pulling his knees up and wrapping his arms around them, "if you're not mad, then why do you look so fucking glum?"

I wanted to laugh, and then I wanted to cry, but I did neither. I also didn't want to divulge. Not when it seemed Todd might actually like me. That didn't seem right. "Don't worry, I'm fine."

He groaned. "Fine, she says. That fucking word is akin to a big fat I'm so far from fine, I can't even with the word fine's existence."

I did laugh then, the sound rattling out in a way that loosened my shoulders and dumped heat into my cheeks. I couldn't remember the last time I'd really laughed. "Funny."

"Evidently, Miss I hardly laugh anymore. What's he done?"

I coughed, almost choking on my next piece of mandarin. "Just go right there, why don't you?"

"You've changed," he murmured. "More sassy-sorrow now."

I swallowed, then fiddled with the remaining fruit in my lap. "He hasn't done anything."

Todd sat with that a moment, then said, "Which I'm gathering is the problem."

That, and the numerous parties he seemed to be attending, girls like Ainsley often commenting on photos he'd shared from them. I wasn't sure how our parents were allowing it, and I couldn't even ask, being that he'd never talk for longer than ten minutes. If he even answered my calls at all.

I closed my eyes, the hollow feeling inside my chest making it hard to breathe. I wanted to breathe. I needed to. But his absence, the distance that spread wider each day, was suffocating. "I guess things aren't…" I stopped, unsure and scared. "You probably don't want to hear this."

He nudged me with his elbow, and I opened my eyes. "Wouldn't have asked if that were true. In case you haven't noticed"—he blew out a breath, rubbing his short hair with his giant hand—"I care about you. A little more than what is smart, all things considered."

His smile didn't glow, but I appreciated it all the same. Still, I looked away as I continued, "Things aren't good."

"How so?"

"We don't talk. It's always been hard to with my mom and his dad being so controlling, but even when we do, it's brief. And I can't help but feel like he's had all these chances to talk to me lately. He's going out more, partying and seeing friends, but he chooses not to call me."

Todd sucked air in through his teeth, and I didn't need to look over to know he was wincing.

After a moment, I did look at him. "That's not a good sign, right?"

He was staring across the field, lips twisting. "I don't want to upset you, Dimples."

My brows creased, my heart drooped. "You can say it. I already know it's not good."

"It's not," he admitted. "But it also doesn't make a lot of sense."

"What do you mean?" I prodded.

He was still staring forward, at nothing it seemed. "That night outside your place, he was losing his mind. I don't know if I've ever seen a guy with murder in his eyes because of a girl quite like that before."

Like a slow-moving cloud crossing the sun, it cleared. "Shit."

Todd clapped, chuckling. "Hearing you curse is always the best thing ever."

"Shut up," I said. "You think it's that?" He had been different since that night. Yes, things had been going downhill before then, but they'd worsened at rapid speed since he'd found Todd outside my place, trying to kiss me.

Todd hummed, his hands spreading. "I wouldn't be happy, but I really can't say."

We sat in silence until the bell rang a few minutes later, and I stewed over all the things I could've done differently about that night.

I should've apologized or apologized more. I shouldn't have let him drop me off at home without having a proper conversation about it. I shouldn't have gone to that party in the first place.

"Hey," Todd said, standing with his hand outstretched for mine. After gathering my mandarin peels, I took it, then released it once I was on my feet. "You can't beat yourself up over something I did. You might just make me feel all guilty and shit."

I huffed, tossing my trash as we passed a can on the way to the brick building's doors. "We can't have that, can we?"

"Sarcasm, Dimples, really?" He feigned offense. "I'm trying here."

I shook my head. "Sorry, I just... I really don't know what to do."

He was silent as we walked the halls and neared my locker. I thought he'd keep walking to his, almost jumping when he leaned in close, and said, "If you feel like you're going down, start swinging, or you'll always wonder if you should've."

Then, with a kiss to my cheek, he wandered down the hall with his hands inside his pockets.

So swing I did, but it was hard when the person who usually took control and called all the shots decided to leave the ball in a court that was dying without the nourishment it needed to thrive. To find strength and resilience.

Jackson didn't seem to care. More parties and more sleepless nights, yet I kept calling, kept leaving messages to remind him that I was here, that I loved him, and that we were almost there.

Raindrops splattered onto my windshield as I found a parking spot on the outskirts of school. Reaching into the back seat, I grabbed my umbrella and hurried through the parking lot to the auditorium.

It was crowded, as predicted. Teachers, parents, friends, family, and students stuffing the interior to the point of needing to strip out of the blue cardigan I'd donned.

I didn't. There wasn't enough room to move, which was precisely why, regardless of the fact that Mom and Heath would be here, I'd decided to come.

They wouldn't even know if I was careful.

"Sorry," I muttered, slipping behind an elderly couple. The husband was taller than my five feet six by a full head of curly gray hair, and so I peeked between him and his shorter wife, watching as Principal Denham handed a student their diploma and shook their hand.

Once my breath had resettled in my lungs and my heart rate had resumed its normal rhythm, I smiled.

We were graduating.

Well, I was graduating next week, but still. We'd made it. We were getting away from the restrictions this town had strapped around us.

Ten minutes later, Jackson was striding up the steps and across the stage, accepting his ticket out of here with a small grin shaping his perfect lips.

My heart danced at the sight of him, danced and sang as he adjusted his cap and joined his peers at the side of the stage.

Then it darkened as Heath stood and his ear-piercing whistle sliced through the air and my chest.

A knot formed in my throat, and I looked down at my purple suede boots, willing the tears away. I hadn't cried over them in months, and I'd be damned if I did now.

But it killed me, drowned something vital inside me, to know they wouldn't show up to my graduation. That they would probably never clap at any success I'd found without them in my life.

When they neared the end of the alphabetized surnames, I dragged my numb feet outside and waited against the wall by the bike stands, ready to duck away if Heath and Mom exited before Jackson could.

Some type of quiet rebellion rose within as I stood there, the rain splattering the fabric of my umbrella and boots. What did I even care if they saw me? It wasn't like I had anything to hide anymore. Anything to lose.

Besides Jackson.

But he would be leaving in a few months, and I was certain if they decided to punish him too severely, he would leave and stay with one of his friends.

I was so certain that when he appeared, running a hand through his longer, swept back dark hair, with Dash by his side, I stepped out of hiding and called his name.

Dash's eyes widened, then lit with amusement when Jackson froze.

He stalked off, and Jackson, his expression so blank I couldn't read it, joined me by the side of the building.

"Wil," he said, voice low. "What are you doing here?"

I licked my lips, wanting them on his, but I settled for touching his fingertips with mine. "I had to see you graduate."

He recoiled, tucking his hand into his slacks pocket beneath his graduation gown. "You didn't need to," he said.

Frowning, I stepped closer, something prickling as it slithered over my skin. "Jack, what's going on?" It'd been a long two weeks since I'd last heard from him. Two weeks that I'd tried to shrug off because our new beginning would soon be underway.

"Jack!" Ainsley.

I blinked, my hand slipping around the umbrella handle, rain spitting onto my forehead and cheeks.

I righted it as she bounded over then halted, seemingly shocked to see me. "Oh, hey, Willa."

I said nothing, giving my attention back to Jackson in the form of disbelieving eyes. "Jackson..."

He sighed, then looked at Ainsley. "Give me a sec?"

Nodding, she walked away, her diploma tucked close to her chest and her eyes never moving far from us.

"This isn't okay, Willa."

I took an unsteady step back, feeling as though he'd punched me in the stomach. "What isn't?"

"You just showing up here," he said through his teeth, his eyes hard and unfamiliar.

"Why am I getting the feeling this isn't about Mom and Heath?"

His throat dipped as he swallowed, gaze lowering. "Because it's not, and we both know it."

"No," I said, but the word had no sound.

His cheeks billowed, a loud breath preceding poisonous words. "We need to cool this, Willa. Give it some time."

Unable to help it, I glared at Ainsley, who was chewing her thumbnail. She glanced away. "Some time to be with other people?" I shook my head when he didn't respond. "No, no way. And... and but..." I couldn't see, couldn't think. "But why?"

His tone was unforgiving and brooked no room for argument. "You know why. It used to work, but now it's not, and I just…" He lifted his eyes, and mine regained enough focus to discover they weren't even sad. There was no remorse, only clear intent. "I need some time to think."

"You're breaking up with me." I didn't know where those hideous words came from, but they flew from my lips anyway.

Ainsley's gaze became an unwanted audience, a party of one to the eternal damnation of everything I'd believed in when I had nothing else.

Jackson said nothing but roughly palmed his hair.

"For her," I croaked, again, unsure how I'd managed it. It felt like my brain was running the show, asking all the hard questions my heart and soul would never dare to.

All the questions we should've began to ask months ago.

"No," Jackson said, then cursed. "Yes, ugh, fuck. I don't know. Look, let it rest for a while, okay? It's not working, Willa. We need some time." Then he was backing away, mumbling, "I'll call you when I'm ready."

No. He couldn't just dump all those ugly words on me and then leave me with them to rot. "Jackson," I yelled.

A few people turned, but he didn't. He ignored me, and Ainsley tucked her arm in his, offering a guilt heavy smile over her shoulder as they disappeared into the crowd of parents and students.

No.

No, no, no. I wanted to scream it at them, chase after them and demand to know why. Why would they do this to me? How could he do this to me?

But I couldn't. I didn't need to know why.

If I'd relinquished the precarious hold I'd had on hope long enough to open my eyes, I would've seen it. I would've seen how we'd unraveled like a piece of silk that'd aged over time. We'd collapsed into crumbling threads that were all too easy to pluck and discard as something that was once beautiful but no longer shined.

From the tips of my toes to my eyes, I burned. Every part of me turned to ash and just a lick of the breeze on my face threatened to send me to the wet ground.

A few passersby looked on as I stood there, a white-knuckle grip on my umbrella, my eyes unwilling to release their hold on him. Swaying and still, I watched as Jackson and Ainsley headed to his truck. I watched as she turned to him, her head tilted back, laughing as rain hit her face and she tried to keep her hat from flying away. I watched as he gazed down at her, smiling, and I looked away when she rose onto her toes, her lips meeting his.

Coughing to mask the heaving of my stomach and shoulders, the sob that itched to crawl out of my throat, scraping it raw, I turned to go.

And that's when my darkest day turned into a living nightmare.

"Hi, Wil," Mom said, her fingers fluttering.

She and Heath were standing by one of the hedges, mere meters from where Ainsley had been.

How long they'd been there, how much they'd seen, I didn't care to know. All I knew was if I didn't leave, the humiliation setting in would surely have me collapsing into a broken heap.

It was one thing to have your heart broken, and another to be humiliated at the same time those pieces disintegrated, falling like dust on the wind into a goodbye that would never be wiped clean from your soul.

Jackson's truck was gone, and ignoring Mom's touch on my arm, I pulled away and trudged through the throngs of people.

Uncaring that I probably looked like a ghost, I knocked into people and felt water seep through my boots as I took the fastest exit, sloshing over puddled grass to my car.

sixteen

Willa

That night, I pushed through a different kind of crowd, needing something to staunch the bleeding.

Todd found me as soon as I stepped out onto the back porch of Rebecca Derrell's two-story house by the creek.

"He dumped me," I said when his eyes simmered with concern at the sight of me. I stole the bottle of bourbon from his hand. "I went down swinging, though." I took a swig, wincing at the burn. "No regrets, right?" I laughed, then sniffed. "Ugh."

"Jesus." He glanced around at the few people who were watching, then collected me around the shoulders, directing me back inside and upstairs.

The whole time he searched for a quiet, unoccupied space, I continued to ramble about everything that'd happened, unsure if he'd even hear me over the music and loud chatter and laughter.

"Okay, okay," he said, closing the door and pacing the expanse of Rebecca's parents' bedroom with his hands in the air. "Let's retrace our steps here. He said he needed time?"

I kept sipping small drops of bourbon, enough to accompany the burning inside me. "Yep. What does that even mean?" I threw my arms out, bourbon splashing out of the neck of the bottle. "And I tried to call him, tried to ask what the hell I'm supposed to do with that..." I trailed off when I saw Todd had stopped moving, saw that his onyx eyes were glimmering with sympathy, or pity, and his brows were hovering low. "What?" I whispered.

"Come here," he said, gesturing for me.

I folded into his strong arms like a broken and battered building that was sick of housing a heart so weary and weak.

His hand cupped the back of my head as I rolled my puffy face side to side into his black T-shirt, my arms limp around his narrow waist. "It's over," I said. "All those years, all those promises, the plans, all the consequences, and it's just… over."

He held me as I cried, rubbing my back and whispering into the top of my hair, and when I could no longer stand, he set the bourbon on the nightstand and helped me into the white linen-covered bed, and he held me there too.

"Tell me something," I said some time later, tears dried on my face and my nose half blocked, the noise of the party still seeping through the walls. "Tell me something good."

"I'm going to college with you," he said, a smile in his voice. "So I'll be on call for burritos and ice cream whenever you need them."

I pushed off his chest, gazing down at him. "Are you serious?"

He nodded. "Yeah." Smiling, he shifted some hair away from my sticky face, tucking it behind my ear. "Dead serious."

"What about your mom? Your sister?" I knew he'd wanted to stay closer to home in case she'd needed help.

"I didn't get accepted into any of the nearby schools," he said. "Besides, Mom would be furious if I didn't take the full ride."

A smile, real and shocking, took hold. "Why the hell haven't you told me all this?"

He tipped a shoulder. "It was a toss-up between two." He blew his knuckles, rubbing his shirt playfully. "I couldn't decide."

I knew, I just knew, that he'd probably picked Gray Springs because of me, but I couldn't muster the strength to berate him or be annoyed. Not when I felt something I didn't think I'd feel again for a long time. Something that felt a little like hope.

I wouldn't be left to contend with a broken heart, and the reason for it, all alone.

My head flopped back to his chest, and I squeezed him tight. "Congrats, sneak."

"It's his loss," Todd said after a few minutes had faded into the past. "And I know he'll regret it."

With the thud of his heart in my ear, the lines of his hard body began to take shape beneath me. My hand flexed, moving to slide over his lower stomach. It was flat, but there were grooves around his abdomen, outlines and ridges that had my throat constricting and my bleeding heart needing.

"I hope he does," I whispered and meant it. "I'm sorry."

Todd stilled. "Why?"

"For laying my crap at your feet. I mean, I don't know if you actually like me, or if you just wanted to—"

"I more than like you, Dimples. And there's no need to be sorry. I decide what I can and can't handle."

I held him tighter, his shirt rising, silken smooth, warm skin meeting my hand. The image of Ainsley and Jackson kissing next to his car had my eyes closing, my heart darkening, and my hand moving.

When I reopened my eyes, the darkest brown I'd ever encountered stared down at me, questioning as they roamed over my face.

I knew I was using how he felt for me for all the wrong reasons, and that it wasn't right.

But right and wrong had no business messing with a shattered heart.

His lips were softer than they appeared, tasted different than what I'd expected, and moved over mine with a precision that spoke of ceaseless want. The kind of want that'd painted pictures of this moment in his mind's eye and colored his wildest dreams.

His want, his desire for me, was so heady, my reasons for doing this became muddled, lost within the unprecedented lust he'd coaxed to life.

"Say no," I panted to his lips. I needed him to because I'd discovered there was no stopping the horror, no staunching the bleeding wound Jackson had left me with.

There was only revenge, distraction, and the need to feel good enough.

His hands gripped my face, his gaze darker than a starless sky but glittering all the same. "Like hell."

We crashed together, teeth and tongues dueling, hands pulling at clothes and legs kicking them aside.

A condom came from somewhere, and I touched his thick length as he tore it open with his teeth, then whimpered as he pulled away, leaving me cold as he rolled it on.

The whimper turned into a long mewl as he pulled my panties off and spread my thighs, his tongue and fingers driving me to perilous heights.

With every swipe of his tongue, every twist of his finger inside me, then every slow thrust as he loomed over me, pushing deep inside, he blocked it out.

His touch was magic; one hand behind my head, tangled in my hair, and the other caressing my breast, my side, fingertips grazing my thigh that was hooked around his waist.

His mouth was warm rapture, carrying me from comparison and throwing me into wild abandon.

As if knowing it might ruin it, he didn't talk. Not with his voice. His body did enough talking on its own, and I found myself savoring the soft feel of his short hair, the purring throaty sound that climbed from his throat into my mouth when my nails ran over his scalp.

In and out, he worked me slowly and played me expertly, drawing me to the edge with delirious strokes and touches.

He swelled against the most hostile places inside me, his pubic bone rubbing over mine with every deep glide, every slide of his tongue over mine.

I came slow and steady, the pleasure drawn out and leaving me on a hoarse cry. I clutched his head to mine as he panted into my mouth, his eyes never leaving my face, and when his hips jerked in fast, deep plunges, I kissed him as he grunted and groaned, long and loud, against my lips.

I didn't wake with a start or with regret knocking me sideways.

No, I woke with a smile on my face as I heard humming and felt a finger trailing the dip of my spine.

His finger stopped. "You're awake."

I couldn't ignore the trace of fear in his voice, so I rolled over, taking that finger and kissing it. "I am. What were you singing?"

"Duran Duran."

Grinning, I gazed into his sleep-lined face, noticing the sharp square edge to his jaw that his stubble tried to mask. "You'll have to play it for me."

His lips parted, and he blinked. "Sure." He blinked again. "Wait, you've never listened to Duran Duran?"

"No, but I like old music."

"How do you know they're old?" he asked, his finger dipping to swipe over my exposed nipple.

I pushed his hand away, laughing as I snatched the bedsheet over my chest. "I just do."

"Fine. What's your favorite *old* band?"

Memories formed cracks, and light struggled to shine through those dark fissures as I rasped, "Crowded House."

He eyed me for a long moment, then gently feathered his fingers over my cheek. "They're my mom's favorite."

"Yeah?" I didn't recoil from his touch. I didn't see the point. I liked it, and I needed it.

He nodded, then leaned in to kiss my forehead. "You're beautiful, and I want to be inside you so badly right now, but Rebecca's parents are coming home after lunch, and I don't think she even knows we're in here."

We both dressed as quickly as possible, and I freshened up as best as I could in the en suite before we checked to see if the coast was clear.

A few of the girls from school were cleaning up, tired voices traveling from the kitchen, and Todd looked both ways down the hall before grabbing my hand.

We raced downstairs, smothering our laughter until the front door slammed behind us, and we were halfway down the street.

"You didn't drive, did you?"

"Nah, I was planning on getting shitfaced."

His hand was still in mine, and he used his other to tug his phone from his jeans. "Sorry to foil your plans."

"I've never been so happy to have someone mess with my plans in my life."

We stopped on the street corner as he called a cab company.

The sun was shining, bright, warm, and golden, and I probably looked like hell.

I didn't care because looking at Todd, feeling every sharp

shard that'd broken inside me, I was grateful. I was grateful, and I was fascinated. Not just from our time together, but by him.

He'd caught me by surprise, but he'd also caught me.

He refused to let me fall on my own even though it had to have been hard to hear me upset over someone else.

Someone else. Was that what Jackson was now? Someone I never thought he'd be. An ex. A someone else.

A goodbye that never should've been a hello.

A person I didn't want to think about. Todd made that easier to do, and already I worried I'd take advantage of that. Already I could feel myself swaying closer to him on impulse, seeking the soothing balm his attention provided.

Thirty minutes later, he kissed me goodbye in the back seat of the cab after handing the driver a twenty.

"I understand if you don't want to call me or make this a, um... thing." He cleared his throat, his voice sounding vulnerable and cautious. "But I'm here if you decide you might want to, and I'll wait, okay?" Another kiss, a long hard press of his lips, and then he was walking up a steep driveway to a brown wooden home that had a faded yellow swing chair on its porch.

The problem with slapping a Band-Aid over gaping wounds was that they'd eventually peel off, and the blood would flow freely. As fresh as the moment it'd happened.

The taxi driver snuck glances at me in the rearview as we wound through the backstreets, heading to my place.

I ignored him and concentrated on breathing. The farther we drove, the more the tears pushed and my hands shook, but I let my lids flutter over my eyes and clasped my sweating palms together. I just needed to make it home. I just needed to make it inside my house, escape Dad's anger, and crawl beneath the sheets of my bed. There I could let it all replay, let everything I'd done since, create whatever chaos it would.

Only, it wasn't Dad who greeted me.

The sun bounced off the hood of a familiar truck, and I almost told the driver to keep driving as he pulled up and the tall imposing figure that'd been standing against it looked up from his phone.

Handing the driver another ten to cover the charge and a tip, I opened the door, willing myself to get this over with.

I had no idea what he was doing here, but I slammed the door, the cab driving off, and decided I wouldn't take anymore apologies or drivel about anything being for the best.

I couldn't handle it.

"Willa," Jackson said when I walked to the house. "Bug, what the fuck?" My arm was grabbed, and he gently swung me around, his eyes narrowing as they assessed mine, then my face, my crinkled dress and my mussed hair.

"Don't." His touch singed. "Go home," I rasped, pulling my arm free. "It's done, remember?"

He stumbled back, and I turned for the door when his next words stopped me. "Tell me you didn't do what I think you did."

I laughed, caustic and choked, then spun to glare at him. "And what would that be, Jackson? Huh? Spell it out clearer this time."

His skin leeched of color, his mouth falling open as his eyes misted. "You did."

"Did what?" I pushed, almost growling. "Kissed someone else in front of the person I just destroyed?" I shook my head, laughing. "No, I'm not that fucking cruel. But I did more than kiss someone, Jackson. You-you"—I flung my hand at him, disgusted—"you asshole. The difference is, I have the decency not to do it in front of you."

"What did you do?" he said, so quiet, lethal, the words bit at my skin.

"You broke up with me."

"What did you do, Willa?" he repeated.

"You wrecked me, annihilated me, then left me for dead in front of our parents, and then disappeared with *her*." I dragged my hand beneath my dripping nose.

His chest was heaving now, his words roaring into my ears and probably the neighbors' windows. "What did you fucking do, Willa?"

Shocked, I frowned, confused as to how he could be so mad. "I gave someone what you no longer want. That's what I did."

He stared at me for the longest time, a million emotions flickering through his eyes. Then, he turned for his truck, but he didn't make it. He bent over and vomited into the small gardenia bush by the mailbox.

My hands fluttered to my lips, my heart bruising with its relentless pounding. "Are you drunk?" I didn't understand why he'd care that much if he was with Ainsley now.

"No," he coughed out, wiping his hand over his mouth and shaking his head. Hard eyes settled on me, disgust and something else swimming in those beautiful green depths. "You ruined it. Just like that"—he laughed, then groaned—"you ruined everything."

"What?" I moved closer. Vaguely, I was aware of the front door opening, but Dad didn't come outside, so I ignored his presence. "Me? You told me we were done. Then you sucked face with someone else."

He didn't talk, just stared at me with that horrible look staining his features and wetting his eyes.

"Jackson, you've broken my heart."

"Me? You should've trusted me," he said. "They were watching, and you didn't know? They've *always* been watching, Willa."

"Who?" I asked. "Mom and Heath?" I shook my head. "You don't get to ask me to trust you when you never, not once gave me a reason to all these weeks, hell, *months*."

His eyelids lowered, and he blew out a breath that deflated his chest. "I was coming for you. I was…" he choked off, clearing his throat. "I was coming for you. I would never fucking leave you." His eyes opened wide, unveiling clear, iridescent hatred. "Until now."

I ran as he climbed into his truck, but I didn't make it.

I screamed as he turned it on and pulled out onto the road, but he didn't hear me.

I collapsed into a useless, broken pile of flesh and bones on the front lawn when he drove off, but he never turned around.

Time wasn't forgiving.

Time stole everything if you let it.

Days crawled by, and I barely made it to graduation. In fact, I wouldn't have bothered if it weren't for the disappointment and worry that rolled off my father and saddled me with guilt.

More guilt.

I was a barely walking, barely talking, barely breathing, guilt clouded idiot who'd gone and messed up everything.

I hadn't just messed it up, though. I'd thrown gasoline onto a fire Jackson had been trying to put out.

Why he'd done what he did stumped me. As predicted, he wouldn't answer my calls, and he'd blocked me from all forms of his social media.

Maybe I'd never know for sure, but I could guess when a large check arrived mere weeks after I'd graduated and summer began. A large check from Mom and Heath, along with a small note, congratulating me on the completion of school and a new beginning.

Right. A beginning where their prized possession would no longer be tainted by his stepsister's presence in his life.

Dad hadn't touched it, and neither had I. "The choice is yours, but I know what I'd do," he'd said, eyeing the check with clear disdain after taking me out for ice cream on graduation. I wasn't up for huge meals, so he'd often bring me fries, salads, fruit, and lots of junk food after work.

I didn't want the choice because I wanted nothing to do with it. With them.

But that would mean Dad would take most of the responsibility for my tuition himself.

"Knockity, knock, knock," Flo sang, then scrunched her nose in the doorway. "Shit, this place is gross."

If she was saying that, someone who kept pet rats in her bedroom, then I really needed to pick up the piles of clothes and food packages already.

I grunted, sitting up and pushing my hair off my face. A glance at my phone said it was only two in the afternoon. The nights might've been unbearable, but I longed for each one. The setting sun was a sign that life went on, and however reluctant I was, it'd carry me with it into a brand-new day.

It was going to be the longest summer of my life.

She sat on the bed. "Todd's been worried, asking about you almost every day."

I knew he was. He'd even come by twice, but Dad had sent him away, knowing he wasn't what I needed. He might not have been what I needed, but I could sure do with his company. Though I wasn't sure I could stomach it after what I'd done.

"Tell him I'm sorry," I whispered.

"I've told him you're sorry five times now, Willa." Her red

curls bounced as her head shook. "He doesn't need apologies; he just wants to know how you're doing."

"So lie," I said, trying to smile. "Tell him I need some time, but I'm okay." When she frowned, sighing, I urged, "Please, Flo."

She nodded once. "Fine."

"How's Green?"

She bit down on her lips. "Over. He's headed to Ohio after all."

"I'm sorry," I said, knowing she was attending Edmond Ross. "It seemed like you liked this one."

She laughed, kicking off her pink Converse and crossing her legs. "I did, but life happens, right?"

I peered down at the dirty tissues littering my bedding. "Yeah." Pulling the scrunchie off my wrist, I began to pull my hair up onto my head.

"So I heard something. At this party I was at last night."

I quit fussing with my hair at the caution tugging her lips, the freckles over her cheeks shifting as she wriggled them.

The scrunchie fell to the bed, my hair to my back, and I demanded more than asked, "Heard what?"

She seemed to steel herself, her cheeks puffing as she exhaled and grabbed my hand. "He's going to Texas, Wil."

"Jackson," I said, not feeling the warmth of her hand, only seeing the remorse in her blue eyes when she nodded.

Of course, he was.

And I had no one to blame but myself.

PART TWO

Unforgiving are the memories
that find you in your sleep
they won't bother waking you
especially if you weep.

seventeen

FIVE YEARS LATER
Willa

I was coming for you. I would never fucking leave you.

I woke sweating and panting from the same dream that visited at least once a week, no matter how much time had passed. Skin damp and prickling, tears lacing my cheeks, I pushed the patchwork duvet off and stumbled into the bathroom.

The hot water failed to rid the ice cresting my skin, and after washing my hair, I stood beneath the spray with my head tilted forward. It rolled down my neck and chest, and I remained upright thanks to my hands braced against the wall.

The sun was still half asleep, its bronze and gold slow to chase away the dark that could be seen through the tiny window above my head. A bird flapped by, followed by a flock.

Dressed in a red button-down dress, I slipped my feet into my white Converse, then threw my damp hair forward to gather it into a ponytail.

A few strands escaped to fall around my face. When out, the brown tresses bobbed around my shoulders in unruly waves. I didn't miss my long hair. I didn't miss a lot of things about that time, and the things I did miss only poked at the bruise that refused to heal, so when I'd turned twenty-one, I said goodbye.

That was the time I'd also quit using Todd so completely and had said yes to taking a chance on him.

"*You don't want this,*" he'd seethed, his chest heaving and his eyes filled with hurt. "*I've waited, Willa. I've waited two whole fucking years and then some.*"

"*I'm sorry,*" I said for the hundredth time. "*Don't,*" I said when he backed up toward my dormitory door. "*Please,*" I'd rasped, breath failing me. "*You can't leave me.*"

I had no idea where the vulnerability had come from. Not when I'd been nothing but a shell since the summer that stole my soul.

But it showed up and snuck out, and it made him stop.

With his brows low and his shoulders rising and falling, Todd stared at the ground, groaning. "I'm in love with you, Willa. I've been in love with you for years, and I…"

My knotted throat made it hard to ask, "You what?"

He shook his head, lifting his defeated eyes to mine. "I deserve more."

Time stole moments from me as we stared at one another. "Todd," I said, at a loss. He was right. I'd known that for a long time, and it was time I stopped being such a selfish bitch.

But I didn't want to. Pain sliced through me anew, cold and swift, as I struggled to speak. So I didn't. I merely nodded, ducking my head to hide what was happening inside me.

Then he was gone, and I was nothing but a slave to a handler called heartbreak. All over again. You didn't need to be in love with someone for them to break your heart. Or who knows, maybe I had been, perhaps just not enough.

I wasn't sure it would ever be enough, so that was why I didn't fight.

Hours passed, and still, I laid there, in the very same spot he'd left me on my bed. Tears had created sticky streaks on my face, and every so often, a new round would wash them away.

Rinse and repeat.

A pounding echoed through my skull, but I ignored it.

Then, a second later, I heard, "Damn it, Willa." Rough hands lifted me from the bed, and I could smell bourbon on the breath that coasted across my face in a harsh exhale. Todd cupped my cheeks and brushed my hair away.

"You're back," I tried to say, but my voice didn't work.

He caught it, his face crinkling with concern, dark eyes filled with too many emotions to name. "I'm back."

"Why?" It was all I could think to say.

He dropped his forehead to mine, whispering, "Because I'm fucked up. You've fucked me right up."

"I'm sorry."

He reared back, moaning. "Stop saying you're fucking sorry, Willa. Jesus Christ." Standing from the bed, he paced the small space, laughing roughly. "You know what I did tonight?"

I frowned.

"I went to a bar, had a drink, and caught up with Elain from physics. I thought about fucking her."

Elain was blond with huge boobs and small blue eyes. Elain reminded me of Ainsley.

Speechless and winded, I tried to tame the dizziness that took hold.

Todd laughed. "She showed me to her car in the back of the lot, and I couldn't even get in the damn thing before I was backing up and apologizing."

Relief swept in, warm and welcome. Until he pinned me beneath the accusation in his eyes.

"You've fucked me. You've completely messed me up, Willa, and I wanted out, but I couldn't fucking do it."

Faced with the idea of losing him, with the sickening image of him and Elain, I held my arms out. "Come here."

He shook his head.

"Todd," I said. "You belong with me, and I need you. Come here."

He fell over me like a blanket, my back hitting the bed as his mouth hit mine. "You don't need to say you love me," he whispered, undoing his fly and pulling at my panties. "You don't need to lie to me, but please, just commit to me."

"There's never been anyone but you, not for a long time." I gripped his face. "You know that."

His eyes closed briefly, then he sat back to push down his jeans and rid me of my panties. "Be mine. Not just to fuck, Willa. Be mine in every way you can."

I wasn't positive I could do that, but I was sure I couldn't survive without him. "Todd, you do deserve better." My voice was tear-strained.

He sniffed, falling over me and wiping at my cheeks. "Do you want me to have better?"

"No," I said instantly.

"Good," he rumbled, then fucked me with his fingers while his mouth slid over mine, "because there's nothing better than this."

Heartbreak was capable of many things, I'd discovered, but most of all, it had the power to rid you of morality, granting you enough desperation to become a selfish coward.

When we graduated, I finally broke the toxic co-dependent spell and ended things with Todd. I hadn't seen or heard from him since, but I heard he was still in med school and back to playing the field.

After coating my lashes in a layer of mascara and dabbing some concealer beneath my sleep-starved eyes, I grabbed my purse and rushed through my one-bedroom apartment.

Old but with a classic beauty I appreciated, the apartment was dressed in every color I loved. Yellow throw cushions lined the secondhand brown cracked leather couches my dad had bought online. A purple and gold patterned rug lay beneath a chipped oak coffee table that had once been painted a solid white. A small flat screen hung from the wall, and beneath it were three rows of wooden bookcases, each one filled to the brim with books, knickknacks, a photo of me, Daphne, and Peggy at one end, and one of me and Flo at the other.

In the middle sat my favorite picture of me and Todd.

He was smiling at the camera, rain splattering his graduation cap, and I was smiling up at him, my eyes shut and my hand trying to keep my own cap in place while the wind attempted to steal it.

The rain had this uncanny way of showing up when I most needed sunshine.

Grabbing my keys from the coffee table, I brushed my fingers over the photo, wishing I could've given him so much more. That I could've given him what he'd given me.

It was past time I admitted to myself that perhaps I did love him. It was a love that'd grown steady over the course of years. A love that'd survived many insecurities, many arguments, and ultimately, time.

While that love didn't threaten to send me up in flames the same way love had done to me before, it did threaten me all the same, and so it needed to die.

He'd been my haven, and not a small amount of risk came with admitting you were at someone's mercy.

I'd learned the hard way what giving yourself so freely to someone could do.

It destroyed lives.

Long after the flames had finished dancing and the ash was settling into dust, it still wreaked havoc on all those involved.

Swallowing, I wiped a tear from my cheek, backing away from the memories.

My hand skimmed the knitted gray afghan that hung over

the arm of the recliner on my way through the open space. One of the few items I'd taken from Dad's place.

The old floorboards creaked, no doubt alerting those downstairs that I was on my way.

It was no easy thing, being your own boss, but the people I worked with helped make it easier.

Locking and pulling the door shut behind me, I wound down the old metal staircase and into the small foyer below.

Shivers assaulted as I stepped out onto the street, where above my head hung a rusted corrugated metal sign swinging above the neighboring blue door to my apartment. On the sign, the name Dimples was painted in cursive blue script with two smiling cupcakes on either side.

"What should I name it?" I'd asked, standing beside my dad and Todd out on the street as we'd gazed at the empty building, still swiping away tears.

"Dimples," Todd whispered, his hand squeezing mine. "Do you need—"

"Dimples," I'd said, blinking at him, the tears drying and a small laugh erupting in their wake. "That's it."

Todd frowned, but after staring at me for prolonged seconds, he then grinned. "Really?"

I'd known then what I needed to do, and I could think of nothing better than to honor him in that way.

In one of the only ways I could.

I nodded, squeezing his hand before turning to Dad, who'd been plucking weeds from the empty green planter boxes. "What do you think, Dad?"

"I think it's yours, so you can do whatever the hell you want."

Mine.

Never in my wildest dreams did I think I'd be able to take something like this on. That I'd be able to make a dream like this happen. Not with the student loans and the lack of savings and job experience.

But I didn't make it happen.

Dad had surprised me when Todd and I had been at his place for dinner, handing me an envelope, stating it was my graduation present since I never let him pay for college.

I'd burst into tears when I'd pulled out the deed to the building that sat tucked away in a busy old corner of town.

I told myself I had twelve months to start turning a profit, and although Dad told me not to worry about it, he still had faith I could.

Five months after we'd opened the doors, I was already beginning to do that, and I'd put a nice chunk of change aside to repay Dad and tackle the student loans.

The corroded bell above the door chimed as I pushed it open and stepped into warmth and the scent of Flo's vanilla frosting.

Where the exterior was run down, a white painted brick building with planter boxes housing gardenias hanging from the windows, the inside was renovated with some leftover old rustic charm.

Behind rows of glass casing sat half of today's wares. Cupcakes, brownies, muffins, lunch rolls, and loaves of bread. All that was missing were the pies, which were due in the oven in the next thirty minutes.

"Did you leave the trash in last night? Or was that me?" Flo asked, tugging off a pair of gloves while I tucked my purse beside the microwave.

"Good morning to you, too." Flo was Dimples's manager, and though it'd taken her months to learn how to bake, I now couldn't live without her. She'd remained in the cove after college, under the guise of wanting to be there for her sick great aunt. The aunt she apparently loathed and was saying goodbye to tomorrow.

"Mornings are never good; we've been over this."

I smirked. She knew I disagreed. Mornings signified hope. It was when the sun reached its highest peak for the day that I began to feel my energy wane, and long buried memories would eventually sneak in.

Thanks to Todd and a therapist Dad had recommended I see during my junior year of college, I'd gotten better at controlling what ruled my thoughts and what I allowed to visit. I had a feeling that was why the dreams—I refused to call them nightmares for it gave them too much power—still stole me at least once a week.

Virginia, my therapist, had said that as with all things, time would help with that. Then she'd winked and said, "And maybe a glass or two of red before bed."

I got to work, kneading, rolling, and indenting dough while Flo served the customers out front.

I'd just slipped the miniature pies into one of the two industrial-sized ovens when Dennis walked in through the back door and retied his frilly purple apron. "Sorry, gorgeous. I had a fight with a stray, and I lost."

Flo walked in the back, then promptly dumped herself onto the stool next to the phone. "Ruh-roh. Do tell."

Dennis bent low to retie one of his platform shoes. He was in his fifties, loved anything that glittered and enhanced beauty, and he was totally straight. Married with a little girl named Margie. "That old guy who's been walking through town with his shopping cart?"

We both nodded, knowing who he was talking about.

"Anyway, I bought him a coffee, and the jerk threw it at me

while screaming about all the ways I'm a blight upon Earth." He swung his arm out theatrically. "A plague that needs to be wiped out." With a flick of his blond hair over his shoulder, he then dug in his apron pocket for his bright yellow scrunchie.

"Asshole," I said, my limbs tense with anger.

Flo was up and heading to the back door. "Where'd you last see this shit-stain?"

I choked on a laugh while Dennis hurried after her. "It's fine. He missed. They didn't call me the star quarterback in high school for nothing." He flashed me a grin. "Twinkle toes, baby."

My smile made his widen, and he walked over, his fingers pinching the air, coming for my cheeks. "Let me at 'em."

I indulged his odd fascination with my cheeks, standing there while he did his usual prodding and squishing.

"Where's Flo?" I asked after a minute of his cooing had passed.

His hands fell, and he darted for the back door. "Son of a fucking gun."

It slammed behind him, and I quickly checked on the pies before moving out front, my chest feeling lighter.

The morning rush usually began at eight, and I served three customers before the pink framed clock on the wall above twin sets of white metal tables and chairs ticked closer.

I was serving a woman with a monobrow and two screaming kids when I saw her.

Right on time, as per usual. Every Friday morning, Mom—or Victoria as I now referred to her—would drop by on her way to work and leave a basket outside.

The first time, a month after we'd opened, I'd stared at her with an odd sense of disbelief, relief, and horror, wondering what the hell she was doing.

The few times I'd visited home during college to see Dad and

Daphne, I hadn't seen her. Not after the first Christmas of freshman year when I'd knocked on the door of what used to be my home, only to be welcomed inside a house that now felt anything but.

The air felt wrong, blowing warm over my skin from the A/C, and the silence seeped inside my pores, growing stale as Mom, Heath, and I had struggled to finish a cup of tea and open the presents we'd bought for one another.

I hadn't set foot inside that house since.

I suppose she'd heard, as she would have in this town, that I'd opened up a shop, and therefore, I was now a resident once more.

"I'll just leave these here," she mouthed, pointing at the basket she'd propped on the metal table outside beneath the overhang. She then wiggled her fingers, gesturing and mouthing, "Call me."

I wouldn't, and she knew that, yet she still came by every damn week.

I watched her go, feeling nothing, and then the woman I'd been serving cleared her throat, and I apologized.

When the rush began to dwindle, half our stock was already gone. I headed into the kitchen between customers to check the pies cooling on racks. After the last customer had left just after nine, I began mixing a fresh batch of brownies.

The back door opened and closed with a boom, and I didn't bother to glance up.

"You can't chase people down the street, Florence Nightingale." He always called her that, which, of course, drove her nuts when he'd first been hired.

"Why?" Flo demanded. "He's lucky he's sprightly and that's all he got after what he did to you."

Dennis, heading for the sink to wash his hands, sighed. "Because it's bad for business."

Flo's hands met her hips as she gave me a look that said, "Can you believe this guy?"

Then she saw the basket of fruit and recipes on the stainless countertop in front of me and cursed. "Again?"

I nodded.

Dennis pouted. He didn't know the full story like Flo did, but he knew enough. Still, I suppose being a parent himself, he never hid how the nonexistent relationship between Victoria and me saddened him.

"God," Flo spat, tying her apron and fixing her unruly curls into a messy bun. Her face was flushed, likely from running through town. "When will she take a fucking hint?"

"She's her mother," Dennis said, taking the brownies from me. "A mother's love knows no bounds." He shooed me, and I turned for the coffee machine to make a tea.

"That's not an excuse to act like a cruel, crazy bitch." Flo moved out front.

Dennis whispered, "You okay?"

I stirred my tea, staring down into its murky depths as I pondered that loaded question. "Yeah, I'm good." I was. For so long, I'd taken Victoria's and Heath's punishments and had worn them with a little honor and a healthy dose of shame.

I'd thought I'd deserved their wrath, their embarrassment, and their hurt.

And maybe I had, but now I knew better.

I knew they could feel all those things without doing what they'd done to me.

Picking up the basket, I took it to the storeroom and dumped it in the far corner. Dennis took them home with him to a women's shelter near his townhouse.

Then I closed the door and dusted off my hands.

eighteen

Jackson

I'd never been allowed up here as a kid.

Nestled along the edge of town, the high-rise gave view to most of Magnolia Cove. Of the creeks that split and wound through town, eventually joining with the lake, which connected with the sea.

Closing the drawer that housed a bottle of top-shelf whiskey, cigars, and two porno mags, I smirked, realizing they were probably the reason. I doubted Victoria was permitted to enter the large space either.

Dressed in rich brown leathers, red velvet rugs, and state of the art technology, this had been Dad's sanctuary and institution all in one.

Shifting from the sleek black desk, I tucked my hands in my pockets and gazed out the floor-to-ceiling windows that lined the wall behind it.

The sun tried to peek through the tiny gaps in the clouds, but they moved too fast, blanketing the cove in gray.

Home.

I was back in the one place I never wanted to call home again.

A dream I'd harbored years ago was now coming true, but it was too early and too late. I no longer knew if I wanted it.

The past week had been a blur of phone calls, removalists,

and fear. So much fucking fear. It splintered, arcing wide over so many different reasons, the main one I struggled to even think about.

I'd been happy. Content. I'd moved on.

Then one phone call from Victoria in the middle of the night had changed everything.

But... only if I let it.

Steeling my shoulders, I released a long breath, and said, "Come in," when a knock sounded on the door.

I didn't bother turning, my gaze, unseeing, remained planted on the blue and green scenery beyond as Ainsley's heels clipped over the marble floor. "Thought you might still be up here." Her arms came around me, the scent of Chanel enveloping. The overpowering perfume used to drive me mad, but I'd learned to accept it, just as I had the woman who wore it.

My hands found hers over my stomach. "News?"

"Your mom thinks he should be home by next week."

Eight days ago, Dad had been in a car accident on his way back into town after a meeting.

Trying to avoid a fresh pileup on the highway, he'd apparently swung the wheel too sharp, and he was hit by someone in the next lane over.

Both cars lost control and had ended up in the pileup anyway. When Dad had come to, he'd discovered he had no feeling in his left leg. It'd been crushed thanks to the other car's front-end caving in the left-hand side of the footwell.

His leg had been torn open so badly that he could've lost it. They'd reconstructed his shattered tibia; the other fractures would need to heal on their own. He'd recently left the ICU, which was promising. They were hoping for a full recovery, but there was a good chance he might need assistance to walk for the rest of his life.

"Rehab?" I asked.

"Victoria's arranged it. He'll be working with some of the best in the state."

While that should've been comforting, numb was all I could feel.

My relationship with my father hadn't been strained since I'd left for Austin. It simply hadn't existed. As soon as I could get into a dorm, I'd packed up and driven for two days straight, and I never once looked back or answered their phone calls.

"There's one problem."

It took everything I had not to stiffen in her embrace. "And what is that?" Even without the cautious lilt to her voice, I knew what it was, or who it was.

"Willa." The name left her on a rushed exhale, as if she were annoyed she even had to utter it.

I couldn't blame her. It'd taken years for Ainsley to shake her paranoia and jealousy where Willa was concerned.

It wasn't something I could sweep away with words and the coupling of our bodies. Not after she knew. She knew, back before we'd graduated high school, what Willa had meant to me.

It was a risk to involve her in my botched attempt to keep our parents at bay, to keep as much peace as possible, but yearning doesn't provide a great deal of headspace for assessment.

I'd been desperate enough to ask for Ainsley's help, and for whatever reason, after she'd called me crazy with tears welling in her eyes, she'd agreed to give me it.

We hadn't skipped off into the sunset when Willa destroyed me. I'd been single and making the most of it throughout freshman year while remaining friends with Ainsley.

Then one drunken night turned into many repeated nights

over the following years, and before I knew what was happening, we were talking about sharing an apartment during our junior year.

She'd been a distraction from destruction. But you couldn't spend months, years, with a person and feel nothing for them.

Distraction can grow if you feed it. And I kept feeding it, at first just enough to satiate and do a quality job of chasing ghosts from my mind and heart.

But she wasn't just a distraction. She cared for me, she was in love with me, and after what I'd put her through and the fact she was still willing to keep trying me on for size even though I'd never fit, her patience and that love had my eyes opening to possibilities I'd never once thought of.

Something healthy. Something that wasn't innocence wrapped in sin. Something that could last and flourish if given the right attention.

Squeezing her hands, I murmured, "What's the issue?"

"She's blocked Victoria's number. At the bakery and to her cell. Her colleagues won't even let her enter the shop."

It was rolling over my tongue, gaining speed, to ask about this bakery of hers, but I smacked my lips shut just in time.

Humming, I turned. Sliding my arms around Ainsley's back, I felt her shiver as they glided over the curve of her spine. "So she doesn't know."

Ainsley's teeth released her lip, her red lipstick still perfect as she stared at my chest, her fingers toying with the buttons on my dress shirt. "I don't think so. Victoria wanted me to ask if you could..." She stopped, mascara loaded lashes fluttering as she exhaled a sigh.

"It'll be fine," I said, my tone and hold of her slender frame firm.

Her chin tipped back for those blue eyes to meet mine. Uncertainty and hope swam within, coating them in a glossy sheen. "You promise?"

I no longer made promises I couldn't keep, but if there was one thing I knew with a certainty to rival that of the rising sun, it was that Willa Grace couldn't touch me anymore. All that remained was scorched earth. A barren, dead, and useless wasteland.

Taking Ainsley's chin, I brought her lips to mine and reassured her.

nineteen

Willa

Shoving the phone between my shoulder and ear, I flicked off the lights in the kitchen and headed out the front, doing the same there. "I can always change the premium later."

"It would be better to make sure you're covered now, Wil."

I wanted to groan, but as always, he was right. "Okay, I'll call them tomorrow." I locked the door and pulled it closed behind me, then locked the deadbolt. "It's just hard to find the time. I'm on hold for ages."

"What have I told you about making sure you schedule proper break times for yourself?"

I did groan then. "I know, I know." I didn't bother unlocking the door to my apartment. I'd gone there half an hour ago to grab my dinner from the fridge to eat at work while I finished up prep for tomorrow.

"It's important." Dad cleared his throat while I locked the door behind me, heading upstairs. "Listen, there's something I need to talk to you about. Victoria called."

"Nothing good is about to leave your mouth, and I'd rather live in blissful oblivion." I opened my apartment door, kicking off my flats, then almost dropped the phone.

"Willa?" Dad called.

A figure, bathed in moonlight, was seated on my couch, a

leg propped up and draped over his knee. "It'll have to wait. I'll, um, call you later," I managed to mumble, then hung up.

My phone clattered to the entry table, every air particle in the room drifting from reach. All that remained was that scent. Minty cedarwood. His scent.

"Jackson?"

The lamp on the side table came to life, and my heart began to roar in my ears as his face appeared. A face that hadn't changed much, save for the light layer of stubble residing on an even sharper jaw. His green eyes were fixed to something on his lap, but I couldn't remove mine from him to see what it was.

"Do you always leave your door unlocked?"

That voice. My knees quaked, my stomach somersaulted and backflipped, and my eyes stung with the urge to cry.

Unable to clear the emotion building in my throat, I could only blink. "W-what are—"

"Stuttering, Willa. Really?" His eyes swung up then, colliding with mine, and the cold detachment within had me taking a step back. Sighing, he set the photo frame he'd been holding on the couch, then rose to his full towering height, and buttoned his suit jacket. "I'll cut to the chase. Heath was injured in a car accident. No one could get a hold of you, or they were too chicken shit to really try, so"—he spread his hands—"here I am." His lips curved. "Lucky you."

I frowned. "Lucky me?" Then I stepped closer. "Wait, *what?* Is he okay?"

With his gaze flicking over my apartment, he said, "He'll live. Victoria wants you to at least visit him in the hospital." Giving me his eyes, he stared down the straight slope of his nose, indignant and stoic. "Or do you think yourself above checking in on the man who helped raise you after such an ordeal?"

His words, the cruel manner in which he'd uttered them,

combined with his overbearing height, broader shoulders, and intimidating presence... I could scarcely think let alone respond how I wanted to. "I'm not above anything."

Glancing around again, he puckered those perfect lips. "Could've fooled me." Then, turning and walking behind the couch, probably to avoid passing me, he was striding to the door.

Panic, and something too indescribable to name, had me saying, "Wait."

A dark rumble of laughter was all I received before the door to my apartment closed, and I heard him descend the steps outside.

It was almost one in the morning by the time I dragged myself to bed.

Setting the photo frame, the same one Jackson had been holding, back in its home, I readied myself for bed, willing the tears to stay gone.

Silent and untamable, they'd arrived the second I'd seen Jackson climb inside a new black truck out on the street, and I'd let the lace curtains fall back into place.

I hated that even after all this time, I still had tears to shed. I hated that he'd come here, invaded the home I'd made for myself, and had managed to make it cold and uninviting, all in the span of five minutes.

His presence was everywhere, and after tossing and turning half the night, I woke early and dragged the vacuum and mop through the apartment, trying to rid it of his scent.

It wasn't possible it had lingered, and I knew it had to be my imagination, but it made me feel better all the same.

The halls of the hospital were sterile as nurses flitted between rooms and a family passed by with a little boy in a wheelchair.

I smiled at him, and despite his arm and leg both being casted, he smiled back.

This is fine, I told myself. *Just make sure he's okay, that he sees you for five minutes, and then you can leave.*

I'd almost decided not to come, but Jackson had been right. Despite all that'd happened, before that, there was a time Heath had loved me and cared for me as if I were his very own.

I would honor that by ignoring the lingering hurt long enough to see how he was doing.

Pausing outside the door the receptionist had given me directions to, I closed my eyes and drew in an extended breath. Behind the confines of my eyelids, the beeps and soft murmurs of the hospital faded, and memories vied for center stage.

Popsicles in the summertime, and secretive smirks during church when he'd sneak me candy. Yelling, disappointed familiar green eyes, a drill meeting wood, and then silence. So much silence when I needed noise to match the chaos brewing inside.

"Are you lost?"

My eyes opened to find a nurse with a kind face standing before me.

Shaking my head, I prayed my eyes weren't wet and offered a weak smile. "No, just, um… processing." I had nothing else to say that wouldn't have her look of pity turn into one of baffled concern.

"Call out if you need anything."

I nodded, and then it was just me and a white door with an oblong sheet of glass giving view to the patient inside.

Grabbing the cold door handle, I pushed it down and walked into the room.

I couldn't bring myself to look at the bed until I'd closed the door behind me and taken another fortifying inhale, releasing it through my nose as I waded closer.

Heath was staring at me, those eyes, the ones his son had inherited, wide open and heavily lined. I wasn't sure if this had exhausted him or if the past six years had aged him.

Even so, his features were no less striking, and after seeing Jackson last night, it was clear he'd inherited both Heath's and Kylie's best genes.

"Willa Grace."

My name was a rasped exhale. He wiggled his elbows beneath him, propping himself up higher in the bed.

My muscles itched to move, to offer assistance, but my heart kept my feet planted to the glossed floor. "Hi," was all I could say, my gaze floating down his blanket-clad body to the leg that was casted. Swallowing, I nodded to it. "Does it hurt?"

Heath chuckled, a cough rattling from him. "I've had far worse." Frowning, I let my eyes reach his, and he sighed. "The pain is somewhat manageable, but yeah, it's been pretty horrific at times, that's for sure."

I wanted to ask how it'd happened, but my tongue was too thick.

As if knowing, he explained, "Car pileup on the highway home."

"How many?"

"Nine." Clearing his throat, he added, "Two casualties."

My chest squeezed, and when he reached for the pitcher on the nightstand, I found myself moving.

A tremor shot through my hand as I refilled the cup and passed it over.

He took it, offering his thanks, but I couldn't meet his eyes.

I stepped back to the wall, tugging at my floral sundress and staring at a black streak on the white floor. "How long will you need to stay here for?"

"I should be home by next week." I tracked the cup's descent to his lap, where he clutched it. "Not that it'll be much better than being here."

"What do you mean?" I couldn't believe I'd asked.

He huffed. "Look at me, Wil. I'm useless, and I'll be this way for a long fucking time."

Hearing him curse wasn't exactly foreign, but it was still an oddity, something he always tried to refrain from doing unless he was really pissed off.

"You're otherwise okay?" I was proud of how detached the question sounded.

"Yeah," he said. "Guess so."

I nodded, still unable to look him in the eye, and turned for the door. "I need to go, but I'm glad you're okay."

"Wait," he said.

I wasn't sure why I did, but I paused with my hand on the door handle. No, I knew why. I knew I waited because not once, whenever I'd been hurting and I'd needed someone to wait, to listen, had they done the same for me. "Yes?"

"Come back?" He rushed on in a ramble so unlike him, "I mean, just to see me while I'm here? I know you probably won't come to the house, but I'd like to see you again, at least once."

That was the moment I realized, as if I was having some type of out of body experience, that I could've said nothing and walked away for good, or I could do something I never thought myself capable of.

Perhaps time was the answer. Or maybe the spirit grew so heavy from other's transgressions and your own mistakes that you knew holding them close enough to make decisions for you would be something you'd one day regret.

Still, I could make no promises. "I'll think about it."

Out in the hall, I ducked my head to swipe at a rogue tear and walked briskly until I met the end of the hallway that neared the elevators. There, I stood with my back against the wall, and my head tilted to the blinding fluorescent lights above, and I swallowed profusely.

I swallowed every raging, screaming, crying part of me that wanted out. That demanded justice and penance for what it'd made of me.

But maybe, as my offer to think about returning came back to me, what it'd made of me was exactly who I was supposed to be.

Broken, scarred, but still forgiving. At least, forgiving enough to move forward.

Hushed murmurs infiltrated my staccato thoughts, and I turned my head just enough to see a couple talking by the elevators.

Every thought I'd had, every feeling that'd began to resurface since he'd shown up in my apartment last night, dissolved into a puddle of despair.

With his hands framing her face, he said something to her I couldn't hear, but the intensity in which they were staring at each other said more than words ever could.

This was no sick joke; they were together.

Which was further confirmed by the joining of their lips.

I tucked myself back around the corner when their heads tilted, taking it deeper, someplace I never wanted to be privy to.

Anger ignited, faster than I could've predicted. All those years ago, he'd made out as if I'd had the wrong idea, as if I was the one who'd betrayed him and had ruined everything.

Yet there they were, two peas in a heartbreaking pod.

I had to leave. I had to move. Eyeing the hall back to Heath's room, I contemplated finding an emergency exit, and then the sound of heels clipping over the floor had me plastering myself to the wall.

A pointless endeavor as another glance to my right showed Ainsley walking inside the elevator.

I watched, couldn't stop myself, as she adjusted her cream sweater over her skintight high-waisted jeans, and then tugged her hand through her longer, blond waves.

That was when I saw it. The sun streaming in the windows in the waiting bay, and the lights overhead, caught the diamond band around her finger, and made it glint.

Then she was gone, and I wondered if I'd melt into the wall or simply collapse.

As if the first blow hadn't been bad enough, I had to be dealt two in one cruel sweep.

"You cut your hair."

I hadn't realized I'd closed my eyes, and I hadn't even thought about the fact that he hadn't entered the elevator with Ainsley.

"Um, yeah." Blinking furiously, I straightened and gazed at the ground to keep him from seeing what the past half hour had done to my heart. "Some years ago now."

"You looked better before."

My eyes snapped to his, glaring. "Excuse me?"

"You heard me." There was no inflection in his tone, no expression on his face. He was a blank canvas, and I was the paint he refused to soil himself with.

Tucking some of said hair behind my ear, a wet laugh escaped. "Wow."

He hummed. "You've seen him?"

"Why else would I be here?"

A thick brow rose. "I don't know. Perhaps you enjoy loitering in hallways in your spare time now and eavesdropping on other people's conversations."

This man. This cruel man. He knew me, and he knew his words were complete bullshit. "I didn't hear anything. I was just waiting for you to leave."

"Why?"

"What do you mean why?"

His jaw twitched with annoyance. "I mean exactly what the word implies."

Unbelievable. I had no idea why I was even still standing there. "I should go."

"You should."

"You're engaged?"

A nod, his hands sliding into the pockets of his slacks. "We are." My weighted eyes dropped to the streaked floor. "Not going to congratulate me?" The question was so dry, it mocked and dared.

Forcing enough air inside my nose to fuel words that wanted to tear at my tongue, I said, soft and rough, "Congratulations, Jackson."

His eyes thinned, observing and calculating, and I decided I'd already experienced more than I could handle for one day. Hell, for an entire year.

I made myself move, my arm brushing his as he stood statue still.

As I bypassed the elevators to the stairs, my head and heart throbbing, I wondered if maybe forgiveness was overrated after all.

twenty

Willa

"Engaged?" Flo spat, crumbs shooting out of her mouth.

Daphne frowned, her nose scrunching as she leaned back, thanking me as I set her coffee down.

I dragged a seat over, tearing at the croissant I'd snatched from the display cabinet. "Yep."

Daphne stared at her coffee for a moment, seeming lost in thought. "He was rude?"

Remembering our exchange, and the one the night before, I scoffed. "He wasn't just rude. He was…" I observed the pastry in my hand, remembering. "He was horrible."

"He's always had that in him," Daphne said.

"Had what?" Flo mumbled, licking her fingers. "The ability to be a raging dick?"

Daphne smirked. "Precisely."

After leaving the hospital, I'd gone home for an hour, which was how long it'd taken to dry my tears and wash my face and pretend nothing had happened.

I should've known Florence would see right through it the moment I entered the bakery.

So when Daphne had shown up this morning, opening the door with, "What's he done?" I'd glared at Flo, who'd shrugged and began gathering treats for this impromptu coffee date.

I got up to serve a customer who'd walked in, then returned to catch the tail end of Daphne's sentence. "… always wanted him."

I knew they'd been talking about Ainsley.

Sorrow rushed in, fisting my heart. "He made his choice long ago."

Daphne hummed. "As did you."

I scowled, ripping more pastry and eating it. "We've been over this a hundred times."

"Yeah, yeah." Flo waved a hand. "So you thought he'd dumped you. Still, you didn't put up much of a fight before he left."

I felt my face drain of color. "What?"

"I'm just saying."

"She's got a point," Daphne said. "But that doesn't matter now. *None*"—she gave me a hard look—"of this should matter now. So quit showing him that it obviously does. Judging by what you've said, it's probably giving him some whack power trip hard-on."

I thumbed my apron, wiping my greasy fingertips. "What am I supposed to do then? Just hide away and wait until he leaves?" The idea of running into him again was more than I could bear. I didn't know what I'd do if I had to endure another encounter like the two we'd already had.

Flo considered that. "How long do you think he's in town for?"

Daphne made a noise, sipping her coffee.

Flo and I both said, "What?"

Daphne sighed, lowering her mug. "Lars said something."

"So you knew Jackson was back, and you didn't think to warn a girl?" I asked.

Her green eyes shined with impatience. "Shut up. I didn't

know until late last night after he'd gotten off the phone with him. Then this morning, this one"—she jabbed a finger at Flo—"is already blowing up my phone."

Flo grinned, then stole Daphne's cupcake.

I waited, unsure if I should run out the door and back upstairs to the safety of my bed.

"He's taking over the company."

My stomach hollowed.

"But he's like, what, twenty-four?"

Daphne raised a brow at Flo. "Willa has her own business."

Flo snorted. "Not a multi-million dollar one." Sheepish, she smiled at me. "No offense, Wil."

"None taken," I mumbled, trying to process. "For good?" I asked Daphne.

She lifted a shoulder. "I don't know, but for the foreseeable future."

It had been his plan, his dream, to one day do just that. I didn't know how he might feel about it all now, though. It was possible during his years in Texas that he'd collected new dreams and aspirations for himself.

"Well…" Flo licked her fingers once more. "This small town is about to get real cozy."

I whimpered, and my head dropped to the table with a thud.

twenty-one

Jackson

My hands tightened around Ainsley's hips, bringing her body to mine with every violent thrust.

She moaned, her back arching as she began to rub herself. I let her go, too focused on finding my own pleasure to stop now.

Her damp blond hair dripped down the valley of her spine. I'd cornered her on the way out of the bathroom after waking in a cold sweat and said nothing as I'd tossed her towel to the floor and began feasting on her cunt.

Her cries grew louder, echoing off the tiles, adding to the roaring in my ears as our skin slapped and my heart galloped.

Perfect. She was fucking perfect. All bronzed skin and glazed blue eyes staring back at me in the mirror, her huge tits swaying.

As she came, I threw my head back on a groan, expecting to follow as she squeezed my cock. I didn't and forced my eyes shut as acute need warred with the restless, reckless desire to come. To unload and rid the tension that'd crawled inside my body since arriving back in this god damned town.

Blue eyes were replaced by hazel, and I growled, shaking my head, opening my own to a damp ceiling. Still, they remained, the pucker to her top lip, the collapsing of her shoulders as she'd folded into herself with every word that left my mouth.

Those huge eyes, surrounded by naturally long, dark lashes,

gazing at the ground before finally meeting mine with the force of a thousand knives to the chest.

I'd hurt her.

Good, I thought, my climax within reach once more.

I'd crushed her.

Even better, I groaned, my hands bruising slick flesh, and my body trembling.

I would destroy her.

With a shouted curse, I came, breathing as if I'd just ran ten miles. On and on it went, and I grew dizzy, struggled to stay upright.

Warm hands slid over my chest, and I shook my head, staring down into deep blue jewels as my blood ran cold. "You needed that."

I blew out a breath through my nose, unable to talk, and just nodded.

Ainsley pressed her lips to my sweat-misted pec, then used the toilet while I disposed of the condom I'd filled with a fuck ton of cum.

I was in the shower, the water raining down over my cold skin, when what'd just happened dug its claws in. My hand slapped against the wall, that old rage returning with a vengeance I was too scared to even try to tame.

Even here, while I was balls deep inside a woman who'd been by my side through all my bullshit, Willa was able to sneak in with the potential to fuck it all up again.

Not this time, I vowed silently.

She might've been able to penetrate my thoughts, but she could no longer get near my heart.

Ainsley had left for work by the time I made it out to the kitchen, dressed and ready to leave myself.

We were leasing a two-bedroom villa by the beach. A nice

slice of calm to help with resettling, Ainsley had said when she'd found it online. There was nothing calm about it. In fact, I hadn't even had the time to open the doors to the back verandah that overlooked the sand and bay.

Ainsley had found a job running one of the local preschools, which wasn't her dream, but she'd said it would do for now.

She'd made no secret of her love for children, nor of her desire to have as many of them as she could.

We were still young, thankfully, so talk of that was easily shelved with a soft, "One step at a time."

I had a long road ahead of me before I even contemplated the idea of raising another human being, and if I was being honest, I wasn't entirely sure I wanted to.

I parked underground in the reserved spot meant for my father and hit the key fob on the way to the elevator.

The new truck had been a gift to myself after completing school in Texas and gaining full-time employment as a scout for an up-and-coming motocross team.

I missed it, not really the place itself, but the freedom and independence it provided. It'd never felt like home, but it was good enough. I wasn't sure any place would ever feel like home again.

Desmond found me before I'd even reached the office door. "Mr. Thorn, your nine o'clock is running almost an hour late."

"That's fine," I told him. I had plenty to do, given I was still finding my feet and therefore, trying to catch up. "Have Freda bring me a coffee when she's got a minute."

Blinking, he nodded. "It's going to make the meeting at noon run overtime, which won't please some of the partners."

"They'll survive," I muttered. "That all?"

Blinking again, he pushed his glasses back and checked his tablet. "Ah, yes. For now."

"Good." I opened the door, breathing a sigh of relief when it sealed shut behind me.

I'd barely drank half my coffee when Desmond phoned. "Sir, I'm sorry, Mrs. Thorn is on her way—"

A sharp knock had me hanging up.

I let her wait for a full minute while I finished my coffee. Gone were the days I did anything in a hurry for Victoria. If it were possible, I wouldn't have anything to do with her at all.

I buzzed her in.

Huffing and adjusting her bright blue suit jacket, she crossed the room to my father's desk, words already vacating her mouth. "She still won't talk to me. She went to see your father, but she won't even allow me inside her kitschy little bakery."

I wasn't sure what kind of test I was being put through, but I was determined not to let myself fail. The hatred and the need for retribution that would never come, it needed to stay buried, or else there was little point in being here.

"Is this your way of asking me to talk to her again?" I lifted a brow, knowing the idea would likely still unsettle her. Besides, I wouldn't. Willingly putting myself in the same place as Willa was a mistake, and if I kept making the same one, I knew I'd be sorry.

Victoria gazed down at the desk, the morning sun bouncing off it, sending dust motes into the air. "I don't know," she said, her tone gentler now. "I just wish she'd give me a chance."

I couldn't help but prod. "For what, exactly?"

She blinked, then shifted. "To make amends, I suppose."

I had nothing to say to that, so I clicked my pen, my shoulders growing more tense with each heartbeat.

She eyed the velvet armchair beside her as if she might take a seat, then reconsidered. "Anyway, I'm organizing a coming home party for your father next weekend."

And she wanted Willa to be there. "Do you really think that's a good idea?"

Her forehead creased. "What do you mean?"

She had to be too hopeful or just plain stupid. There was no way in hell all of us could be in the same room together. If I had to see the asshole Willa ruined me for all those years ago, I'd probably kill him. "Think about it, Victoria."

She visibly deflated. "Do you know how much it hurts when you call me that?"

"Did you know how much it hurt when you gave me reason to?" She'd been ten times the mother than my real one had been. I wasn't even twelve years old when I'd wised up to who Kylie really was. A child stuck in a woman's body who never wanted a child of her own. I was a hindrance, and Dad had no qualms when I'd said I wanted to quit visiting her.

Victoria, for all of her numerous faults, had always treated me like her own son.

Until I misbehaved in such a way that demoted me to family pet.

Silence permeated, thick and constricting, as we both stared at one another.

After a minute, Victoria straightened, adjusted her purse strap over her shoulder, and moved her lips into a passable smile. "I'll be in touch with the details."

When the door closed behind her, I plucked out Dad's whiskey and took a hefty swig.

twenty-two

Willa

D ennis waltzed out from the kitchen, his hair braided today, dressed all in denim save for the checkered Vans on his feet. "Red velvets are ready," he sang, sliding the fresh batch of cupcakes onto a tray from the display cabinet.

I handed Marie Elden, my elementary school teacher, her change and smiled as she and her partner walked out on the street. "I'm going to clean out the storage room."

Dennis straightened, his brows arching high. "For real? You did that two days ago." Eyeing me a minute, he stuck his hands on his hips. "Was it really that bad?"

"What, exactly?" I leaned back against the window beside the till, my eyelids fluttering as the sun warmed my back.

"Seeing the ex, or seeing the stepdad."

My nose wrinkled. Nothing could remain a secret in this place, not that I'd expected it to. Staring at my black flats, I conceded, "Both."

Sympathy tugged at his thin lips. "Are you going back to see him?"

That was the question I'd asked myself time and time again since going to the hospital last week. I knew he had to be going home soon, and there was no way I could visit him there. I wasn't even sure why I felt the need to visit him at all.

When I voiced that, Dennis said, "Because no matter what

he's done, he's still your father, and you're always going to care about him."

And there was the ice-cold truth.

Dennis shooed me ten minutes later, and I climbed inside the same Volkswagen Heath and Victoria had bought me all those years ago. Thanks to my proximity to work, it didn't get used nearly as much as it should and lived behind the bakery in a small carport adjoined to the parking lot.

This time, after some space and letting myself acknowledge the truth, I didn't feel as squeamish as I strode down the hall.

That is, until I knocked on the door and opened it to find Heath wasn't alone.

Jackson sat beside the bed, a laptop open on his lap that they'd both been looking at.

He didn't close it as I walked in. He didn't so much as acknowledge my presence as I stood there, unsure what to do. "I can come back," I offered after an awkward moment.

Heath frowned. "No, no. Take a seat." He gestured to the only other chair left in the room, which was thankfully on the other side of the bed, away from Jackson.

But it didn't matter. We were in the same room, and I wasn't sure how long I could endure it, let alone muster up conversation.

Heath took care of that for me. "Jackson's running the show now, but we've still got contracts and other things to iron out."

I nodded. "You're retiring fully?"

Heath pondered that a moment. "I'll still be present should he need me, but otherwise, yes. Other things matter more."

The clicks of Jackson's typing bounced off the walls, and I cleared my throat. "So, how are you feeling?"

"Good now that you've come back." He smiled, a real genuine smile, and I felt my lips part. "Tell me how school was. Do you have a boyfriend? What's that bakery of yours like? I've heard people will trample their grandmothers for your mini pies and treats."

Struggling to keep up, I struggled with what to answer first. "No boyfriend. I had one, um, in college, for a long while. He's in med school on the West Coast."

"Is that why you broke up?" Heath asked.

I realized then that the typing had ceased, but I kept my eyes fixed on Heath's curious expression. "Sort of." We'd broken up because of my inability to commit to something that was good for me. We'd broken up because I hadn't been fair to him.

We'd broken up because no matter how much time passed, nor how hard I'd tried, I'd forever be in love with my stepbrother.

"And you liked school?"

"I did," I said. I then went on to tell him about some of the classes I'd taken, and the more I talked, the easier it was to ignore the giant asshole in the room.

Heath was all smiling eyes as I explained when I'd moved back, and how I'd come to open the bakery.

"How is Daniel?" Heath asked as I was getting up to leave.

There was no ire or annoyance in the question, only honest intrigue. "Really good. He's been dating." I laughed a little, remembering how I'd set up his profile on one of the dating sites he'd been using. "Using websites and such, though I'm not sure he's using them the way he should."

Heath chuckled at that, then winced, shifting on the bed.

"I need to get back to work, but you're looking a lot better." I smiled. "You can go home soon, right?"

"Two days," Heath said. "Oh, speaking of, your mother's planned this god-awful party for me." Peering up at me, he said, "You'll be there, won't you?"

I swallowed, about to shake my head when Jackson spoke. "She'll be there."

Finally, I looked at him, ready to say… I didn't know. His hair was swept back over top, the sides cropped close to his scalp, making those jade greens luminous. The only vibrancy to an otherwise carefully vacant face.

"Saturday afternoon," Heath said, and I dragged my attention back to him. "Show up whenever you're ready. Stay for as little or as long as you want. We'd just love to see you."

I was tempted to ask what all this change of heart seemed to be about, but I didn't.

It didn't matter what had caused it—whether it be time, regret, a near death experience, or something else.

What mattered was it was happening, and I had to figure out how I felt about it and what to do with it.

With a nod and a small smile, I traipsed to the door, letting it fall closed behind me.

But it didn't close, and a half minute later, I knew why.

"You lied to him," Jackson clipped.

"What?" I stopped, confused. "About what?"

"About the asshole you're with."

"I did no such thing."

He tutted. "Your little bakery is even named after the stupid nickname he gave you."

Observing the tic in his jaw, the curling of his hands at his sides, and the harsh slant of his lowered brows, it finally dawned on me.

It wasn't only the bakery, but the photo of me and Todd in my apartment. The one he'd been holding. "You really believe…" I stopped, laughing. "God, okay. You know what? Keep thinking whatever you want." I waved a hand, then walked on. "Your first assumptions are always the only facts you've ever needed."

My wrist was grabbed before I could reach the end of

the hallway, and I was tugged into a small alcove with a fire extinguisher.

Dark and vibrating, Jackson loomed above me. "You don't get to throw out words like that as if you have the right. You don't get to lie to the people who still give a damn about you, and you definitely don't get to have the last word and then walk away."

I was about to tug my wrist free, but staring up into those haunting eyes, inhaling him with every rushed breath, I thought better of it, and turned my hand over, clasping his.

"I'm not lying." Slowly, my fingers tickled across his skin, and his jaw loosened, nostrils flaring. "And Jackson, I can do whatever I want. I can say whatever I want. And that ego of yours is just going to have to deal with it."

He snatched his hand away, his lips rising a fraction. "You decide to try the sass on now? It's a little too late, and it's not endearing." His eyes raked over my peasant blouse, then returned to mine. "Stick to what you're good at."

"And what's that?" I dared to ask.

"Being meek and stupid." He strode away, brisk and so sure of himself, while I wilted into the shadows of the alcove.

The bell to the bakery jangled, and I rushed out from the kitchen, brushing flour onto my apron. "Hi, what can I..." Words evaporated as I took in the tall blonde bombshell in tight jeans and a fitted emerald green cashmere turtleneck.

"Hi, Willa." Ainsley released the tight hold she'd had on her purse to flutter her fingers. "It's been a while, so I thought it was best I stop by, you know, to see how you're doing." She feigned interest as she glanced around. "You've done a great job with this old place. So cute."

I could hear Dennis returning from his cigarette break, laughing about something with Flo in the kitchen. I prayed they stayed there.

"Thanks," I said, for lack of anything better to say. "Want a cupcake?"

Pursing her lips, Ainsley eyed the pastries before her, then shook her head, tendrils of blond hair shifting over her shoulders. "No, me and carbs still don't agree."

I rocked back on my feet, forcing a smile, and felt my stomach knot as she lifted her hand, the one with the engagement ring, to tuck some hair behind her ear. "So, are you coming to Heath's homecoming?"

It was tomorrow, and I still hadn't decided, but I was leaning toward a definite no. "I'm not sure."

Flo and Dennis walked out, then stopped.

Ainsley made a face, humming in agreement. "I mean, how uncomfortable right?" She laughed. "I couldn't even imagine."

A keening sound came from Flo, and vaguely, I heard Dennis usher her back into the kitchen.

Frowning, I asked, "How so?"

Her laugh was exactly the same, high pitched and breathy. "You know, after everything. It'll probably be awkward is all." She paused as if realizing how she was coming across, then waved a flippant hand. "If you do, though, I'll hang with you and help alleviate any tension."

If I wasn't sure I was wanted there, she'd just given me my answer.

My spine stiffened, my shoulders rising. I pasted on a bright smile. "That's actually real nice of you." Her eyes didn't agree with her smile. "I guess I'll think about it."

After staring at me for a minute that felt as if it'd never end, Ainsley nodded, glancing to the kitchen where hushed words were being spoken, then waved. "Look forward to seeing you, then... if you show."

"Yeah," I said as her hips swayed with each step to the door. "If I show."

"Oh, my god," Dennis said, racing out as soon as Ainsley had hit the sidewalk. "Was that her?"

"Jackson's pretty distraction," Flo said. "Yep." I shot her a scowl, and she shrugged. "It's true. She's always around to be his constant backup plan." She made a gagging sound. "Girl needs some more self-respect."

While I definitely wasn't Ainsley's biggest fan, I didn't know if I agreed with that. If anything, I could empathize with her actions wherever Jackson was concerned.

"She hates that you're coming back into their lives. She was totally just trying to piss all over what's hers and warn you away." Flo quirked a brow. "You have to go now, you know that, right?"

Sighing, I looked from Flo to Dennis, who nodded in agreement, his lips pressed tight. "I know."

twenty-three

Willa

C ars lined the street and spilled out of the driveway, the most noticeable being the large black truck parked right in front of the double garage.

I'd scored a parking spot five doors up outside Mr. McMahon's place, who, judging by the faded garden gnomes, still seemed to live there. Then I'd sat in my car for a solid ten minutes before I finally found enough courage to see this through.

It was strange, almost as if I'd stepped back in time, to be walking up to the house I'd spent most of my childhood and adolescence in. Save for a new roof and updated gardens and plantation shutters, not much about the two-story home had changed. At least, not from the outside.

Being that it would likely be a semi-formal event, even if it was held at home, I'd donned a silken black dress that reached mid-thigh, brown sandals, and a brown floral kimono. My hair fell in loose waves around my shoulders, and I'd kept the makeup minimal with just a touch of mascara and a nude lip balm in case my emotions got the better of me.

Reaching the door, I could hear the laughter and chatter inside, and hesitated with my finger over the doorbell.

I decided against it. The last thing I wanted was to draw anymore unwanted attention to myself than necessary.

As soundlessly as possible, not that many would hear it with the steady hum of music and voices, I closed the door behind me.

Some of my parents' friends stopped talking as I passed the formal living area on my way to the kitchen. I kept my head up, a smile in place, and some familiar faces even smiled back.

I made it to the kitchen without anyone stopping me and thought about running upstairs to hide in my old room. Nostalgia gripped my heart in a fist, squeezing, and then the sound of a drill and the click of a lock scattered any fond memories.

"You made it," a velvet deep voice crooned from behind me.

I was busying myself with pouring a glass of much-needed champagne. "I did."

Jackson leaned against the counter, his scent overbearing and his crisp slate gray dress shirt bunching against the new marble countertop. "I didn't think you'd have it in you."

I chose not to respond, and instead, I drank a greedy gulp of Moet.

"Have you seen your mother yet?"

I shook my head, setting the glass down when I realized I'd drained half of it. I had to drive, and I needed my wits about me to make it through this in one battered piece.

"Where's the sass now?" He continued to poke.

Ainsley's laughter reached my ears, and I finally allowed my eyes to drift up the expanse of his muscled chest to meet his. "I think I lost some when your fiancée paid me a visit yesterday."

Thick brows drew in. "What?"

Licking the sour-sweet from my lips, I slid my thumb beneath my bottom lip. "You heard me." Seemingly dumbfounded, I left him there, my limbs growing warm as I waded through the crowd of colleagues, church goers, and family friends to find Heath in the family room.

Sitting in a wheelchair, he nursed a beer, staring at the TV while Glen, one of his golfing buddies, tried to talk to him. His leg was propped up, a blanket concealing most of it, his gaze weighted with dark shadows.

"Willa?"

My eyes closed, and I sucked in a quick breath before releasing it as I reopened them.

Heath was smiling now, and I smiled back, then felt it droop when the person who'd called my name came into view.

Tears welled in her eyes, and her hands fluttered before her as if she'd reach out and touch me, but thought better of it. "My girl," she breathed.

"Woman," I said, barely a sound, forgetting that other people surrounded us. I said it again when her brows creased with confusion. "I'm a woman now." I held out my glass of champagne for emphasis, taking a sip.

Sucking her lips, Victoria nodded. "And what a beautiful woman you are."

I almost choked, coughing a little. Was she being serious? How could she, after all this time, after the way she'd treated me like I was some abomination, act as though none of it had happened?

"I won't be staying long," I said.

"At least stay for some food. We had a gorgeous cake made, too." Her eyes popped. "I would've asked you, but you never—"

"It's fine."

She nodded again, then glanced around. "Do you mind if we talk?"

"Not here, and I'm not ready." I wasn't sure I'd ever be ready, but for whatever reason, I didn't have the heart to crush hers. For no matter what she'd done, what she'd been capable of, she still had one.

Gazing at me with sorrow deepening the lines of her

forehead, pulling at her mouth, and filling her eyes, she didn't move. Not until one of her friends came and collected her, saying it was time for the speech.

Draining my glass, I placed it on the entertainment unit and ducked my head, giving myself and the tightness in my throat a moment.

Cutlery met glass, and I straightened, turning to find Jackson leaning against the other side of the entryway, mere feet from me.

He forced his attention to my mother, and we all listened as she stood on a chair, her Louboutins below it on the floor, and prattled on about how delicate life was, and how thankful she was that her husband was home, on the road to recovery.

Bile simmered, each word she said creating a storm that refused to pass over. And when it was done, everyone clapping and approaching her and Heath to wish them well, I decided I'd had about enough.

As I was walking down the hall, Heath called, "Willa? Come over here."

Cursing beneath my breath, I backtracked, heading to where he and Victoria were seated in the dining area, guests flocking around them.

Warm and cautious smiles greeted me as I slipped between people and leaned against the wall.

"You must be so glad they're home." Irene, Heath's cousin, patted his shoulder.

"So glad." He grinned, real and bright. "Us Thorns, we need to stick together."

I didn't know why I decided then was the time to burst their bubble, only that there was so much injustice, so much betrayal, and so much hurt, and they'd left me alone to rot with it for years.

"Actually, it's Grayson." Bewilderment swept across the room at large, and softer, more gently, I explained, "My surname. It's now Grayson."

Mom gasped, and Heath's face drained.

I didn't stick around to see what happened next. I didn't run either. Smiling at some of the gawkers, I excused myself for the bathroom but did no such thing.

I'd almost reached the front door, I could almost taste the freedom and fresh night air, when I let my eyes traverse the staircase, the pictures lining the wall.

Pictures of me and Jackson as babies, toddlers, kindergarteners, and the years dragged on as I wound up the stairs, my finger tracing the dusty edges of the gold-embossed frames.

My feet crossed the landing, padding over new carpet to the bedroom closest to the bathroom. The carpet wasn't the only thing they'd replaced. The door with a giant padlock was now gone. My heart pinched as I opened the new one. Inside, I discovered nothing else had really changed.

The items I'd left here were still on the desk and shelves. Books, knickknacks, and a few unfinished scrapbook albums. I made a mental note to get Peggy and Daphne together for a scrapbook date, just like old times, if I survived this mess.

The curtains were open, giving view to the sprawling yard and the rolling hills of the cemetery beyond. When I moved back a step, my legs hit the bed, the mattress dipping as I sat and allowed the burn in my eyes to catch fire.

I'd left the door open, but it was closed a few minutes later, blocking out the noise from downstairs as Jackson entered and leaned back against it. "You changed your name?"

Swiping at the wet streaking my cheeks, I said, "Two years ago. My therapist suggested doing things that made me feel better. That would help me move on."

"Therapist?" Jackson questioned.

I nodded, running damp fingers over the faded bedding.

"And did it? Make you feel better?"

"Yes," I admitted, remembering when I'd gotten confirmation it'd been finalized. "So much better."

"And now?"

Standing, I struggled to make out his expression in the dark, but he was standing next to the light switch, and I wasn't about to get any closer. "What's it matter?"

He lifted his shoulders, slowly prowling forward. "You're crying."

"Not because I regret it, but because of"—I expelled a frustrated breath, waving my hand around the room—"all of it. Everything."

He tilted his head, stopping before me, close enough to notice his tongue slide across his teeth, and how his eyes dipped over every inch of me. "Yet here you are. You willingly walked back into the same hellhole of our own making."

"We didn't make them behave the way they did. That was their choice, and you know it."

He tutted, lifting my chin for our eyes to connect. "Everyone makes choices they feel are best, whether it be right or wrong." With a gleam that spelled arrogance, he added, "You've made quite a few terrible choices of your own."

His firm hold on my chin wasn't exactly comforting, but I couldn't bring myself to remove his fingers. "You've forgiven them?" I couldn't, or maybe I didn't want to, believe that. "Jackson—"

"No," he said. "I might never forgive them, but you're so quick to judge, to trample what they're trying to fix, when you've fucked up in immeasurable ways yourself." He licked his plush lips. "A little hypocritical, don't you think?"

"You," I started, stopping to try to gather words I'd wanted to tell him years ago, if only I'd been given the chance. "You never let me explain."

"What was there to explain? What position you let him fuck you in?"

I sniffed. "Everything. You broke up with me."

"But did I?" His brows rose.

Growling, I shoved his hand off. "Stop it. You know what you did, and you know I would never have done that if you didn't break my heart."

"Oh." He chuckled, the sound void of humor, stabbing a finger at his chest. "I broke your heart?"

"Yes," I said, wanting to scream it at him. My chest was heaving, his eyes heavy on it as I struggled to gather some composure. As I struggled to make my feet carry me to the door.

He caught my hand before I could make it, and then I was against the wall, and his forehead was against mine. "In the battle of who hurt who the most, you fucking won, Willa."

"I won nothing," I breathed, his lips so close to mine, I shivered when I inhaled his exhale.

Then, because I was a fool who hadn't learned anything, I rose onto my toes, and grabbed his head. "I lost everything."

Jackson groaned, deep and guttural, as soon as our lips touched. It wasn't soft, and it wasn't special. It was hard and aggressive, his hands gripping my face as our teeth and tongues vied for dominance.

A knock on the door had him cursing and stumbling back, his eyes filled with the type of horror even darkness couldn't hide.

"Jackson?" Ainsley said. "The food is ready."

She knew. She knew we were both in here. The satisfaction I felt over that was quick to morph into shame.

He didn't wait or even fix his hair. Jackson tore open the door, and without so much as a backward glance, he disappeared.

My fingers opened and closed, seeking the soft strands of his hair, the coarse bristle upon his cheeks. I lifted them to my lips and closed my eyes, flopping against the wall.

Ten minutes later, I walked downstairs and straight out the front door.

twenty-four

Jackson

Heartbreak and peril had never tasted so sweet.

Staring up at the ceiling, I watched the silver blades of the fan twirl as the sound of her fluttering sighs and tiny husky moans planted themselves deeper into my psyche.

Her sweet scent, the desperate clawing of her hands, and the way her lips had fit so seamlessly to mine... I was a fucking idiot.

A fucking idiot who was engaged.

"Jack." The bed dipped as Ainsley took a seat by my feet, braiding her hair. "You okay?"

I hated it when she called me Jack. I'd told her that years ago, and still, sometimes she slipped. Now wasn't the time to remind her. Now was the time to remind myself of what a giant jackass I was.

Clearing my throat, I forced my eyes to hers. "Fine. Just tired."

Nodding, she pressed a hand against my leg over the white duvet. "It's been a crazy month."

She wasn't wrong. I yawned and stretched my arms above my head, wondering if I could erase what I'd done with a long morning run.

"I don't want to add to it," she said, her tone cautious. "But..."

Shit. "But what?"

Her lip disappeared behind her teeth, hesitation wringing her hands. "Well, I want to set a date."

Feigning confusion would be a total dick move, and I was a total dick. I knitted my brows. "For the wedding?"

Her laughter was soft, even as her eyes rolled. "Duh." Giving me a gentle look, she sighed. "Look, I know this has been a hard time for you, and I'm not asking for us to walk down the aisle tomorrow, but it would make me feel a lot better if we could at least agree on a date."

When she'd asked me to marry her, I'd thought she'd been joking. Thankfully, I hadn't released the laugh that wanted out at the time. I'd swallowed it, and my damn heart, when I'd realized she was serious.

I could never tell myself why it was that I'd agreed to it. I loved her, sure. I loved her in all the ways I was capable of loving someone after I'd had my heart and soul stolen by another. Forever halfway in.

But I'd thought, if this is as good as it gets, then I needed to snatch it. I needed the next best thing. The next best chance at living a happy life. For there weren't many women who'd be able to love me the way Ainsley did.

Who'd be able to accept a past that'd robbed me. Who'd be able to love me enough for the both of us.

I never thought I'd see Willa again, and if I ever did, then I never predicted it to go down the way it had. I'd been naïve in thinking she could no longer slither beneath my skin and poison me. Time didn't change someone's effect on you; it merely hid it from you long enough to believe it could.

"I can't," I heard myself saying. "I can't do that," I said it again, as if just realizing the truth inside the admission. "I'm sorry."

"What do you mean?" Disbelieving laughter followed her question. Then she was up, pacing the room, her eyes ablaze with hurt. "Jesus Christ, Jackson. Still? I thought we were done with this."

"Done with what?" I asked because I was a moron like that.

Stopping, she flung a hand at me. "With *her*. You promised me."

I never promised her anything, but I suppose by giving her that ring, I had. "It's over, and it has been for a long time. There's nothing to worry about."

As I sat up, the duvet sliding down my chest, her eyes followed before closing. "Then why were you in the bedroom with her last night?"

I'd thought it strange she hadn't asked about that on the drive home. "She was crying, and I was annoyed she'd changed her surname. I didn't think she'd do something like that." Tipping a shoulder, I shifted to slide my legs out of bed. "So we talked."

"You talked?" she repeated, the words dangerously bland.

"Yes."

"Why would you care about her changing her surname?"

I didn't. That had been a lie. In fact, the teeny tiny part of me that didn't hate her was proud she'd taken such a stand for herself. "I don't really."

"You just said it annoyed you."

I huffed, running a hand over my cheek, containing a groan. "It annoyed me how she'd admitted it. The way it'd all gone down." Dropping my hand, I let out a loud breath. "Can this wait until I've done my run and grabbed some coffee? I'm still half asleep here."

A caustic laugh split her pursed lips. "You're unbelievable, Jackson."

She didn't even know the half of it.

I'd tell her. But not right now. "You're going to be late."

"I'm going to be late?" She seemed to like repeating me, and it was grating, to say the least. "All I want is a date, Jackson. Pick a month and pick a number."

"I told you," I said, standing and walking to the dresser to pull out my running shorts. "I can't do that."

"When can you do that?"

Slamming the drawer, I turned and folded my arms over my bare chest. "I don't know, okay? I really don't fucking know."

"Why agree to marry me then?" She was yelling now, and I blinked, the crazed look in her eyes unsettling. Gesturing to the diamonds on her finger, she almost screamed, "What is the damn point of wearing this stupid ring if you have no desire to follow through with what it stands for?"

Meeting her eyes, I struggled to find words, wishing there was a way I could make her understand the impossible. That couldn't happen. Not when I didn't even know what I was thinking myself.

With tears glassing her eyes, she threw her hands up and stormed out of the room. "Enjoy your run. I won't be here when you get back."

"Ains," I said, following her.

The door closed in my face.

I thought she'd just been trying to piss me off, but I'd thought wrong.

When I returned, I found our closet door open, and half her shit and two of her suitcases gone.

I dropped the bottle of bourbon to the sidewalk, then banged my fist on the door.

I had no idea why I was here; all I knew was the alcohol had done nothing to calm me down. The anger climbed, hot and steady, simmering and bubbling to the surface, and it needed out.

In a purple satin robe with what looked to be hummingbirds on it, her hair in a small mess atop her head, and clean faced, Willa opened the door. "Jackson?"

I pushed my way in, pacing the small foyer in quick strides. "You just have to ruin everything, don't you?"

"Excuse me?" The door slipped from her hand, slamming as she stepped closer.

I stopped, stabbing a finger at her. "You know damn well what I'm talking about. You seem so fucking sweet, so damn naïve and fucking innocent, but it's all a pretty lie," I hissed the last words at her.

Her eyes rounded, her bow-shaped lips parting with a harsh exhale. "Are you drunk?"

"What I am has nothing to do with you. Nothing," I seethed, getting right up in her perfect face. "Yet you've found a way to fuck it all up anyway."

"Are you talking about the party?" She licked her lips, her gaze dropping, cheeks filling with color. "Because I didn't plan on—"

"That's just it. You never plan anything; you act on impulse. On feelings you haven't thought through, and you wreck other people's plans and lives."

Swallowing, she nodded once. "I think you should go." She drifted to the stairs, then raced up them.

Before she could close her apartment door, I was there, pushing it open.

She staggered back, gasping, the soft glow coming from two lamps in her living room highlighting her wet cheeks. "Jackson, please."

"She left. She's gone, and it's all because of you." The words were rough, falling out on a hoarse breath.

Her slender shoulders tensed, her hand moving to her mouth. "I'm sorry, I didn't think—"

"You never fucking think, and don't for one second act like you give a damn." The door squeaked closed behind me as I waded farther into her apartment, the tips of my shoes meeting her bare toes. "We both know you don't."

Her eyes narrowed, her hand falling to her side, as her shoulders squared. "Fuck you." A low, breathy laugh traveled with her next words. "How long can you blame me for something you did, Jackson?"

I scowled, my fists clenching. "Fucking *what?*"

"You heard me," she said, daring to move closer as I moved back toward the door. "How long are you going to peg all the blame for what happened to us, for what is now happening to you, on me?"

"For as long as you're at fault." I smirked. "Forever."

Her hand flicked out, knocking a vase to the floor. Flowers and water flooded the wood, cracked porcelain laying in five different sized pieces. "You're an egocentric asshole. You always have been, and I see now that will never change." She wasn't yelling, but she was growling, emotion and fury drenching each word. "You concocted some fucked-up plan to help me get into college and left me to stew over what was happening to us for months. I was eighteen, you fucking asshole. I was eighteen, lost, confused, and so scared."

With her back to me, she dug her nails into her hair, sending the tie to the floor and her hair around her shoulders. "You could've told me. You think I cheated on you?" She turned around. "You cheated on me first. You lied to me first. You devised a plan to use another girl to hurt me. You," she wheezed, her finger shaking as she pointed at me, "you cheated first, you failed me first, and that's why you're so angry, so full of hatred. Because we both know it's true. We both know if you'd had enough balls and foresight to communicate with me, I never would've done what I did."

"Bullshit," I rasped, even as my chest caved inward, stealing my breath.

"No," she said with a humorless laugh. "Not bullshit."

"You fucked someone else."

"You kissed someone else. You broke my heart on purpose, believing I'd what?" She sniffed, shaking her head. "That I'd just take it? That I'd wait for you to come and fix it?"

I couldn't answer, and we both knew why.

Moving too close, she murmured, "I waited for months, Jackson. I waited, and I tried, and still, we drifted apart. Part of that might have been your intent, to make it believable, but come on." Her smile was sad, her eyes too, as they sank into mine. "We were struggling regardless."

"We would've made it."

She tipped a shoulder, nodding. "We might have." Her lashes fluttered, a bead of salt sitting upon her bottom lash, waiting to be sent down her cheek. "We'll never know, and maybe, we weren't supposed to." With that, she turned away, heading down the short hall into the dark. "You can see yourself out."

I crossed the room, my boots crunching over flowers and further cracking the porcelain. "Don't walk away from me."

She spun back just as I reached her, her brows lowered and a response ready on her tongue.

I grabbed her face, swallowing whatever she was going to say with my next inhale, and forced her back to the wall.

With a squeak, she pushed at my chest, then clung to my shirt, fisting it in her tiny hands as her tongue stroked mine, and I angled her head back, allowing better access.

"We can't," she said between kisses that drugged.

"That's never stopped us before," I said, licking her silken upper lip.

Then she was lifting my shirt, and I groaned as her skin met mine. My spine pulled taut as electricity strangled every muscle, and every breath turned weighted.

I broke away long enough to tear it off, her hands moving to the fly of my jeans as mine fumbled with the tie of her robe, our lips hovering and desperate to stay connected.

Her robe slipped down her arms, and desperation fled in the face of savoring what stood before me.

Her pale skin was unchanged. My gaze absorbed the tiny freckle next to her belly button, the rosy buds of her pert nipples, and the gentle curve of her hips.

They flared more now, creating an hourglass figure that begged to be traced, to be squeezed, to be devoured and appreciated in every way. "Christ, Bug."

At hearing the nickname, her eyes roamed up my chest, locking with mine. A million memories warred with what-ifs, and consequences be damned, I needed her.

Her breasts heaved, heavier, but no less perfect, and her cheeks flushed with want. "Touch me."

My eyes slammed closed, and I pinched the bridge of my nose, trying to shake some sense into myself. All that went to hell when I felt my jeans being lowered, along with my briefs, and I opened my eyes to find Willa on her knees.

"Willa."

Her hand wrapped tight around me, and although her gaze was fixed on mine, she didn't wait. Her tongue snaked out, licking at the want she'd caused to leak from the tip, and then I was sliding inside her warm mouth.

I almost collapsed, my ears ringing and my balls drawing

tight. Her tongue and hand worked together, stroking and pulling, sucking and twisting. I was going to come, and it took every ounce of restraint to keep from doing so.

I couldn't remember the last time I'd been about to explode like this. So quick and with hardly any preamble.

It was her.

Always fucking her.

Bending, I pulled her up and shucked off my shoes and jeans, then I grabbed her hand and tugged her to her room.

It was dark, and though I longed to see every inch of her, I was too far gone to seek any form of light.

At the foot of her bed, I gathered her to me, my hands gliding down her back as our lips slid over one another. Inside her panties, I squeezed her ass, then palmed it, my cock pressing into her stomach as our bodies melded. Her little moans, the tender way in which her hand held my cheek and the other ran down my side, had me shivering and then breaking away.

"On the bed," I croaked.

Lust-filled eyes shone up at me, every barrier stripped bare in the moonlight as I crawled between her legs and paused.

"Jack," she whispered, hands cupping my face, forcing my eyes to hers. "Get inside me."

I didn't even test her opening. I knew she'd be soaked, and I was right.

My head fell to her neck as I slid inside, bare and fucking blind with need. "Shit, Willa." I went to pull out, but her nails scored into my shoulders, and her thighs tightened.

"No," she whispered. "If you're going to fuck me, you do it the only way we know how. Nothing between us."

I was going to combust or cry. My head swam, and I pulled out, rolling out of her hold and off the bed.

"I can't." Dragging my knuckles over my forehead, I left the room.

"You just did," she said, tears in her voice as she raced after me.

"Willa, stop," I said, that anger returning.

"No, you fucking coward. You went too far, and now you need to finish what you've started."

My brows jumped, my dick a rock-hard burn between us as I glared into her hazel eyes. "Did you need to beg that asshole to fuck you too?"

I heard the sound of her hand striking my face before I even felt the sting. "Get out. I'll finish myself off to thoughts of anything but you."

"Real mature," I called, following her back into her room.

"Fuck off, Jackson."

"Never." I pulled her back flush to my chest, then fisted her hair to one side. She moaned as I walked us to the bed, dropping kisses to her neck, my tongue sliding out to skim her delicate jaw. Releasing her hair, I growled, "Bend over."

She did, folding like a flower in the breeze, her back arching.

My finger traced her ass, sliding down until it found her wet cunt, then I slapped the inside of her thigh. "Open up."

Before she'd finished adjusting her footing, I was sinking inside, my head falling back as her wet heat tightened around me.

I didn't care that I was coming within minutes. Fast and hard, I fucked her, my hands gripping those perfect hips as she rocked forward with each brutal thrust.

I kept bringing her back, milking myself as her cries permeated the room, and all too soon, I pulled out, coming all over her lower back and ass. My entire body shook, my knees quaking, and before I could even see straight, she was climbing over the bed.

Shaking my head to help clear it, I quickly grabbed her ankle and pulled her back to me.

Willa squeaked. "Your semen's now all over my bed."

"I don't give a fuck." I spread her thighs. "I'm not done."

Whatever response she'd formed exited on a garbled sigh of pleasure as my hands tightened around her thighs, and my mouth feasted on her.

The sound of a phone ringing opened my eyes.

They then immediately closed against a room lit up with bright rays of sunshine. Groaning, I tried to move, but the body curved against mine had me stilling.

My hand clenched around a smooth hip, and my rock-hard dick... holy shit, it was still inside her.

Willa.

Swamped with a kaleidoscope of filthy memories, it only grew harder, and I heard a soft mewl in response.

In at least four different positions, I'd fucked her. Three of them being during the night, the last one taking place when we'd woken wanting more. Slow and deep, we'd collided and clung, and then we'd passed out. The last thing I remembered before it was lights out was kissing her shoulder and neck, feeling myself soften inside her.

The phone rang again. Realizing it was mine, I carefully moved Willa off me, rubbing my eyes as I stumbled into the small hall to retrieve it from my jeans.

Three missed calls from Ainsley, plus a text saying she was sorry, then asking where I was.

Fuck.

Fuck, fuck, fuck.

Torn, I stared at the screen of my phone when it rang again, then looked back at the room I'd just vacated.

I jumped when there was a knock on the door, then frowned at my phone. There was no way…

After tugging on my clothes, I marched to the door, dodging the water and pieces of broken vase, then paused to draw in a steadying breath. Time to face the music.

Only, when I opened it, Ainsley wasn't there.

About to knock again, Todd lowered his hand, his other holding a tray with two takeout cups. "Um, what?"

"Yeah, my thoughts exactly," I said, throwing the door closed with a bang.

"Jackson?" Willa's sleep-coated voice reached me. "Who is it?"

She was tying her robe, her hair tangled and her lips swollen.

And I was the biggest idiot alive.

Checking my phone was in my pocket, I felt my hands shake with building rage.

"Jack?"

"Don't say that."

Her lips pursed, her large eyes searching, as she reached for my arm. "Don't tell me you regret it?"

Shoulders squaring, I stepped back. "I'd need to feel something in order to feel regret," I said. "And I feel nothing." Staring down the bridge of my nose, I held her gaze, glaring as I backed up to the door. "Thanks for helping me screw loose what little I still felt." I grinned, sharp and sincere. "I'm good now. Enjoy your life."

Her face crumpled, but I was already breezing out the door, shoulder checking the asshole on the other side before racing down the stairs.

twenty-five

Willa

"Tell me again how you just allowed that scumbag back into your life?"

"I haven't," I said, crossing my arms defensively as we skirted people on the street.

After Jackson left, I'd told Todd to come in and said I'd be out soon.

Under the spray of the shower, I'd spent a solid ten minutes feeling like I'd taken a thousand steps backward, the water washing each shredded piece of misery from my face.

"That's not what it looked like to me."

"I was wondering when you'd bring it up," I muttered.

Todd huffed, kicking at a pebble. "It seemed too fresh to bring up this morning."

"It was just..." I crinkled my nose. "It just kind of happened." Remembering his words and feeling the sour ache of regret, I said, "It won't again."

"Uh-huh," Todd said.

The fact he didn't seem jealous, not even a tiny bit, pricked. Not in a bad way, but in a way that made me curious. "What's going on with you?" We'd already discussed med school, his job at the pharmacy near school, and his mother and sister who he'd come to visit. There was something new, though. Not only could I feel it, but I could see it.

Something that brightened his eyes and smile as he looked at me, and said, "What do you mean?"

"You know what I mean. Have you met someone?"

We reached the steak house, and he opened the door for me. "I have, actually."

The hostess greeted us, showing us to a booth in the back. "Well?" I said, sliding my purse off my shoulder to the table. "That's all I get?"

Arching a brow, he asked, "Do you really want to know more?"

I didn't want to hurt him, and I didn't want to hurt myself either, but I wanted him to be happy. I wanted to hear about this person who'd delivered a glimpse of his soul to his eyes. "I really do."

"Todd?"

Todd and I both looked in the direction his name had come from.

Ainsley, looking pale, peered around the restaurant, her eyes and tone accusatory. "What are you doing here?"

Seeming baffled, Todd closed the distance between them, gesturing to me. "I told you I was in town to see family and a friend."

If looks could kill, the one Ainsley sent me would've killed me ten times over.

I struggled not to sink into the pleather seat. "Oh, shit."

"Ains," Jackson called from the bar. Noticing who she was with, he then said something to the bartender and walked over.

Todd's demeanor changed, from confused to defensive, as Ainsley slid around him to Jackson's side. "Ainsley," he said, blinking. "Wait, you're..." He couldn't even finish his sentence, his hand swiping hard over his mouth, his feet carrying him a step back.

HEARTS AND THORNS | 231

Jackson looked from Ainsley to Todd, then to me.

I said nothing. Not that I had anything to say anyway.

"How do you know him?" When all Ainsley did was blink away tears, her hands strangling her purse in front of her, Jackson's tone and jaw hardened as he repeated himself. "Ainsley, how do you know him?"

The few other patrons surrounding us ceased chattering, a strange quiet descending over the restaurant. "I only just met him," she finally said, her eyes stuck on Todd. "Yesterday."

Todd muttered what sounded like, "Fuck this," then walked right up to Ainsley and whispered, none too quietly, "Are you going to tell him what we did after meeting yesterday?"

If I heard Todd, then Jackson did too, yet he didn't move, didn't seem to breathe, as he stared at nothing on the other side of the room. Then, before I could get up, he was exiting the restaurant, Ainsley calling out to him as she followed.

Todd slumped into the opposite side of the booth, waving down a waitress. "Bourbon. Bring the bottle."

I leaned over the table. "You slept with Ainsley?"

He licked his lips, blowing out a gust of air. "Yup."

"Care to elaborate?" I waved a hand. "Given the circumstances and all."

Todd scratched at his cheek, contemplating, then sighed. "Yesterday, I pulled into the rest stop outside of town to take a piss, and there she was, crying at a damn picnic table."

"And you just...?" I felt my eyes bulge.

He chuckled, then coughed. "No. Well, not right away. I spent some time chatting with her. Time got away from us. We ate. We drank." He nodded a few times, making a face. "Then the sun was going down, and we, ah, got a room."

Wow. "She never once mentioned Jackson?"

"Nope, and she said it was over, so I didn't ask what his

name was." Shrugging, he gave me his eyes. "Would've fucking helped."

"Maybe," I said, wincing a little. "I'm sorry." Taking his hand, I squeezed it. "You seemed excited about her."

"Yeah," he said, thanking the waitress who set down a bottle and glass. "Perhaps it's past time to admit I have a fetish for heartbroken girls."

Todd crashed on my couch. We watched *The Wedding Singer* and got drunk, and he left for his mom's the following morning with a nasty hangover to go with his bruised feelings.

Almost two weeks had passed since the weekend that seemed to have upended so many lives.

I'd lost count of how many times a day Jackson entered my mind. I wondered how he was doing, what he was doing, and if I should do anything.

His parting words to me in my apartment had me drowning in indecision and taking no action.

I set the rolling pin down when the bell tinkled. Dennis was busy serving other people, so I knew he could use some help. Dusting my hands on my apron, I pasted on a smile that was quick to wilt when my eyes found Victoria.

She twisted side to side in her navy blue sundress and matching peacoat, her gaze bouncing over the interior, so it took her a moment to notice I was watching her.

"Oh." She tittered, her hand flapping to her chest, feet carrying her forward. "You scared me."

Words failed me, so I stood, silent, allowing her to further ruffle her own feathers.

"You've done a brilliant job with this place," she said, her smile shaking. "I remember when it was a cheap diner. It always had this strange smell, do you remember?" Laughing, she nodded to herself. "Never mind. I see you've remedied that situation."

"Dad and some of his friends helped." I decided to put her out of her misery. "How's Heath?"

Her teeth tugged at her cherry red bottom lip. "He's good."

She was lying, but far be it from me to dig deeper. "That's good."

The chatter of customers drifted, fading out into the muted sunlight as we struggled to find words to blanket what we really wanted to say.

Dennis jumped into the fray; his hand stuck toward Victoria. "You must be our lovely boss's mother. I'm amazing, also known as Dennis."

Victoria tilted her head, then let her hand slip into his gentle grip. "That's a beautiful shirt."

Dennis grinned, releasing her hand to tug at his bright pink T-shirt.

Victoria drank in his tight jeans and the hot pink high tops on his feet, struggling to keep her expression neutral.

"The recipes you dropped by, I took some home." Dennis paused, scratching his bent nose. "I hope you don't mind."

Victoria's eyes swung to me, then back to him, smiling. "No. Of course, not."

"The chicken curried pie?" Dennis groaned. "My wife just about proposed to me."

Victoria's smile grew warm, real, as the two talked about Dennis's daughter and his wife, and the small firm his wife worked at in the next town over.

Grateful for the distraction, I returned to the counter and tidied up the crumbs and receipts around the till.

On the way to the door, Victoria stopped. "Would you consider coming to dinner this Friday night?"

Dropping tongs into the tin of sanitizer, I looked up. "Um…"

She floated over, gripping her purse in front of her. "Ainsley and Jackson have been coming by these past few weeks. We'd love to make it," she faltered, shifting, "you know, a family thing."

A family thing.

Ainsley and Jackson…

"Wait, they're still together?" I knew it was a stupid thing to say the second the words vacated my mouth, but the panic sliding down my body, tugging at every organ, didn't give a damn.

Victoria laughed. "Of course." Frowning, she said, "But you knew that already."

Florence thankfully chose that moment to return from her break, waltzing in the door with fake cheer. Sensing the tension, she immediately introduced herself, and she and Dennis saw Victoria out as I faded on the spot.

Victoria waved, trying to say something over her shoulder, but as soon as the door closed behind her, I was gone.

Inside the bathroom, the whirring fan overhead hid the heaving breaths that escaped, scraping my throat and lungs raw.

Flo and Dennis were banging on the door a minute later, and after giving myself another minute, I opened it.

"Well, she didn't seem so bad," Flo said.

"A little uptight," Dennis said, bobbing his head. "But nothing some sugar can't fix."

I wanted to laugh. I wanted to cry. I wanted to scream. I did nothing but stand there, listening to them prattle on.

Then, finally, Dennis's brows knitted as his eyes studied me. "You okay?"

"She has this nasty effect on her," Flo said.

I shook my head. "It's not her."

Dennis took me by the shoulders, directing me to the stool in the kitchen, and pulled a batch of brownies he'd made from the oven.

"What is it?" Flo said, then her eyes bulged. "Oh, hell. What's he done?"

Wiping his hands, Dennis leaned over the counter. "Spill."

"It's not so bad, kind of like chicken." Dad held up a forkful of his roasted chicken, grinning.

I crinkled my nose, smiling. "Still a snail, so it's still disgusting."

Coming over for dinner was the last thing I'd wanted to do, but I'd promised when he'd called a few days ago. Plus, I hadn't seen him since before finding out about Heath.

"Okay," Dad said, dropping his cutlery and grabbing his beer. "That was the most pitiful attempt at a smile I've seen from you in months." Taking a sip of beer, he said, "What's up?"

He knew Jackson was back, but he didn't know of our tumultuous encounters. I wanted to keep it that way.

I stared at my half-eaten dinner for a moment before saying, "Victoria came by the bakery today."

"As she often does."

I shook my head, struggling to meet his assessing gaze. "She came inside this time."

Dad whistled, watching me a moment. "She know you call her Victoria?"

Frowning, I pushed my plate away. "I don't know, maybe. Why does it matter?"

Lifting a shoulder, he downed more beer, sighing as he set the bottle on the table. "I imagine it'd matter a great deal to her."

"I can't just forget it," I said. "And that's what she wants me to do."

"What she's done?" Dad pushed.

I nodded.

He hummed, scraping a nail over the label on the glass bottle. "Maybe she's not expecting you to forget. Maybe she's just after forgiveness."

"She hasn't said sorry."

Dad quirked a brow. "She's been saying it in other ways."

Frustration heaved a loaded breath from me, pulling at my brows. "Since when have you been her fan?"

"Never," he said with a chuckle. "I can't stand the woman, but that doesn't mean I don't respect her to some extent."

"Why?" I said, pushing my chair back. "Ugh, don't worry. I should head home."

"Not yet," Dad said, and I looked back at him, noticing the wary look in his eyes as they danced over me. Sighing, he muttered, "I need another beer for this."

I waited until he'd returned, wondering what his deal was, and why everything seemed to be upside down when I so desperately needed for it to be right side up.

You couldn't fix or change other people's opinions, decisions, or actions, and I was growing tired of feeling as though I could no longer predict what would happen next.

As soon as he'd taken a seat, he dropped the bomb. "She's not your mom."

Four words. Four rushed words entering the air and my ears.

"What?" I wheezed, blinking, as if doing so would help me hear better. I had to be losing my mind.

The lines framing Dad's mouth deepened, and when his eyes met mine, they shined. "Your mother's name was Sara Elizabeth

Dean. I met her while on leave, spent a solid two months with her. It was fun until it wasn't." He pinched the bridge of his nose. "She had a voice that would knock you off your feet. Sweet and airy. I could listen to her talk for hours." A wistful smile chased some of the darkness from his eyes. "Her heart was ginormous, and her sense of adventure..." He chuckled, shaking his head. "I've never met anyone like it."

Shock and fear and sorrow crowded within my chest. I couldn't move if I wanted to, could scarcely draw a breath without my throat swelling each time.

"You're a lot like her," he said. "But I'll give Victoria the chance to tell you about her. They were close. As close as two opposites can get." Taking a moment, he stared at our plates, then cleared his throat. "She wrote me while I was away, telling me that she was pregnant. I couldn't leave, and she didn't ask me to. She said she'd be fine, and that hopefully one day, I could meet you."

"One day?" I managed, bewildered.

"We weren't..." Dad stopped, scratching at his beard. "We had fun, Wil. But for as carefree as she seemed, she was troubled. With the help of Victoria, she managed to get clean while pregnant, but then she relapsed—"

My chest exploded. "She was a drug addict?"

Dad nodded. "Yeah." He nodded again, the dining chair creaking as he shifted. "She, um"—he blew out a breath—"she relapsed and overdosed when she was around eight months pregnant. You were born five weeks premature."

But the name change. He'd been there. He had helped me gather what was needed for the process.

Seeing the question in my eyes, he added, "Victoria was her sister, her next of kin, so she signed your birth certificate."

"She overdosed," I muttered, staring unseeing at the table.

I knew she was gone. I'd known it since he'd uttered those four words, and perhaps somewhere deep down, I'd known it all along too. Still, the blow rattled something loose inside me, sending ashes of grief sailing through my veins.

"They kept her on life support for two weeks, waiting for your lungs to develop further, and then…" He didn't need to finish. "It's one of my biggest regrets. That I couldn't be there. I didn't know," he said, his voice breaking. "I had no idea until it was all over, and Victoria contacted me with the funeral arrangements."

Dad let me sit with all he'd said for untold minutes as he finished his beer, his gaze heavy on my head as I stared at my hands. I squeezed them together, over and over, watching my skin turn white, then redden, trying to lessen the tremors.

"Your grandparents had written Sara off years before you arrived. Victoria was all she had, and in turn, all you had. In a sense, she rescued you, raised you when I couldn't, and loved you like you were hers and hers only."

Dad huffed. "I was thankful, at first. So fucking relieved you had someone to look out for you and to be there when I couldn't be. But as the years passed, I began to grow up, and she grew more possessive, and I knew." He put his bottle down with a thump. "I just knew she'd never tell you. That she'd cover your existence in pretty lies and dress it up as normal."

"Would she have ever told me?" I looked up then, my blood running cold. "How can someone live with a secret that huge?"

Dad mulled over that for a few beats. "The way I see it, no. And though how you came to be might have been a secret, one thing shouldn't be forgotten here." His eyes met mine, solid warmth and unyielding sincerity. "For all her faults, she is still, and will always be, your mother."

"She's a liar," I exhaled.

"True, but she loves you. She loves you as if you're hers. I've often wondered if it's because she believes that to be true, or if it's because she loved Sara with a devotion I've never encountered from siblings before." Dad tapped the table. "You ever wonder why someone as fancy-pants as Victoria purchased a house that sat atop a cemetery?"

My eyes rounded, a tear trickling down my cheek. "Oh, my god."

Dad's lips pressed together. "They grew up here. Moved away in their teens."

"Why now?" I heard myself ask. "Why tell me now? So I'd what, go easier on her?"

"Something like that. You know I never knew my own parents, have no idea who they are." He'd grown up in foster care. "I didn't want that for you. I'd always planned on telling you when I thought you were ready. But planning and doing are different things. When was a good time to upset you? You've already been through enough."

I was up and out of my chair, making a beeline for the door.

"Willa." Dad followed, grabbing my car door when I'd climbed inside. "Jesus. What are you doing?"

"Whatever I need to," I said, yanking on the door. When he wouldn't budge, I glared at him. "You need to let me."

Moonlight washed over his grave expression, defeat sagging his shoulders and loosening his grip on the door. "Drive carefully, and at the very least, text me when you get home."

The drive was a blur, my mind in overdrive as everything Dad confessed tried to settle within my head and heart.

A crazed laugh shuddered out, tears dripping down my cheeks, as I wound through the backstreets of the cove. It all made so much sense. So much dizzying sense.

Since I'd known how children came into being, I'd always

thought Dad and Victoria had some type of one-night stand. I was never corrected, and I was never steered in another direction when I'd implied as much to Victoria before Dad had moved to the cove.

I didn't notice the extra cars in the drive. I didn't care. I parked on the street and crossed it, heading straight for the door and letting myself in.

Ainsley's laughter filled the hall, and I followed it to the dining room, where she, Victoria, Heath, and Jackson were eating dinner.

"Willa," Heath said, beaming and dropping his fork.

Jackson's eyes shot up, but I ignored him, my focus, all my frantic energy trained on the woman with the perfect updo and drooping smile. "Willa." She pushed her chair back, standing. "What's the matter?"

"You might want to remain seated, Mother." A strange sound left me, maybe a laugh, maybe a wail, maybe both, as her forehead scrunched. "I know." I nodded. "I know everything. Everything you never thought I deserved to know."

Victoria swallowed, her eyes welling, her question strained. "How?"

"What's going on?" Ainsley asked.

I wanted to scream at her, but I wasn't here for that.

I was here to watch the blood drain from the face of the liar standing before me. I was here to make her feel even an ounce of what she'd made me feel. Years ago when I was eighteen, reckless, and in love, and now, twenty-four, hollowed and defeated. All thanks to her.

"This isn't the place," Heath spoke up. "Willa, you and your mother should talk. How about you two—"

"You knew?" I said to Heath, my eyes still fixed on Victoria. A humorous huff departed my cracked lips. "Of course. Everyone but me." I didn't remove my gaze as I said, "How about you, Jackson? How long have you known my entire life has been a lie?"

Jackson cursed, a chair screeched over the floor.

"Don't," Heath said. "He doesn't know, Willa."

My brows jumped, tears sliding down my cheeks. Victoria was shaking her head now, inching a step closer to me. "Don't you dare," I whispered.

"Willa," Jackson said. "What's happened?"

"She happened." I sniffed.

"Please," Victoria murmured, her lips wobbling. "You can judge me all you want, you can hate me, but we need to talk about this properly."

"Talk about fucking what?" Jackson hollered, out of patience.

"Jackson," Heath warned.

"Either tell me what's going on here, or shut the fuck up, Dad."

"She's not my mom." I slid back a step, smiling now. "She never was. Not only because mothers don't treat their children how she did, but because her dead sister, the one practically buried in our backyard, is my real mother."

Victoria screamed as I raced out of there, and I heard something smash.

Inside my car, my heart thundering through every limb, I could hardly see. I pulled over on the next street and turned the ignition off, my head falling back against the headrest.

Cars zoomed by, the streets growing quiet as the time on the dash neared nine.

My eyes cleared. Eventually, I unleashed enough sorrow to ease the weight on my chest and to take note of my surroundings.

Wiping my nose on my sleeve, I snickered as I thought of what Victoria would say, and then I saw it.

There were no streetlights looming above, but there were

solar lights scattered throughout the hills and dips of sprawling green. I stepped out of the car, wrapping my cardigan tighter around me, the wind drying the damp upon my cheeks.

It didn't take me long to find her. Two houses down from ours, she sat upon the hill, overlooking the mass of memories beyond. With trembling fingers, and a heart to match, I trailed them along the grooves of her name.

Sara Elizabeth Dean.

She was twenty years old when she died. Already, I'd lived more of a life than she had, all the while never knowing who she was. "I'm sorry," I whispered.

She might have been an addict, but the thought of having a child, and of that child not even knowing of your existence had me saying it again. "I'm sorry."

Wilting flowers were tucked close to the headstone. Victoria's favorite. Daffodils. The silken texture crumbled within my fingers, and I rested my head against the cool marble, watching the breeze carry the remains downhill.

Soft swishing, and then an exhaled breath, as Jackson sat down beside me. His hand was warm in mine, a tether to something real.

If it had been broken, it was real. For perfection, I'd learned, was often the lie.

For minutes, or maybe hours, the moon a white button against a dark gray sky, he said nothing, and I didn't even try.

When my lips finally cracked apart, my voice was low and hoarse. "How can you forgive Ainsley, but not me?"

He answered instantly. "Because I don't, and I never will, love anything the way I love you."

Then he was gone.

twenty-six

Willa

A week passed before I finally let myself acknowledge what I needed.

And what I needed wasn't explanations or apologies.

It was knowledge.

Next door to the same ice-cream parlor we'd visit after church as kids, Victoria waited outside the café.

She didn't remove her sunglasses as I approached, but she did offer a weak smile. She went to stand, but I motioned for her to stay seated.

With a calm I'd practiced inside my head on the walk over, I lowered into the opposite metal seat, set my purse in my lap, and asked, "Have you ordered?"

"I can't have kids."

My exhale faltered. "I'd really rather we order a—"

"I had a hysterectomy when I was sixteen. Endometriosis. My parents were sick of the constant hospital visits."

My lashes fluttered closed, and I sucked in a fortifying breath. "Victoria."

"Please," she said, and the way she'd said it, without desperation and without weight, made me pause. It was just a word. An empty, resigned word.

Looking at her, I nodded, and she continued. "Sara was my

best friend. She was two years younger than me, but she was my person. She was my person even when I got annoyed with her energetic, risk-loving personality. She was my person even when she got caught up in the wrong crowd, and I tried desperately to get her back. She was my person even when our parents jumped states for work and left us to our own devices most days. She was my person even when I gave up on her and began a life of my own after school. And she was my person even when she got knocked up by a Marine and needed help."

Tears collected, fast and strong. I didn't blink for fear of setting them free.

"She was nothing like me, and it used to drive me insane." Victoria choked on a laugh. "She was wild, but she was the sweetest soul I'd ever known." Her bare lips curved. "Until you."

The waitress arrived, and I cleared my throat, but Victoria ordered for us. She got halfway through requesting a tea for me when she paused.

I nodded, thanking the waitress. Her smile was dimpled as she tucked her notepad in her apron and left.

"Did she pick my name?" I had so many questions, but it seemed the least important were the ones I most wanted answers to.

"She did." Victoria sat back, retrieving her wallet from her purse. "I didn't have the heart to change it. She knew she was having a girl, and it excited her to no end."

Before I could ask my next question, she opened her wallet. Her finger dug behind a picture of me and Jackson taken in the first grade to retrieve the one hidden behind it.

My eyes remained on me and Jackson, tracing our red cheeked smiles, the too large and missing teeth, and the arm he'd flung around my shrinking shoulders.

"You two," Victoria said, noticing where my attention was.

"We couldn't take you anywhere without people commenting on how adorable you were."

We'd had no idea. Those innocent faces, the innocent affection and scorn we'd shown one another, and our unbruised hearts. It was impossible to predict a future, but even when ours took a turn we didn't see coming, I was certain we never imagined it would turn out like this.

My thoughts receded, the bruised organ inside my chest swelling as Victoria slid a picture of myself over the table.

It was me, but with different eyes. Everything else—the hair, the smile, the eyebrows, and the shape of her jaw—it was all me. I was all her.

"She had deep dimples," Victoria said. "Yours are more faint, but even so"—I heard her swallow—"twins."

My hand reached out, hovering then retreating, my heart screaming in my ears until Victoria said, "Take it. I have plenty more."

The waitress arrived with our drinks, and I coughed to rid the emotion in my throat, quickly depositing the picture inside my purse.

In silence, we readied our drinks, passersby drifting in and out of the café, families walking down the street.

"How long has Heath known?"

"I told him when you were ten."

That morning before church slammed into my addled brain as I remembered Dad showing up, and Heath's confusion during all the yelling.

The fighting that'd transpired the following week.

"You're not sorry," I said the obvious, taking a big gulp of too-hot tea.

"Far from it," Victoria said. "I've hurt you in ways I'll always be sorry for, but not for this. This," she said, her tone steel, the mother in her rearing her head for the first time in years, "was a decision made from love."

"It was selfish," I said, meeting her eyes.

She didn't even flinch, just sipped her coffee. "I know. My love for you makes me selfish. When it comes to you, that will never change."

We stared for a minute, and although I was certain I'd had a million and one things to ask, I couldn't seem to remember a damn thing.

I drank my tea, stewing over what had been said.

"Will you come for Christmas?" she asked, then finished her coffee.

I choked, patting my chest as I tried to swallow some tea. "I don't think that's a good idea."

Victoria handed me a napkin to wipe my chin. "I know it might be a lot to ask, and I know you have a lot to think about, but I'm not about to just fade out of your life." Her chin tipped up, the stubborn set grating. "I refuse to."

Dropping the scrunched napkin, I set down my tea, the cup shaking the saucer. My stomach began to quake, and I knew I'd swallowed about all I could handle for now. "I need to go."

"At least think about it."

It wasn't even Thanksgiving, and though I would think about it, I was reluctant to give her anything else today. With a nod, I plucked up my purse, and I left.

Inside my car, I traced the picture I'd carried everywhere with me.

From Victoria's wallet to mine, Sara's smiling face was transported, tucked away beneath folds of leather.

I wasn't sure why, when I spoke of her with Dad, Flo, and Dennis, I still called her Sara. Perhaps it was because, even if she was my biological mom, I already had one of those.

Looking at the house, the lights draped from the windows, the tree visible in the large arched window of the formal living room, I pondered whether I could do this.

"It's just Christmas," Dennis had said.

"Shut up." Flo had shoved him. "Text me. I'll call you and then you can say you'd forgotten you were supposed to have dessert with me."

Flo was spending Christmas with Dennis and his family. Now that her great-aunt was gone, her parents had left the cove and were traveling around the country with their inheritance.

Slipping the photo away, I checked my reflection in the mirror. My cheeks had pinked from the cold, and I hadn't done much to my hair, which now sat beneath my shoulders. My eyes were bright circles, my lashes bare of mascara.

I couldn't bring myself to care much about makeup, though I did make some effort with my clothes. Climbing out of the car, I pulled down my red sweater and tugged up my black skinny jeans, my ankle boots losing traction on the rain dusted driveway.

Carefully, I moved to the door, shivering as I rang the doorbell.

Victoria opened it, a huge smile lifting her cheeks and eyes. "Willa." Before I could say hello, I was drawn into a tight hug, one of her hands petting my hair. "Thank you," she whispered, her voice thick.

Nodding, I pulled away, then offered the gift bag filled with gift cards and baked goods.

"You needn't have worried. You should save your money for that shop of yours."

"It's doing fine," I said, meaning it. I could stand to raise my prices a little higher, but I was making enough to keep us afloat, pay my debts, and save a tiny amount.

"Good, come in." She grabbed my arm, tugging me into warmth. "It's freezing out. Where's your coat?"

"In the car." I kicked off my boots, my fuzzy pink socks slippery over the hardwood. "Where is everyone?"

"Family room. I should've put the tree there, but I like—"

"How it looks from the front window," I finished for her, my smile wane. "I know."

Smiling, she led the way, and I tucked my hands into the pockets of my jeans.

I knew they'd be here and still the sight of them together on the couch, Ainsley fussing over Jackson's new sweater, the annoyed slant of his jaw, still clawed at my insides.

I hadn't heard from him. I hadn't seen him. Nothing.

It'd been two months, and it wasn't that I'd expected him to have a sudden change of heart after what'd happened, but I had expected the boy who'd once been my friend to see if I was okay.

I should've known his stubborn streak ran far deeper than any of us knew.

He didn't so much as smile, just jerked his head, then returned his attention to the game on TV.

Ainsley smiled, but it was insincere, to say the least.

That was fine, for mine was probably similar. "Merry Christmas," I said, turning to find Heath. He was at the dining table, glasses on as he pored over the pages spread before him. "Hi."

Tearing his glasses off, he looked up, his eyes lighting. "Willa, Merry Christmas."

I walked over, offering a brief hug, and eyed his leg, which was no longer in a cast, but sat in what looked to be a sore heap beneath the table. "What are you doing?"

"Just checking next fall's helmets."

"Isn't that Jackson's job now?" I untucked the chair next to his, taking a seat.

Smiling sheepishly, he nodded. "I'm just looking."

"Uh-huh." I grinned. "How's the leg?"

His eyes seemed to dull. "Ah, pretty useless. I've just started rehab."

I nodded. "I hear it gets easier."

"Yeah," he said. "Me too."

We settled in to eat ten minutes later, and I hadn't realized how much I'd missed Victoria's cooking until I took my first bite of slow roasted pork and homemade gravy.

I ate in silence, fielding any questions that came my way but mostly just listening.

Conversation with Heath and Jackson was stilted, not that Heath didn't try. Unless it concerned work, Jackson approached any subject with such boredom that Heath didn't stand a chance at receiving anything but cold, hard detachment.

Ainsley talked about her job at the preschool, the upcoming trip she and Jackson were taking with her parents, and their plans for New Year's.

As soon as she mentioned the trip, I began mentally categorizing all the items I needed to order for the bakery on Monday.

Unscathed, and feeling like I should leave so I could remain that way, I rose from the table before dessert was served, explaining that Dennis and Flo were expecting me.

Victoria beamed. "Oh, take some for them."

I said my goodbyes to Heath, muttered one to Jackson and Ainsley, then waited as Victoria cut up some fruit cake and set it in a Tupperware container. I gave her a brief hug before saying I'd see myself out.

"Your presents." Victoria flitted to the front room and

handed me two heavy gift bags. "I wish I could've seen you open them."

I wasn't sure what to say, guilt a little nudge at my full stomach.

She gave me a hopeful smile. "Just... tell me we'll talk soon?"

"Yeah," I said, meaning it. "I'll call you, okay?"

She flicked her hand. "Whenever you're ready."

Opening the trunk, I tucked the cake in the corner where it wouldn't roll around, sandwiching it with the presents, then almost screamed as I closed it.

Jackson's lip curled. "Leaving so soon?"

"Yes," I said. "Now if you would be so kind..." I gestured to my car door, which he was blocking.

His nose twitched as he chuckled. "Just like that."

"Just like what?"

"You give in. You give up so easily with everything."

I felt my brows pucker. "What are you talking about?"

"You find out your mother isn't actually your mother, and two months later, you're having Christmas dinner with the very same woman." Prowling closer, his eyes flitted over my face. "You cheat on your boyfriend, and then you hide away until he leaves town for good."

"Jackson," I said, sticking my hand out, feeling the rough fabric of his coat.

"You had me," he said, voice gentle, deceptively so. "You had me eating out of the palm of your hand, and you just let me run off." His head lowered, warm breath washing over my lips and cheek. "All. Over. Again."

My fists balled, my eyes stinging. "You don't know anything."

"I know you, and you're the same as you've always been," he said, voice heated and dark. "*Weak.*"

"I'm not weak," I said through gritted teeth.

His chuckle singed my skin, the rapidly beating idiot in my chest. "Your actions say differently. You stand for nothing, Willa Grace. You refuse to fight for anything."

"There's a difference," I said, my chin lifting, our lips an exhale apart, "between fighting and picking your battles."

He hummed. "So true. So," he whispered, taunting, "are you going to fight for what you want, Willa? Or will you submit to the idea of a future without me all over again?"

"You're engaged."

"Exactly." He floated back, his eyes daring, and his hands tucked inside his coat pockets. The searing wind caught and fluttered it as he headed back to the house.

Exactly.

For days, his words had cooked up a storm inside my head. Gone was the misery that usually accompanied thoughts of him, and in its place, a fury born of frustration and disbelief took hold.

Who he thought he was, I didn't know, but I was sick and tired of the whiplash.

"Hey, whoa," Flo said, taking the bowl from me. "Sufficiently mixed, my friend." She peered inside, making a face. "Or dead, maybe."

"Ugh." I ripped off my apron and marched to the coffee machine.

"That's your third one this morning," Dennis said.

Flo pointed out, "And you stopped drinking coffee months ago."

Groaning, I spun around, glaring at my two friends. "Can

I not be in a mood without everyone pointing out that I'm in a mood?"

"You're in a mood," they both said, then snickered.

Digging my hands into my hair, I filled up my lungs, then sent air out with, "I'm taking the day off."

"Oh, thank god." Dennis raised his hands heavenward.

Flo bit her lips, her eyes laughing. "Get gone, cranky one."

I flipped them off, their cackles chasing me out the bakery door.

I didn't bother slipping into something sexy. I didn't even bother checking my reflection in the car. It wasn't until I'd crossed town, parked out on the street, and asked the receptionist to see Jackson that what I was doing began to sink in.

Like a weighted brick in the stomach, my nerves ignited, and my racing heart began to pound a slow and sluggish beat.

The receptionist eyed me over the counter, the phone pressed to her ear, murmuring something I couldn't hear. As she hung up the phone, perusing me none too subtly, she said, "Top floor. He's expecting you."

Nodding, I thanked her and made my way to the elevator behind her desk.

The emergency exit beckoned, its bright light tempting me to throw this stupid idea down the toilet and hit flush. For it wasn't really an idea.

It was a reckless, spontaneous act of defiance.

Are you going to fight for what you want, Willa?

The doors dinged, and I steeled my shoulders. I had no idea if what I was doing could even be considered fighting. In fact, I grew increasingly disgusted with myself as the elevator doors closed and carried me up to the lion's den.

He was engaged. He was engaged, yet he was goading me. Why? Jackson had always had a mean streak. He could be cruel, but he knew the difference between right and wrong, and was well versed in every shade of gray.

This, though, whatever this was he was playing at, was too dark to blend into any blurred lines.

"Finally, I'm starving." His first words to me as the door opened pulled me up short, every insult and question I'd wanted to hurl at him disintegrating.

Peering around the huge, sleek room, I felt the door close at my back, and slowly crossed to where his desk sat, front and center, before the floor-to-ceiling glass windows. "I didn't bring any food."

Meeting his gaze was a mistake. Undoing the top buttons of his dress shirt, he grinned, all predator, no mercy in sight. "But you did. Come here."

The haze that settled over his eyes, the speed in which my heart began to race, and the way his teeth sank into his lip, made me pause. "I didn't come here for that."

"Well, I'm afraid my tolerance for chitchat has been exceeded today."

"You're an asshole."

His head flopped to the side, his chuckle silent. "And you're making me so hard it hurts, even with gunk on your cheek." My hand reached up, and he tutted. "Come here. I won't fucking bite."

As if I could control it. I never could.

I was before him in seconds, a squeak escaping as he deposited me on his desk, and then licked his thumb.

Trapped within his punishing gaze, I watched, my stomach warming and dipping as he dragged his wet thumb over my cheek, then popped it in his mouth. "Chocolate chip."

"I murdered it."

His brows jumped. "Interesting. Lie down."

"What?"

With a gentle push of my shoulders, I was tipping back, catching myself on my elbows, papers scrunching beneath me.

"Feet up on the desk."

When I didn't move quick enough, he lifted my legs, positioning them where he wanted them, and then he tugged my panties aside.

I gasped as cool air hit slick flesh and heard a low curse before hot silk was traveling through me, sucking and licking.

My elbows went lax, and I ended up on my back, gazing up at the checkered white ceiling with its fancy light fixtures.

Within a minute, maybe less, my hips began to rock, and I felt his laughter rumble against me.

I came apart, shattered into splinters that imbedded in my chest, pricking and stabbing.

Vaguely, I registered the sound of a fly being unzipped, and then I was being hauled up and helped off the desk to the floor.

Dizzy from the euphoria that was slow to leave, and a sense of shame that hugged so tight, it became hard to breathe, I lost the desire to please him.

He didn't care, or he didn't notice. His cock nudged at my mouth, thick, long and so hard. Closing my eyes, I reached out and grabbed it, then opened my mouth.

Giving Jackson head was something I adored. The ability to render him a needy, cursing, mess, to cause his legs and lungs to shudder, made me feel powerful. Pleasuring him made me feel important, irreplaceable.

But as I sucked and bobbed my head, I felt nothing. Only the growing slime of shame that worsened with every harsh breath he expelled.

"I'm a taken man; you're going to have to work harder than that."

At those words, I choked, and he groaned, fucking my mouth. I let him, and I swallowed as a collection of throaty curses fogged the stifling air.

The sweet and sour taste of him eroded over my tongue, taking its time to disappear down my throat. Falling to my ass, I sat on the floor as he grabbed some tissues from his desk and cleaned himself up.

"You can go now."

My head snapped up from where I'd been staring at his dress shoes, wondering if Ainsley had picked them out. It finally clicked, and that insidious old and new friend of mine, shame, laughed and threatened to send his semen back up my throat. "You never wanted me to make it up to you. To fight."

"To be honest, I really couldn't give a shit what you do."

Though those words might've sounded honest, I knew he didn't mean them, not entirely. Still, I now knew his game, and every hateful word was part of it.

"You're doing this on purpose." Grabbing the desk, I used it to assist my shaking legs to stand. "You have no intention of marrying her, do you? And all you're doing is messing with me. You're just trying to hurt us both."

We'd both betrayed him.

We'd both destroyed this idea he'd had in his head. That if you loved someone, truly loved them, then you remained perfect. For anything less than wasn't true love.

"Nothing is perfect, Jackson. Nothing. People fuck up and make mistakes. You, especially, have made many of them." I refused to cry. I wasn't even sure if I could. But somehow, that made it worse. There was no release for the poison that was now multiplying inside me.

There was no way to rid myself of this bad day.

"It's probably a bad time to say this." Jackson wiped his

bottom lip, eyes finally finding mine, and licked his thumb. "But your cunt tastes even better with age."

Rage funneled through me, fast and all consuming.

Walking behind his desk, I grabbed his chin, hissing, "Unless we're seated at a table with our fucked-up family, don't talk to me, don't even look at me." His smirk slowly slipped as I continued. "I hope you feasted enough for a lifetime because you won't be touching me again." My eyes flicked between his, hatred and revulsion causing my thumbnail to pierce his skin.

I shoved him away, my flats eating the floor in quick strides.

"Willa, don't walk away from me."

"Shut up." I flung my middle finger over my shoulder, then opened the door. "You fucking disgust me."

"Bug, fucking stop—" The closing door cut him off.

I dived into the elevator and hit the first floor button repeatedly, Jackson jogging out of his office.

Keeping my finger on the door close button, his vivid eyes disappeared as they collided.

twenty-seven

Jackson

The wind had picked up her hair, twirled it, then resettled it over her hunched shoulders. As if it'd decided not to bother her.

After sitting with her, I'd watched from one of the many exits, watched and waited until she'd climbed inside her car, and only then did I do the same and drive home.

There was something about seeing someone's world split apart that made you forget the pain, the memories, and the ache, long enough to remember. To remember who that someone was to you, at your core, even if they were no longer that person.

She'd always been my person, and now, once again, her world had exploded. The bleak tone of her voice, the defeated set of her shoulders, and the spirit that'd departed her once lustrous eyes, caused a multitude of conflicted feelings.

So, I'd watched—I was always watching—not that she knew, as she'd slowly pulled on the tattered seams of herself, studied the new pieces, and began to make something with them.

You fucking disgust me.

Such strength in horrific words. Such venomous accuracy. I was still trying to extract the barbs from my chest.

"Don't turn into me," a gruff voice muttered.

Looking up from the contracts in my lap, I found Dad's heavy-lidded eyes on me. "I would never."

He held my gaze and didn't flinch, just nodded, seemed to take some kind of comfort in my honesty. "Have you spoken to Willa?"

Annoyance trampled over my skin. That he could ask me that with a straight face and think I'd tell him anything only further proved what an asshole he was.

You fucking disgust me.

Enough. "You know what?" I said, tucking the files away and setting them on the seat next to me. "You've got some nerve."

As if he'd been waiting, Dad's eyes widened with interest while the rest of him remained the same. Broken, unmoving, and miserable. "You never talk about her."

"Because you made it abundantly clear, many years ago, that the two of us had ruined our family."

The clock in the room framed with mirrors and gym mats ticked in the silence.

Dad's eyes shifted from me to his hands, then back again, his jaw hard. "That's what you think?"

"That's what I know." I tapped my temple. "Memories don't lie."

"Damn it, Jackson," he snapped. "When are you going to learn?" Shaking his head, he said loud and rough, "I wasn't mad at you. I was furious with *me*. With the decisions we made in anger that we couldn't undo." His voice gentled some. "I'm still furious with me. And some asshole rams his cruddy car into mine, and all I can think is, I can't die like this. I refuse to die with all this, this…" Nostrils flaring, he smacked his chest, sputtering, "Self-hatred and regret inside me."

My jaw came unhinged, every clenched muscle drooping.

With a stare more solid than I'd seen since I was a teenager, he continued, "My issue wasn't you. For the longest time, it's never been you. But even so, saying it, telling you I've behaved atrociously and that I love you, I can't even do that," he cried, his tone loaded with frustration.

My eyes closed over the emotion I felt gathering. When I opened them, I said, "You just did."

He froze, save for his face, as anguish leeched from the tense lines, his lips going slack.

The door creaked open as the nurse finally returned. "Okay, let's get you on that bar. Are we ready?"

Our eyes remained locked, but when I smiled, still hurt but already healing, my father nodded.

"Yeah," he said with another nod. "We're ready."

Arriving home, I dumped my keys and computer on the dining table and wondered if maybe Ainsley was out.

A slight noise sounded from the bedroom, and I marched straight for it.

"We need to talk," I said, untucking my shirt from my pants.

Ainsley huffed. "I'll say. We haven't had sex in months."

"Because we've been over for months," I blurted, impatient, but mainly with myself.

At Ainsley's silence, I paused in unbuttoning my dress shirt and turned.

In the center of the bed, she sat in lingerie, white and translucent in the glow of the moon.

Fuck.

"What?" Her lips made the shape, but there was no voice to accompany it.

Exhaustion ate at my limbs, the stumbling beast in my chest. "I can't do this. Not anymore."

"What do you mean?" She scrambled off the bed, snatching

her robe from the ottoman and pulling it on. "I moved back to this rotting town for you. I've watched you pine and lose yourself to your own sister all over again for months, and you tell me you can't do this?"

"I'm sorry." I was. She'd hurt me, sure, but it was nothing compared to the hurt I'd carried with me for years. It was almost embarrassingly easy to say those words. I said them again, frowning at the bureau. "I'm sorry."

A slipper was tossed at my head. "Fuck you and your stupid apology."

I nodded, staring at the cream satin slipper by my feet. "I'll go—"

"You sicken me." My eyes pulled up at those words, my fingers curling. "You took me back after I'd found someone who actually gave a shit about me. Why?" She was crying now, her breasts straining the flimsy material covering her chest. "Just so you can use me?" When our eyes met, her features went lax as apprehension spread. "You bastard."

"I know." For I did. I was well aware of my tendency to bite twice as hard as the person who'd bitten me. I was aware, and still, I continued to do it.

"Is she really worth all this?" When I didn't answer, she prodded further. "Was she worth destroying your own family all those years ago?" I bit my tongue so hard, copper filled my mouth. "You know"—she laughed, bitter and low—"I never should've agreed to help you. I should've told you right then and there that I was the one who'd followed you two and took those photos because what you were doing was wrong. Instead, I stupidly believed that it was ending, that it would never last, and I was going to be your new beginning."

My spine locked, my jaw and neck tensing.

Laughing again, she said, "Yeah, it was me, and you know

what?" Stepping closer, she smiled. "I'm not sorry. I never have been."

"I know."

Her brows lowered. "You knew?"

I nodded, my tone blank and matter of fact. "I found out a month after we came back while I was looking for something in Dad's email."

Silence slithered into the room, cold and screaming.

Staring out the window to the water beyond, I heard her swallow, heard her draw an uneven breath, and then I heard her say, "Would you have gone back to her if you hadn't known?"

Yes, I wanted to say. Instead, I grabbed my keys and headed back out. "Leave whenever you're ready."

twenty-eight

Willa

"Ahoy," Dennis crowed to the young boy who giggled with frosting smeared around his mouth. "That's a mighty fine eye patch you've got there, matey."

"I'm not a pirate," he stated, licking more frosting. "I got an eye infection."

"Pirate sounds way cooler, no?" Dennis asked.

The boy grinned and so did his mother, who took his hand and walked to the door.

We waved when his little hand, still clutching the cupcake, lifted as the door jangled closed.

Before I could blink, the door opened again, and I felt my heart squeeze as Jackson stalked inside as though he had every right to.

His eyes, smudged in shadows, fixed on mine. "We need to talk."

Dennis made a noise, backing up to the kitchen.

"We don't," I said, tearing my eyes from his.

All that got me was pressed back into the wall as Jackson rounded the counter, quicker than a flash of life-changing lightning. "She's leaving."

I planted my hands behind me, inhaling that maddening scent. "Ainsley?" At his quick nod, I frowned. "And what, you came here to blame me again?" Straightening, I glared up into his face. "I won't let you."

His lips twitched, a speck of humor dancing in his gaze. "I ended things."

"Oh," I said, deflating, then remembered what a gigantic dick he was, and not the good kind. "That's nice." I slid down the wall, trying to move away.

Warm skin encircled my wrist. "Not so fast, Bug."

"Don't call me that," I snapped, irritated at the ease in which he'd said it, in the way it wrapped every bruised part of me in warmth.

"You know, not once have you said you were sorry," he said, those eyes flashing.

Disbelief had me sputtering, "Neither have you."

"I didn't sleep with someone else." His grip loosened, his feet shifting closer to mine, the taste of mint on his breath, searing. "That was you."

It wasn't that I couldn't own up to the mistakes I'd made; it was that I was sick of having to relive and rehash them, only to wind up winded, even years later. "We're not doing this."

"We need to."

Those words surprised. "Why?"

His teeth dragged over his bottom lip. "We'll never not do this, and it's time we stop running from it."

"I never ran," I reminded him. "That was you."

His nostrils flared, and he looked away, assessing the shop. "Let's go upstairs." Grabbing my hand, he started to take me with him to the door.

I tore free when we'd rounded the counter. "No. You don't call the shots anymore, Jackson."

Smirking, he looked at his empty hand, then at me. "Don't I?"

I feared I would've screamed if it weren't for Flo. "Oh, hell to the no. Is that who I think it is?" Jackson didn't remove his eyes from me as Flo stormed through the shop, dumping a takeout coffee on the counter and grabbing a caramel slice. "Excuse me."

Jackson sighed, then finally, gave his attention to Flo.

"Thank you. I'm Flo, short for Florence, short for your worst enemy, if you don't use the door behind you and to your left."

Jackson looked as though he was struggling with the decision to argue or laugh.

Flo stood, unperturbed, with a hand on her hip, then huffed. "This"—she gestured up and down his tall frame—"doesn't work on me. It no longer works on her, either, by the looks of things. So leave, buddy."

"Buddy?" he repeated. "I thought I was your worst enemy."

"Oh, you are now."

Biting his lips, he gave me his eyes, then asked, "Do I no longer work for you, Bug?"

"No," I lied. "The lies, the games, and the misery never worked for me."

"Dear Lord, if you can hear me..." Dennis began to pray.

"That's enough," Flo said, shoving at Jackson's chest.

He didn't move; his gaze, assessing and tormented, remained glued to me. There was no sound, but I heard the silent word loud and clear. "Liar."

My stomach twisted, my hands itching to reach out as he finally backed up to the door, then disappeared through it.

Flo launched the caramel slice after him, but missed as onlookers gawked. "Don't come back, you great big idiot waste of perfectly good male!"

"That was the last one," Dennis whined, rushing to the closing door. "I was saving it for morning tea."

"Too bad." Flo wiped her hands. "So worth it."

"But you missed," I pointed out.

Flo raised a brow, breezing by us into the kitchen. "But did I?"

Dennis and I both looked at each other, confused.

twenty-nine

Jackson

"If the wind changes, will your face stay like that?"

I stopped the swing chair from moving so Lily could climb up. "Would that be bad?" I asked, turning to her.

She set Borris, her rainbow bear, next to me and shrugged. "I don't know. I suppose it depends."

"On?"

She made a face, her tiny brows low and her eyes squinting, jaw all crooked.

I couldn't stop the laughter that barreled free. "That's what I look like?"

Relaxing her features, she nodded. "Yup, well, most of the time."

"Right. Well, I don't know if I want to look like that forever."

Lily giggled. "You would scare all the pretty ladies away."

"Not you?"

Her chin doubled as she sank back, grinning with pink cheeks. "Nah, I'm not afraid of no monster."

We both laughed then, and Lars cursed as he came outside and tripped over Lily's Barbie campervan. "Lil, what did I say about keeping this thing out here?"

"It's just easier," she said.

Lars handed me a beer, and I popped the top. "Easier?" I asked.

Lily jumped down, sighing. "Than having to bring it back out every time I want to play."

"You don't want to play with it inside?"

She gave me a look that suggested I was clueless. "Look around, Jackie." She'd called me that since I'd arrived here three days ago. "It doesn't look like this inside."

Gazing around the estate—which had belonged to Daphne's grandmother—they'd recently moved into, I found I had to agree. "Good point." I took a long swig of beer.

Lars opened the door for Lily to wheel her campervan inside, Borris hitching a ride on top.

As soon as she was through, he pulled both doors shut and then sank down beside me, making the chair rock.

Expelling a huge breath, he raked a hand through his hair. "She kills me."

"She gets her smarts from you."

"And her sass from Daphne," Lars added, meaning Lily's stepmom.

Nodding, I drank some more.

"She left yet?" Lars asked.

"Sick of me already?"

"Nah, but I'm not down with my daughter's googly eyes for you." Shaking his head, he chuckled. "It's fucking weird."

"It wouldn't have happened if you'd trained her to call me her uncle instead of Dash."

"Dash," Lars said, pointing his beer at me, "for all his many fucking faults, actually made an effort to see her while she was growing up."

Shame blistered, hotter than the setting sun edging the distant fields. "I know."

"Was it that bad?" he asked after a minute had dragged by, taking more of daylight with it.

"Yeah," I said, my voice rough. "That bad."

Lars sighed. "Say you're sorry and I'll work on the uncle thing."

My eyes shot to his, blinking. "Yeah?"

He twisted his lips. "I said I'll work on it." Looking back at the setting sun, he muttered, "She's probably too far gone."

I chuckled, then sobered. "Yeah, Ainsley left." She'd texted me that morning, saying the keys were in the front garden and not to call her again. "I'll get out of your hair tomorrow."

"There's no rush," Lars said. "But what are you going to do?"

I scratched at the heavy stubble on my jaw. I needed to shave. "With Willa?"

Lars belched in response.

"She's being stubborn." He made a sound that had my eyes narrowing on him. "Something amusing, Bradby?"

Grinning, he muttered around the mouth of his beer, "Just you."

My nose twitched in agitation, and I knew if I didn't ask, he wouldn't divulge. After two minutes, I groaned. "Fuck, just say it."

"I just find it funny that you call her stubborn. In case you haven't noticed, you're the biggest grudge holder of the century."

"She fucked someone else."

"When she'd thought you'd dumped her. Six years, and you still don't want to remember that tidbit, do you?"

I grunted. "Still happened. And I'm trying, okay?" I admitted. "I've been trying. I went to see her today, but she and her spitfire work friend sent me away."

"So go back," Lars said. "And take it from someone who's failed to do so, leave that ego at the door when you do."

I lowered my beer. "What?"

"Ego. Your pride. Get rid of it. It has no place in trying to fix something broken." Tipping his beer, he shrugged. "Unless you want to get to the point of no return, then sure, keep going as you are."

thirty

Willa

Wiping dots of sweat from my brow, I stretched my back, then bent over.

"Giving everyone a nice view there, Bug."

My hands slipped off the bag of flour, and I whispered a curse. "Get lost, Jackson."

We had a new delivery driver this morning, and instead of taking them around the back, as they all tended to, he'd dumped them at the front of the shop. Now, I was hauling them inside, wishing Dennis wasn't on his scheduled day off.

Hands tugged at my waist, and I was tempted to stomp my foot as Jackson hefted the bag over his shoulder and marched it inside and out to the kitchen.

I followed, hands on my hips. "I don't need—"

"Here?" he said, opening the stockroom door.

I didn't answer, but he saw the two bags inside and dumped it beside them.

"What are you doing here?" I asked, chasing him back out front.

He picked up the remaining bag, trudging past me in a cloud of delicious cologne, indifferent to my ire.

Giving in, I waited in the doorway to the kitchen, crossing my arms over my chest.

Jackson emerged, reaching behind him and pulling out a thick envelope he'd tucked in his jeans. "Here."

Removing my eyes from his black Thorn Racing T-shirt, I stared at his offering, then at him, and slowly unfolded my arms. "Jackson, stop it."

I didn't know what it was, but I did know that he couldn't just show up like this and look at me like that. The affection, the longing, it wasn't fair, and it wasn't fun. It was all for sport, and I was tired of playing.

"Just take it." He shifted close. "Please."

I grabbed the large envelope and opened it, peering inside.

"What are these?" I asked, eyes darting from a stack of what appeared to be email drafts to his.

"Everything I didn't say." With that, he slid his hands into his pockets and left.

With my lip between my teeth, I watched him go, then flipped the break sign on the door and locked it, retreating to the kitchen.

I hate you because I could never actually hate you, and that makes me hate you so much.

———

I'm drunk.
And you're every unfinished song I couldn't listen to.

———

Hey,
Still hate you.

———

Did you think of me at all? Was I all you thought about when you did it? I want to know. I want to know because knowing beats wondering. The wondering never seems to end. Knowing will end it.

Do I want it to end?

It never ends.

Each unsent email contained the date and time it was written. Most in the early hours of the morning or in the late hours of night.

I miss you.
I hate that I miss you.

———

Do you remember on my seventh birthday, you won this stupid stuffed goldfish at the fair, and I won nothing? It was orange, covered in sequins.

Yeah. Well, I stole it from you when you were sleeping.

I didn't actually want it.

I wanted what it did for you.

I wanted to feel the way it seemed to make you feel.

I felt guilty, sure, but not enough to give it back.

It didn't work.

The next day, I tossed it in the trash outside.

And I'm not sorry.

———

Heartbreaker,

For the first time since you ruined it all, I slept with someone else to-night, and I don't even remember her name.

It's been six months. I hadn't planned to wait this long, but it was harder than I expected it to be.

So why was it so easy for you?

That's what I wondered. Drunk as fuck, balls deep inside some girl who had talons for nails, and all I could think was, How. The. Fuck. Did. You. Do. It.

The answer came when I eventually did.

You didn't love me.

Not as much as I loved you.

———

Bug,

I didn't think it would be this hard.
Trying to breathe without you.

———

I couldn't stay.

I couldn't face what we'd become.

I could have done many things, but I couldn't fix something that bro-ken, Bug.

And you didn't ask me to.

I walked into my favorite cafe before school today, and as I was waiting in line, Crowded House came on.

Needless to say, I went without coffee.

But it didn't even matter. It was too late.

You invaded.

Or maybe, you never fucking left.

———

I don't know why I keep doing this, or what I even plan to do with these.

Sometimes, I imagine what it'll be that makes me finally hit send.

Sometimes, it's when I'm ninety years old, dying in a bed somewhere.

Sometimes, it's when I picture you the morning of your wedding.

Sometimes, it's when I imagine you imagining me.

I should just delete them.

———

Why?!!!?!

———

I think of you most when I'm with someone else.

No one smells like you.

Then again, I doubt I could handle it if they did.

———

I love you.
I loathe you.

———

I'm not sure how it happened, but somewhere along the way to our forever, I lost track of right now.
And I ask myself, all the time, if things would've been different had I just stopped and breathed with you.

———

It's been storming for three days straight.
Just a bad day, right?
I can still hear you giggle.

———

Come find me

please

———

They scattered to the countertop when I lowered my head to my hands, tears flooding too hard to see through.

Tucking the last daffodil in the stand by the headstone, I then thought better of it and plucked it out. The breeze carried my hair from my face as I leaned forward and laid it before the headstone.

Sitting back, I pulled my knees up and stretched my dress over them.

The grass crunched beneath the soles of shoes, and then the scent of cedarwood and mint cocooned. "Thought I might find you here if you weren't at work."

I pondered not talking, leaning forward to rest my chin on my knees. "Shouldn't you be at work?"

"Should be, but I'd rather be here."

"In a cemetery?"

Like the briefest touch of fingers skimming skin, his gentle laugh caressed. "You should know that." I swallowed, closing my eyes. How like him to find me when my emotions were circling high, brimming the edge of their confines. "You never hid over here," he said.

I blinked, gazing back at the weather worn stone. "I didn't?"

"No," Jackson said, then gestured to the hills with fat gray clouds perched above. "Always over there or down among the bowl."

We'd called the center of the cemetery the bowl, being that it was surrounded by slow rolling hills on either side.

"Sara Elizabeth Dean." He read her name aloud. "No wonder Victoria never wanted us playing back here."

I snorted. "The fact it's filled with dead bodies wasn't reason enough?"

Humor coated his words. "Yeah, there's that. Crazy," he said, stretching his legs out, dress shoes shining against the stone. "That she picked this house because…"

"Because her sister was buried behind it?" I asked. "Yeah, I know."

"Have you spoken to her?"

"Not for a few weeks." I tugged some grass from the ground, rolling the gritty blades in the palm of my hand. "She's tried to call, but I don't know."

"It's a lot," he said.

I hummed, not sure where he'd left the attitude he'd become so fond of carrying, but not in the mood to ask.

"Do you know what she looked like?" he asked, quiet, cautious.

"Me," I said and heard the distant rumble of thunder grow closer. "Just like me."

Jackson released a loud breath, and I could feel his eyes probing, but I kept mine where they were. "I wonder what else about her was like you."

In the weeks since I'd discovered someone who I'd never met, I'd wondered many things. Rolling the grass some more, I said, "I wonder too. But most things feel stupid to wonder about."

"How do you mean?"

"She was my mother, and instead of wanting to know if she could have one day changed the world or have changed mine, I want to know silly things." I smiled, my eyes growing wet. "How did she sound when she sang? Did she sing off-key like me, and so preferred to hum her favorite songs?"

Jackson cleared his throat, his voice rough. "That's not stupid, Bug. Far from it." After a moment, he added, "I bet she was a far better singer than you."

I breathed out a laugh, then tucked my head to my knees as rain began to drip from the gray clouds hovering overhead.

Jackson quit probing but scooted closer to drape a heavy arm behind me.

Some minutes later, our clothes began to soak through, and I lifted my head, splatters of rain washing the salt from my cheeks. "Just a bad day," Jackson said.

Turning, I watched him for a moment, the tiny dent in his chin less prominent with his jaw, all his features, relaxed. "How's your mom?"

Beads of water were collecting on his cheeks, his lashes, his upper lip. He licked it, gazing toward Sara's headstone. "I wouldn't know."

"How long has it been?"

"Three years and five months." His throat bobbed.

He'd never had all that much of a relationship with Kylie, and when we were kids, he used to blame Heath for that. He learned better long ago.

"What happened?" I dared to ask.

He shook his head, then sighed. "She asked for money to bail her latest boyfriend out of jail. Again. I said no. She said it'll be the last time I hear from her if I don't help." His jaw turned rigid once more. "And I said..."

"Fine," I finished for him.

His hand squeezed my side. "Probably wasn't wise, but I couldn't handle it anymore."

"You didn't think she was serious. As you shouldn't, that's your mom."

His lips tried to rise. "Guess I don't get the stubborn streak from Dad."

I had to agree with that, and as the rain began to turn to mist, I shivered, remembering all the times he'd said *don't walk away from me*.

As if he knew I'd found that dark piece of him, he said, "I didn't think I cared, for so many years, and maybe, I didn't. But still"—his gaze snatched mine—"I don't do well with losing people."

"None of us do," I told him. "But that doesn't excuse what you've done, Jackson."

Reaching out, he cupped my face, thumb stroking my damp cheek. "I was wrong. I was hurt, and I was wrong. I've been wrong this whole time. I know that."

"Knowing doesn't change anything," I whispered, needing to pull away, but the sheen in his eyes held me immobile.

"I disagree," he said with a thoughtful hum. "We have the ability to change everything." Stunned, my heartbeat stalled as our wet lips sealed. Breath rushed from us both as they rubbed and roamed, gentle and scared.

When his arm tightened around me, I gasped. "Stop." When he sucked my lip instead, I shoved my hand between our faces, pushing him back by his forehead.

He laughed, watching as I scrambled to my feet, then laughed some more as I stormed off. "Later, Bug."

"No. No later, Jackson."

More laughter.

I wasn't sure if it was noticing the anguish Jackson had tried so hard to keep hidden regarding his own mother, but when I thought about what it would be like to keep stumbling through life without my own, I picked up the phone.

She was seated outside a small restaurant on the street below her office where I'd said I'd meet her, two blocks from the bakery.

Awkward small talk about the bakery, one of her new high-profile clients, and Heath's rehab, kept us busy until our lunch arrived.

"You really should've gotten some salad," Victoria said. "So many carbs."

Some things would never change. "I'm not fat." I had some curves, sure, but I liked my body, and I loved carbs.

"Of course, not," she said, her cheeks flushing. "I'm talking about your health."

I waved my fork. "Point made." I scooped up some more penne soaked in mushroom sauce and bacon.

"Ainsley has returned to Texas."

I swallowed, keeping my eyes trained on my food. "Yeah, I heard they broke up."

"Don't play coy," Victoria said, though it was gentle. "I know Jackson's been seeing you. Heath told me."

I coughed, then grabbed for my water, swallowing half of it.

When I set the glass down, she had her brows raised. "Really?"

I said nothing.

"Look." She dabbed at her mouth with her napkin even though it was clean. "I don't care."

"You don't care?" I repeated, finding that hard to believe.

Her lips pursed. "I did. I hated it, as any parent would, but after all that's happened..." she rambled off with a tilt of her shoulders. "Besides, most of the town knows by now anyway."

Shock had probably painted my face white, but after a minute, I gathered enough composure to say, "There's nothing to care about."

She gave me a look that said she wasn't stupid, then began spearing pieces of her salad with her fork. "Well, be that as it may, I just want my family. It no longer matters how or in what shape. I just want us all here, together and happy."

I waited, my hands squeezed in my lap, and I waited some more, and finally, she lifted her eyes from her food, and said, "I'm sorry. I'll never forgive myself for how I treated you, and I know Sara probably wouldn't either, but I hope that maybe one day, you can forgive me."

I was trying, and she knew that, so all I managed was a soft smile.

Her answering smile shook, and she reached across the table, her hand upturned for mine.

Plucking one from my lap, I laid it upon hers and felt my smile grow.

We finished eating five minutes before her next appointment, and for the first time in six years, we hugged. Neither of us had dry eyes as we pulled away, but as I walked back to the bakery, I noticed my chest felt the tiniest bit lighter.

All too soon, it filled with dread when I saw the truck parked outside.

Cursing, I raced inside, ready to give him hell for ruining what had been a good day when I was pulled up short by the sound of a bang.

"What are you doing?"

Jackson was on the floor, the top half of him under the sink. "Fixing your tap. That drip is probably costing you an extra hundred dollars each quarter."

My purse plonked to the countertop, and I looked around, noticing the tools and plaster kits. "And the back door?"

"Well, yeah." He grunted, dropping something. "It had a huge dent in it."

"And the molding?"

"It was chipped as fuck."

I didn't know where to look next or if I even should. "How'd you learn to do all this?" He'd helped Heath some growing up, but fixing walls and wooden fixtures was something Heath hired people to do.

Jackson eased out from below the sink, wincing as he rose and tried to stretch out his back.

Heat began to flutter throughout my veins, my mouth falling open at the sight of his dirtied white shirt, plastered to his chest with grime and sweat.

Then the toilet flushed, and Lars walked out.

My jaw unhinged further, and I raised a brow at Jackson.

Lars lifted his hands. "He mainly just needed me to tell him what to do."

"Thank you." I smiled at Lars, who winked and began to pack away their things.

Jackson guffawed. "What about me?"

It was Flo's day off. I had no idea where Dennis was, and I didn't care. "You, outside." When Jackson just wiped his hands on some towel, smirking, I growled, "Now."

Taking my purse with me, I tore off my cardigan as Jackson followed me out onto the street and inside the stairwell to my apartment. Turning on him, I snapped, "You're unbelievable."

"Do you mean that in a good way or...?"

Stomping upstairs, I fumbled for the right key. "How did you even get Dennis to let you do all that? Not to mention, the customers who couldn't come in." I stabbed the key into the lock, shoving open the door. "That's money lost, Jackson."

"Since when do you care so much about money? It was an hour, tops."

Dropping my cardigan, purse, and keys to the floor, I spun to glare at him. "Since my dad bought me this building, and I need to pay him back."

"I was trying to help," he said, walking inside.

"Oh, no you don't." I gestured back outside. "Stay on that side of the door."

His lip had the audacity to curl. "A door won't keep me from you." His eyes swam with something untamable. I knew that look, the one that dripped from my face, drenching my body with its presence, before meeting my eyes once more. "Nothing can."

Then he was in front of me, an arm banding tight behind my back. "Get off." I shoved to no avail as the door slammed closed.

His maddening half smile and that predatory glint in his eyes didn't leave. "If you really wanted me to, I would." His finger landed upon my cheek, coasting down, reaching my neck and stopping right above my pounding heart. "But I can feel you don't want that."

My outrage was snuffed when he kissed me, my hands taking their frustration out on his stupidly silken hair, and tugging.

His landed everywhere, one behind my head, the other unbuttoning my blouse just enough to palm my breast. I moaned, and his tongue seized the opportunity, dipping inside to touch mine.

Inside my room, clothes ripped, and our breathing grew labored. Hot kisses were scattered over my chest, breasts, stomach, and finally, my mound, as his hands pried my thighs apart for his fingers to play.

I was writhing, a puddle of heated need twisted up in the sheets, when he finally crawled over top of me and plunged inside.

My back arched, and I felt the bittersweet sting of his teeth in my neck, and then he moved, hard and way too fast.

With my nails scoring the slick flesh of his back, I forced out, "Jackson, wait."

He slowed, his head lifting from where he'd buried it in my neck. Yet when he met my eyes, the fiery lust, the mischievous want, anything I'd expected to find, wasn't there.

"What's wrong?" I asked. Somewhere, some distant part of me thought it insane I was even asking, considering I'd had no plans to do this. That I shouldn't even be doing this. But we were doing this. As always, we'd fallen under, but I couldn't be in it, in whatever we did, alone. I never could.

"You read my emails." His voice was hoarse.

Dread seeped in, but he knew I had so lying would be pointless. Lying to him was always pointless. "Yes."

"Did it feel this good?" he asked, his Adam's apple shifting when he swallowed. At the puzzlement I could feel crinkling my eyes and brows, he explained in a toneless voice, "When he was inside you."

Ice traveled over my skin, raising goose bumps and sinking my stomach. I looked away, wanting him off me, feeling my eyes pool.

He grabbed my chin, forcing them back to his. "Tell me."

"No," I croaked.

He studied me a moment, his cock twitching inside me, broad, heaving shoulders covered in a sheen of sweat. "Show me."

"What?" I almost shouted.

"Show me," he stated, as if it were the most reasonable request in the world. "Show me how he fucked you."

Horror engulfed me, and I felt a tear fumble free of my lashes. "No."

I tried to move, but his weight settled over me, his breath fogging my ear as he whispered, "Every time I imagine it, I die a little more inside. So just fucking show me, Willa."

"No, please. I'm sorry, Jackson." Gripping his forearms, I

struggled to breathe. "You know I am. I've been sorry for years." When he didn't say anything, I cried, "Knowing won't help. It'll only hurt us more."

A gruff exhale of breath had me shivering. "It needs to do more than hurt. It needs to kill me, so the thought no longer holds the power to paralyze me."

I was shaking, shaking and crying, but I knew, if I really wanted him to, he would get off me and leave. He needed this even if it destroyed us even more.

And damn it all to hell, I could never deny him anything he needed.

Swallowing a thick wad of emotion, I could barely recognize the rasping sound of my voice as I said, "Take my right leg and hook it behind your back."

They'd both been wrapped around him, but when he'd stopped and suggested this lunacy, they'd slipped away.

He did.

"Now," I said, but no sound came out. I tried again. "Now, fuck me deep and… and touch me."

"Where?" he said, voice guttural.

"M-my breast." I squeezed my eyes closed, memories of that night burning like fire against the ice I was now encased in. "Yes, there. Caress my side." He did. Slowly, he began to thrust, touching me in all the same places Todd had. "A little faster," I mumbled.

He cursed, doing as I said. A minute later, I began to feel him swell. "Open your eyes."

"No."

He paused. "Willa, did you let him fuck you with your eyes shut?"

"I didn't," I whispered.

"Open them," he said, harsh and impatient.

"No!" The shout echoed through the room, and then my tears were escaping my closed lids, racing down my cheeks into my hair.

"Fuck, Willa." He rolled off me. "Fuck." I felt him punch the bed. Once, twice, and I curled into myself. Then warm hands were pushing damp hair off my cheeks, and his lips were kissing my eyes. "I'm sorry. Open your eyes, Bug." Over and over again, he rasped, "I'm sorry. Open them, please."

When I finally did, green eyes, drowning in tears, stared back at me, and I reached up, catching one before it rolled onto his upper lip. "What have we done?" I wondered aloud.

He searched my face, desperate arms pulling me close. "We fell in love."

"Why does love have to be like this?" I whispered against his lips, my hands framing his face, thumbs seeking more of his grief.

"It won't be anymore," he tried to say, but his voice kept cracking.

I smiled, my soul weary and defeated, then looped my legs around his back as he sank back inside me. "Then is it still love?"

"If it's us, always."

Our hips and lips fused. We rocked, and we clung to each other, and to every last drop of a forever never found.

When we crashed back into reality, our hearts and bodies spent, I crawled off the bed. "Get dressed and go, Jackson."

"Willa, don't—"

"Stop," I gritted, every breath cutting. "I mean it. I won't let you punish me anymore." My hair tickled my bare shoulders, my head shaking.

As I locked myself in the bathroom and slid down the other side of the door, I wondered if the regret that shone in his eyes and the slow drag of his feet to the door would haunt me forever.

thirty-one

Willa

Sleep was elusive, chased away by every moment I couldn't recapture and every feeling Jackson had uncovered until I gave up and got ready for work.

The moon was still a solid ball of distant light in the sky as I dragged myself downstairs. Locking the door behind me, I fumbled to open the bakery door. The keys hit the sidewalk with a rattling clang, and I bent down.

A large hand grabbed them, opened my palm, and folded them inside while a scream scraped up my throat. Red rimmed green eyes connected with mine, and a stunned exhale sailed from me. "It's four thirty in the morning, Jackson."

"Couldn't sleep." His thumb brushed my chin, tracing the underside of my bottom lip, as my eyes studied the darkness pillowing his. "I didn't tell you something."

I began to rise. "It doesn't—"

"I love you." He stood with me, holding my face. "I'm still and will always fucking be in love with you." Soft and lingering, his lips pressed to my temple, his harsh intake of breath and his shaking hands causing my chest to burn. "I love you."

Then, he left me there on the sidewalk with the fading moon.

"Nice doesn't mean good," Daphne said, adjusting her phone on the table.

We were scrapbooking in my apartment the following night with Peggy on FaceTime.

Peggy huffed. "So he probably hated it then."

Daphne folded her sheet of indigo paper in half. "I didn't say that."

"Willa?" Peggy said.

"Huh? Oh." I looked up from the box I'd been perusing. "I don't see what the big deal is. He said he liked it." I shrugged, giving my attention back to the photos. "So he liked it."

Peggy groaned. "You're no help."

"You're overthinking it."

Daphne conceded. "She's right. Forget it. Just buy the house and move back here already."

Dash and Peggy were still in New York, being that Peggy had landed an internship right out of school at some type of virtual gaming place. It was coming to an end, though, and she still hadn't been offered a paying job. Dash was working for his dad, which would be easier if they were back in Magnolia Cove.

I paused on a picture of me and Jackson, plucking it from the box to study it closer.

He was wearing his motocross gear, save for the helmet, which was pinned at his side, and I was pinned on the other.

Our smiles were contagious, and not a speck of space lingered between us. I didn't care that he was covered in mud and sweat. I was holding the trophy he'd been awarded for coming in first place, and he was holding me.

"Is that from when he raced?" Daphne asked.

"Yeah," I said, then coughed a little to empty the thickness from my throat. "He stopped when he turned seventeen." When things got more serious, more complicated with us.

"It's fun, and I love it," he'd said one night in his room. "But it's not my future, and if I treat it that way, I begin to feel myself slipping away from it, losing the excitement."

I'd thought it an odd thing to say at the time. I'd been too focused on me, on us, and I felt my eyes flutter as I remembered my response.

"But if I'm your future, will you slip away from me?"

"Bug." He'd laughed, poking my cheek, then cupped the side of my face. "You're not only my future." His forehead pressed into mine. "You're one half of my soul. If you slip away, then a huge part of who I am goes with you."

"You're crying," Peggy said, sounding panicked. "She's crying, Daphne."

I swatted at my cheeks, then waved my hand. "I'm fine, it's just..."

"Memories," Daphne finished.

"What am I supposed to do here?" I found myself saying what I'd asked myself countless times.

"Whatever feels right," Peggy said.

Daphne gave her a look, then set her scissors down. "The way I see it is, once upon a time, you guys had every reason not to be together." She spread her hands. "You did it anyway. But the odds were stacked against you, and like so many of us, you folded."

Peggy hummed in agreement. "But what's stopping you now?"

"You," Daphne answered for me. "Just the two of you."

"I don't need new door trim," I told Victoria for the sixth time the following morning.

She continued to prance around the room with her tape measure, a few waiting customers eyeing her and scuttling out of the way.

"Dennis," she called, ignoring me. "Hand me my phone, would you?"

As if he were a puppy infatuated with his new owner, Dennis had waited on her since she'd walked through the door an hour ago.

He riffled through her purse, plucked it out, then held the chair for Victoria to stand on while she snapped a hundred photos.

After I'd tended to the customers, two of whom chose to sit outside in the sun, I marched over. "Don't you have a job to get to?"

"Rude," Victoria said, taking Dennis's hand to climb down from the chair. "I rescheduled a few things."

"A few?" I frowned. "Why?"

Perplexed, a small laugh tittered out. "Why? Because I want to make this place shine as much as its owner." Her brows puckered, and she reached out, smoothing some rogue tendrils of hair off my face.

The sound of a picture being taken had us both turning to Dennis, who shrugged and eased back, setting Victoria's phone on the table. "I'll just, ah, go check on those pies."

"You do that," I suggested.

"You look tired."

I was exhausted, but I didn't admit it.

An ear-piercing shriek dragged our attention to the street. "Willa Grace Grayson."

My stomach dropped and dunked, quaking my knees.

Victoria hummed. "Now, there's the reason for those unsightly bags." She snatched her phone. "About time," she muttered, tucking her phone away and sliding her purse over her shoulder. "And Thorn sounded much better. Just saying."

"Willa," Jackson called again, standing right on the edge of the sidewalk, collecting even more onlookers by the second. "Will you do me the honor of accompanying me to dinner and a movie?"

The room began to shrink, taking every sound, scent, and shape with it, creating a tunnel that contained only me and the boy I used to know.

"He's causing a scene," Victoria said, nudging me. "Get out there and end it." Flo made a hissing noise, and Victoria added, "I mean, you know, put him out of his misery."

But my feet had become two blocks of concrete. I couldn't move them forward, even if I wanted to, and I wasn't sure I did.

"Bug?" he called, the whine of the megaphone echoing. "Don't make me come in there."

Laughter sank inside the tunnel he'd created, laughter and hushed murmurs.

Backing away from the windows, I felt my head and heart shake.

The megaphone protested, hitting the sidewalk with a crash as the door opened and closed and I entered the kitchen.

An arm wrapped around my waist before I could close myself inside the bathroom, heated words rushing into my ear. "Bug, talk to me." Turning me in his arms, he pressed me into the counter, then lifted me to sit atop it, and moved between my legs.

The hope and fear in his eyes caused my heart and mind to riot further, my fingers fluttering to his face, rubbing the stubble cresting his lower cheeks and jaw. "This, us, isn't what you hoped it would be. It's been broken now. We'll never be perfect, Jackson."

"I know," he said. "I know, but there's no one else I'd rather be imperfect with." When I didn't respond, he continued, "I fucked up, okay? There were so many things I should've done differently. We were both so young and so fucking sure of ourselves."

I laughed at that, offering a sad smile. "We really were."

"I'm a stubborn asshole, and I'm painfully aware of that." His hands squeezed my waist. "We made a huge mess, Bug, but we're almost done cleaning it up."

"Why now? What makes you think we can do this?"

His lashes lowered, lips parting. "Because we tried to go without, and it didn't work." Eyes opening and searching mine, his voice was ragged. "Because in trying to forget, we lost six years." His hand skated up my back, holding the back of my head, as his dropped down to rest on mine. "I won't make it another six without you." Smirking, he linked his fingers with mine over his cheek. "You can't do that to me."

A hoarse breath of laughter left me. "You can't guilt me, you toad."

"No, but I can love you." Earnest greens held me suspended. "If you'll let me."

"There's nothing stopping us now," I said, as though it were a bad thing.

Jackson grinned. "Just us."

My eyes closed, my heart a stampede of butterflies trying to escape the thundering cage encasing them.

I wasn't sure if we could make it. I wasn't sure if we could endure much more than we already had. I wasn't sure if we'd survive any more damage.

And I wasn't sure I could live without knowing if we could.

My eyes opened. "One date. But if you screw it up, Jacks—"

His kiss was hard and firm, a promise and a thank you. "I won't."

Wrapping my arms around his neck, I tucked my nose against his skin, inhaling, coming home, and I felt him do the same.

We didn't leave the kitchen, our only movement the rise and fall of our chests, but we didn't need to.

The sound of the door opening reached us, then Dennis yelled, "It's a done deal!"

Cheers erupted, the clapping, whistling, and laughter loud enough to find their way inside.

"Bug?"

My eyelids fluttered. "Hmm?"

"You really need to rename this bakery."

His arms, holding me impossibly close, tightened as I laughed.

epilogue

One date turned into three, and then it was as if nothing had changed, and the sun had decided to shine over our small pocket of the world once more.

But that wasn't entirely true. Many things had changed. And with those changes came new discoveries, fresh arguments, and strange family dinners.

The trees curved, the wind gathering speed as nightfall approached.

Willa raced around the trunk of a looming oak, her hands raised, button nose scrunching as she snarled.

"Wrong mouse, Bug."

She splayed her hand at me, hissing, "Or is it?"

I laughed as she launched onto my back, and I hoisted her higher as we waded through the ankle-deep grass.

"They better have stayed away from the creek," I muttered, eyes skimming the water up ahead, and the woods beyond.

"You only told them a hundred times." She nibbled my earlobe. "They know."

Shivering, I squeezed her thighs. She was always poking fun at how pedantic I could be. One of us had to be. Willa was more inclined to let them explore. Let them be kids, she'd say.

No thanks. I remembered exactly what we'd gotten up to as

kids when our parents weren't looking. "Since when have they ever listened to a word we've said?"

Her hands tightened around my neck, her giggle warming my ear and chest. "True."

Willa screamed, and I jumped back a step, almost dropping her, as Drew and Dane hurtled out of the dense sprawl of thicket before us.

"Shit," I hissed, my heart pounding.

Willa was in tears, climbing down my back, stumbling with laughter to our three-year-old twin tyrants.

"We scared ya's!" Drew held his belly, laughing, while his brother ran over to see if I was okay.

Dane patted my cheeks, his huge green eyes narrowed with concern. "You okay, Daddy?"

"Yeah, bud." I nodded, laughing a little now that the shock had worn off.

"We scared you good, huh?" he asked, a hesitant smile causing his lone dimple to appear.

"You sure did." I pulled him to me, rubbing his waves of brown hair.

"Can't believe we scared Dad," Drew kept repeating to his brother with a little too much glee for my liking as we walked back.

Willa's hand squeezed mine as I helped her over a log. "Are you thinking what I'm thinking?"

I snorted, watching Dane stop to inspect a mound of ants. "Dane, don't touch."

"Oh, cool!" Drew raced over and crouched down.

"That they're soon going to be devising ways to scare the piss out of me?" I asked Willa. "Yeah, I know."

She giggled, and I tugged her to me to steal her bottom lip with my teeth.

"I don't thinks they are sleepin' after all," I heard Dane say.

"Fuck." I tore away and collected Drew and the stick he'd been trying to prod the ant's nest with. "I said don't touch."

Willa laughed but grabbed Dane's hand, and we headed back to the tents.

"Honestly," Mom said later as she exited the twins' tent, slapping at her arm. "I thought you bought the best repellent they had."

Dad hid his smirk behind his beer, and I dropped my cards once Daniel laid his out.

He grinned. "Should've put more money down."

Dad grunted, then began collecting them all and reshuffling. "Another round."

"I'm good," I said, rising and stretching my arms over my head.

"Well, I'm not. I've been bitten three times," Mom said, standing above Willa, who was laying on the picnic rug, staring up at the stars.

Willa sighed. "You won't die, Mom." At our wedding rehearsal, four years ago, Willa began calling Victoria Mom again, and I soon followed suit. Victoria had cried, and then blamed it on the upcoming nuptials.

"We'll see," Mom responded.

I couldn't help but laugh, and she pursed her lips, turning to me. "Oh, shut it."

"Didn't say a word."

"You never have to," she said, but she was smiling. She brushed my arm, walking over to join Daniel and Dad by the fire.

I gestured to the woods, and Willa bit her lip, nodding.

They didn't ask where we were going, and we didn't tell. The boys were asleep, so my only concern was getting between Willa's smooth thighs as soon as fucking possible.

We were on day two of camping and weren't leaving until tomorrow.

It'd been Dad's idea to invite Daniel, much to Victoria's dismay.

She and Willa's dad still didn't exactly see eye to eye on a lot of things, but they were civil. It was Dad who'd formed a friendship with him after randomly suggesting we invite him for Christmas.

The first Christmas we'd all spent together had been awkward at first, but eventually, once everyone had relaxed, it was pretty awesome.

It was there that I'd proposed. Dad had helped me set up the old tent outside, and Victoria had bought new fairy lights.

We were married the following Valentine's Day.

"Don't waste any time, do you?" Daniel had said when I'd asked his permission two weeks beforehand.

"I've wasted too much."

At that, his brows had jumped, and his smile was all the confirmation I'd needed. He'd nodded, then clapped me on the shoulder with, "Nothing too gaudy. You know she'd hate it."

Willa's rings glinted beneath the moonlight as I reached for her hand and tugged her into the trees.

She was Willa Thorn once more.

After smiling and nodding for months every time I reminded her about changing the bakery's name, I took matters into my own hands and had a new sign made. It was now called Bug's Bakery. She'd caught me installing it the morning after it'd arrived, but just smiled and walked by the ladder I was standing on and headed inside. We lived above the bakery until we found out she was pregnant with the boys. Now, we owned a four-bedroom home overlooking the bay, five minutes from town.

"If we go much farther, we might not find our way back."

"I know what I'm doing."

Willa laughed. "I'm having major flashbacks here."

"Of?" I held a cluster of prickly branches back for her to pass.

"Of you saying that a million times, right before we landed ourselves in trouble."

"Well," I said, figuring we'd gone far enough. "To be fair, this kind of trouble will be worth it."

"Don't sound too smug."

"You doubt me?" I pulled her close, lifting her summer dress, one slow inch at a time.

"Never," she whispered, throwing it to the ground.

Our mouths joined, our hands busy ridding us of every barrier, and then we were on the leaf and twig strewn ground. "On top."

She didn't object and tossed her bra to the grass as she swung her legs on either side of my hips.

Brown waves fell to her waist and curtained her tits. My back protested the hard earth, and a rock dug into my ass, but I wasn't about to move for anything unless it involved loving her.

My hands grabbed her hips, squeezing, then roamed up her chest, gently pushing her hair back over her shoulders. I loved her hair any length. I'd love her if she had no hair at all, and I made sure I told her that when I noticed she was growing it longer again.

"I miss it," she'd said, "but that's nice to know."

I'd laughed, then attacked her lips.

"What are you smiling at?" she asked me now.

"I have a goddess straddling me." I raised a brow. "What sane mortal wouldn't be smiling?"

Her answering smile glowed, and she leaned forward, her lips tickling mine as her hair tickled my chest and cheek. "I love you."

I'd never grow tired of hearing that. Holding her face, I nipped her lips. "I love you more."

Reaching between us, she grabbed my cock. "I loved you first."

I groaned. "Keep telling yourself that." Then I cursed as she took all of me in one slow drop. "Jesus," I wheezed out.

She grinned, humming against my lips as her hips rocked.

I let her do her thing, absorbing every rough breath while palming her ass. When I couldn't take it anymore, I sat up, holding her chest tight to mine so I could better access her mouth.

Together, we unraveled but stayed joined in every way. My fingers lost to her hair, and hers tracing my cheeks and shoulders.

And as the stars glittered between the gaps in the giant treetops overhead, we moved to the creek to clean off.

Willa's legs tightened around my waist, her hands wiping water from my face as my fingers slipped down her ass and toyed with her entrance. Rock hard, I lifted her higher to fit myself inside.

"Again?" She laughed, incredulous.

My hands tugged her hair, exposing her neck to my mouth. I licked the curve of her throat, inhaling. "Not done."

My hips jerked, stealing a moan from her. "I thought you were."

"Bug," I whispered, lips skimming her jaw. "I'll never be done."

Smooth hands gripped my face, tilting it back, as hazel eyes connected with mine. "Every good day."

My throat thickened as I whispered the other part of our wedding vows. "And every bad day."

For there had been, and there would be, many of both, but nothing, not even our own reckless hearts, could separate us again.

We weren't only soul mates.

We were stitched at the seams, unable to part without losing fragments of ourselves.

And I'd learned the hard way just how impossible it was to live with pieces when I could've been whole.

In a world filled with mistakes just waiting to be made, I was thankful we'd already made all the wrong ones. Now, we could make all the right ones.

Together.

The End

Enjoy *Hearts and Thorns*?
It would mean the world to me if you could please
leave a brief review. <3

Did you know Dash and Peggy have their own story?

Dashiell Thane wasn't a nice guy.
He was an abrasive, demanding, conniving, intolerable brat.
Yet somehow, we'd been best friends our whole lives.
Until our senior year when I finally decided to dip my toes into
the dating pool.

All it took was one kiss for jealousy, lies, and betrayal to sweep
in and propel us heart first into dizzying, hostile depths.

You're not supposed to kiss your best friend.
You're definitely not supposed to kiss your best friend while
you're dating someone else.
And the absolute worst thing you could do is fall for your best
friend.
Unless, of course, you want to ruin everything.

Kiss and Break Up

Lars and Daphne do, too!

Lars Bradby was supposed to be my forever.
That was before we found out he would become a father at the tender age of eighteen.

For years, he'd watched me.
For months, he'd wanted me.
For weeks, he'd chased me.

Relentless and infuriating, he turned my stubborn heart into something pliable and weak.
Sly and honest, he worked his way into my life as though he'd always planned to be the focal point of it.

In love and naïve, even when our future seemed bleak, I believed in us.
Heartbroken and desperate, I tore my bleeding heart from my chest, wanting only the best for him.

In doing so, our forever wasn't just interrupted. It was chased away with one irreversible decision after another.
And now, we could no longer see it beneath the heaping piles of debris we'd left in our wake.

Forever and Never

about the author

Ella Fields is a mother and wife who lives in Australia.

While her kids are in school, you might find her talking about her characters to her cat, Bert, and dog, Grub.

She's a notorious chocolate and notebook hoarder who enjoys creating hard-won happily ever afters.

www.ellafields.net

also by
ELLA FIELDS

Bloodstained Beauty

Frayed Silk

Cyanide

Corrode

Serenading Heartbreak

GRAY SPRINGS UNIVERSITY:

Suddenly Forbidden

Bittersweet Always

Pretty Venom

Made in the USA
Columbia, SC
07 June 2022